# The Case of the Dearly Departed

## A Richard Sherlock Whodunit

By
Jim Stevens

ISBN: 978-1-942424-08-6

Dedicated to Alan Smithy

# The Richard Sherlock Whodunit Series

The Case of the Not-So-Fair Trader

The Case of Moomah's Moolah

The Case of Tiffany's Epiphany

The Case of Mr. Wonderful

The Case of the Woebegone Widow

The Case of the Missing Milk Money

**Also by Jim Stevens:**

WHUPPED

WHUPPED TOO

Hell No, We Won't Go,
A Novel of Peace, Love, War, and Football

Certain instances in this novel are based on actual facts and events, others not so much.

# CHAPTER 1

According to certain psychologists, a human's greatest motivator is fear. According to certain other psychologists, a human's greatest motivator is pain. According to me, a human's greatest motivator is the fear of pain, which may explain why, at the present time, I am hanging at a sixty-seven-degree angle, head down, face-up, strapped into the pulsating-ion, electric, elliptical, rotating inversion device known as the Spine Tingler.

My back has been acting up, and I can feel the big one on the way.

So I go into my *I'll try anything* mode.

"The end of your back pain once and for all! The Spine Tingler, a revolutionary, high tech medical marvel will cure any and all vertebral pain. After only one treatment, you'll be back on the golf course, serving aces on the tennis court, or salsa dancing with the best of them. No more aches, discomfort, shooting pains, or embarrassing bend-overs. Forget the pills, stretching, exercises, yoga, surgery, or anything you've tried before because with the Spine Tingler's space-age electronic infusions of ionic beams of healing, you'll be as good as new!" There's a pause in the video's audio, followed by "But wait, there's more. If you sign up now for treatment, you'll also receive a free Asian Oriental Oscillator designed for those minor, pesky backaches that arrive at the most inopportune times."

Yes, when you have a bad back like I do, you'll believe pretty much anything.

"Are you ready?" the voice coming from behind the glass at the Tingler command and control center asks.

"No."

"What's the matter?"

The image in my mind is of my entire body being launched out of this modern-day Spanish Inquisition contraption at Mach 2 speed, and thrust through the control room's glass skylight faster than a poorly aimed circus clown fired out of a

1

cannon.

"I'm scared."

"We can abort the mission if you want."

"Well—"

Is discretion the better part of valor?

"But since you're already strapped in and you're scheduled to go, your payment is no longer refundable," the voice reminds me.

"That's not good."

"What do you want to do?"

I have no other choice.

"Blast off."

The room goes dark and quiet; the only sound is from a fan starting to spin. Soon, frigid air hits me like a Chicago winter squall. A vibration hits my spine, starting with the lumbar vertebrae, and works its way up to the base of my neck, then repeating with stronger and stronger shots of pulsating ionic electrons. I hear a buzz beneath me and see the room's control board light up like a disco ball.

Oh, no, here it comes.

Goodbye, cruel world.

My body begins to move. Feet go down, head goes up, twisting to the left in an over/under/sideways/down spin that would make a physicist dizzy. No wonder they told me not to eat in the previous twelve hours. I hope the granola bar doesn't come up and prove me a person of little willpower.

The spin starts to increase, as do the electrical shocks to my back. I don't know what to think and I don't know what to do. If, in fact, I could do anything, strapped inside this Disneyland torture ride from hell. I get to what must be maximum speed, and I flip around faster than a Cirque de Soleil acrobat on a meth bender. The pulses are hitting my back faster than bullets from an AK-47. The restraints holding me tighten to the breaking point. The constant motion is forcing blood into my head with such pressure I fear parts of my brain will explode through my eye sockets, out my ears, and blow out of my nose like a spring allergy.

And I paid two hundred bucks for this treatment.

Oh, the things you do when the fear of an upcoming bad back attack rears its ugly head.

Just as I reach the point of no return, where death seems

preferable to this torture, the machine slows down, the wind tunnel's whoosh diminishes, the shots to my spine lessen in their severity, and I begin to regain my senses. My blood seeks its own level, the pressure on my brain decreases, and my eyes find their way back into their sockets.

All motions stop.

I lie flat on my back, level with the ground.

"How do you feel?" comes from the man behind the proverbial curtain.

My immediate response would be "Awful" but I'm unable to speak. I'm spent. My body has the rigidity of a wet dishrag. I can't feel my feet, my tongue lies in my mouth like beef tongue before it becomes a sandwich, and I wonder if all my body parts are still attached.

I also can't feel any pain in my lower back.

What? No pain? No ache? No bruising spasms? No horrible debilitating, slicing agony, as if a switchblade is being thrust between my L4 and L5 vertebrae?

None.

It's a miracle.

"Please lie still for a few moments," the voice tells me, like a yoga instructor introducing Shavasana.

I enter a realm of absolute calm. My body isn't working but my brain is. Have I finally found the cure for my aching back? Can I give up my daily floor stretching routine? Finally quit the constant search for the bad-back magic bullet? Stop worrying about unexpectedly crumpling to the ground like a worn-out Gumby doll?

I lie totally still, relishing the joy and wonder that it has finally happened. The pain is gone. I can live free. My new life begins today. Maybe I'll take up golf.

It is said that true, absolute joy and happiness are as elusive as winning lottery numbers, but lying here, I feel I have attained the impossible. The mother of all smiles comes across my face.

And then my world of peace, happiness, joy, and contentment is shattered as I hear the words I detest more than any others.

"Oh, Mr. Sherlock."

Tiffany, my so-called assistant, protégé, and babysitting assignment, rushes into the room and stops at my side.

"Mr. Sherlock, you have to come quick. Some dead guy, who isn't really dead, is trying to scam my daddy for a million bucks, and we have to stop him."

"What?"

"Hurry. We can't let him get away."

"Tiffany, how did you find me?"

"What does that matter? We have to go now."

Tiffany starts to unstrap me from my harness. "What are you doing in this thing anyway? You look like the victim in one of those tie-me-up and tie-me-down slasher movies that I've never watched, but heard about."

The so-called *Doctor of Back Pain Eradication* rushes into the room, ordering, "No, don't get up. You must rest and allow the electrons to finish their work."

Tiffany doesn't listen and continues to free me from the device. "No, we gotta go. A million bucks is on the line."

I tumble out of the machine and hit the floor like a dead trout flopping out of a creel. I crumple into a heap. I try to straighten up and it hits me. "Ouch!" Both my hands grip my lower back as I return to where I started the day.

"Oh, my aching back."

*** 

My name is Richard Sherlock. I spent nineteen years in the Chicago Police Department, sixteen as a detective. I got kicked off the force due to an uncharacteristic temper tantrum. My fist collided with the face of my commanding officer after he OK'd a plea deal for a guy I spent ten years trying to put behind bars. I lost my job and my pension, and couldn't find another gig. Not a lot of suburban Chicago police departments were in need of a guy with a right cross aimed at his superior. I ended up as an on-call investigator for the Richmond Insurance Company, where I am forced to investigate settlement frauds or any settlements that can be proven fraudulent.

I hate my job.

I am also a divorced dad of two girls, thirteen and almost fifteen, going on twenty. I have no savings and an ex-wife who hates me. I live in a crummy, currently sweltering one-bedroom apartment. I'm a lousy dresser. I can't find a steady girlfriend and I drive a 1992 Toyota Tercel.

Am I having fun?

No.

A big portion of my job with the insurance company is mentoring (aka babysitting) the twenty-something, spoiled heiress of the Richmond fortune, Tiffany Richmond. On the surface, Tiffany is a vapid, spoiled-rotten, rich, self-centered, egotistical girl who will never experience an "I can't afford it" moment in her life. Deep down, Tiffany is a vapid, spoiled-rotten, rich, self-centered, egotistical girl with a good heart. I have found in life if you have the latter, all other frailties diminish. Plus, my kids think the world of her. I suspect they like her more than they like me. I really can't blame them because even I like her more than I like me.

***

"Tiffany, can't you give me a moment's worth of peace?"

"No."

Tiffany helps me to my feet. I somewhat stand, hunched over like a flower bent in the rainfall.

"Couldn't this have waited?"

"No." Tiffany explains as she helps me to the door. "I know a million dollars isn't what it used to be—"

I interrupt, "It is if you've never had a million dollars, Tiffany."

"Well, that's not my problem. The point here, Mr. Sherlock, is that someone is trying to cheat my daddy."

Which would be extremely hard to do, seeing that Jameson Wentworth Richmond the Third not only has used every trick in the book for cheating people out of their money, but he's come up with quite a few new ones of his own.

"But didn't you say the guy was dead?"

"He was, but now he isn't."

"His name wouldn't be Jesus, by any chance, would it?" I ask.

"Who?"

"J E S U S," I spell it out for her.

"No, he's not Hispanic, Mr. Sherlock."

I'm walking better, not well but better, as we reach Tiffany's Lexus 430, parked in a handicap space in front of the building.

"And you're not going to believe who uncovered the scam."

"Try me."

"The last in the long line of Daddy's dumpees."

## CHAPTER 2

B ree Bisonette, which is pronounced "Biz-o-nay," works as a claims executive at the Richmond Insurance Company. Bree's office is one floor beneath the massive corner office of Mr. Richmond, who at one time she was dilly-dallying with, in the adult sense of the word; at least until Jameson threw her to the curb like an empty Big Gulp cup, and Bree imploded into a mass of grief-flavored gelatin, worse than any teenager dumped the night before prom.

"If Bree's doing this to get back on Daddy's good side and she's lying, she's going to find herself in a world of corporate hurt, Mr. Sherlock."

"Tiffany," I whisper so the rest of the occupants can't hear, "don't talk in elevators."

"Why not?"

"Because you don't know who may be listening."

"Why would I care who's listening?" Tiffany says in a normal voice. "I didn't do anything wrong. It's that no-good Bree who could be trying to pull a fast one."

"Tiffany, quiet."

"If people didn't want to know everybody else's business, Mr. Sherlock, they would have never invented Facebook."

Tiffany does have a point.

The doors open, and we exit on the Claims floor.

"Hello, Miss Tiffany," Jasmine, the receptionist on the floor, immediately says with a big, phony smile on her face.

"Oh, hi."

There is a bit of an awkward silence.

"Tiffany and Sherlock to see Bree Bisonette," I announce.

"I'll call."

As the nice lady makes the call, I back up into the waiting area, taking Tiffany with me.

"That wasn't very polite, Tiffany."

"What?"

"If she greets you with your name, it's polite to respond in kind."

"Mr. Sherlock, I can't be expected to remember the names of all the little people that work here."

"Her name is sitting right on her desk."

"Jasmine?" Tiffany says incredulously. "I thought that was

the name of the cheap perfume she was wearing."

"Hello, Richard."

If you were to look up *Career Woman* in the dictionary, you'd see a picture of Bree Bisonette. Tall, statuesque, impeccably dressed, carrying herself with an air of corporate confidence.

"How nice to see you." She comes forward to shake my hand firmly.

"Bree, how are you?" I ask.

"Better than the last time we met."

"Hello, Miss Bisonette," pronounced "Bizy-o-net" by Tiffany.

"Oh, hello... Tiffy."

The air conditioning must have kicked in because there is a sudden chill in the room.

We follow Bree to her office.

"Won't you please have a seat?"

Bree sits behind her large desk. We sit in the facing chairs.

"What can I do for you?"

"Tell him what you told my daddy," Tiffany says.

"The Crouch case?"

"The dead guy that ain't dead case," Tiffany qualifies.

Bree rolls her eyes before beginning. "Some time ago, a claim came in for payment on a whole life policy of a million dollars. After careful scrutiny on my part, the claim was refused on the grounds of no death certificate being issued. It seems the man, a Leonard Crouch, known as 'Buck' to his family and friends, suddenly disappeared. One Monday morning his wife got up and Buck wasn't in bed, in the house, on the property, or in the neighborhood. Nothing was missing, not his clothes, car, wallet, jewelry, or toiletries. Nothing. All were exactly where he left them the previous evening. The man simply vanished into thin air. The police were called, an APB went out, a Missing Person report was sent to all the surrounding towns, and the investigation began. There were no signs of a break-in to the house, no odd footprints or fingerprints, no sightings by neighbors, and no one from his workplace had seen or heard from him since he had resigned two Fridays before.

Buck simply poofed into thin air."

"So what did you do?" I ask.

"Nothing. Without a death certificate, there could be no

payment on the policy. Richmond was free and clear of any benefit being due. And let me tell you, Buck's wife and brother were none too happy hearing the news." Bree takes a breath before continuing. "A few months later, I was contacted by a credit card company and asked about the disappearance. There was a fourteen-thousand-dollar balance due on a credit card in Crouch's name. A personal card his wife knew nothing about. Evidently, Buck had not been paying any monthly interest or the payment due."

"Has the card been used since his disappearance?" I ask.

"It was cancelled."

Tiffany interrupts, "Ah, could you cut to the chase?"

"No, Tiffany," I say, "let her continue."

"This is boring, Mr. Sherlock."

"Patience is a virtue, Tiffany."

Bree interrupts, "Tiffy possesses no such thing."

"Patience?" I ask.

"No, virtue," Bree answers.

Tiffany glares. Bree glares back.

"Whom did you hear this from?" I ask.

"The credit bureau hired a skip tracer to find the guy. They wanted their money, plus the interest, which was now much greater than the original balance."

"Did the skipper have any luck?"

"As far as I know, no."

"Then what happened?" I ask.

"Nothing, until months later they refiled the claim."

Tiffany pipes in, "Boring—"

"And—"

"A packet of material arrives in the mail," Bree says. "It includes the death certificate, reports from a coroner in Wisconsin, and photocopies of the evidence collected by the sheriff of Washington County, Wisconsin. Buck Crouch's body was found in a remote section of hill country, buried in a pile of dirt and forest debris. The report said the body was discovered horribly ravaged by wild animals and mutilated by the normal forces of nature. Cause of death was listed as: Fall from a height of at least 1,000 feet."

"How did the county tie this corpse to the death of Buck Crouch?"

"They didn't at first. He was a John Doe."

"That John Doe guy certainly seems to get around," Tiffany says.

"When they finally got around to putting their findings into the missing persons' database, one distinguishing factor matched," Bree continues.

"What was the factor?"

"An upper-arm tattoo," Bree says. "It was a three-by-two-inch image of a blue and red Chicago Cubs logo.'"

"Fingerprints?"

"None."

"Blood?"

"Not to my knowledge."

"Was an autopsy performed?"

"The report says there wasn't enough left to autopsy. Don't forget, Mr. Sherlock, this happened way out in the sticks where the morgue facilities are not sophisticated, and lots of critters are in the woods looking for a free lunch."

"What happened to the body?"

"Cremated."

"Cremated?" I question. "They can't cremate evidence before proper identification."

"He was cooked in the interim between the report being filed and the match being made. He wasn't someone they wanted taking up space in their one freezer for months."

Tiffany is now twiddling her thumbs to relieve her boredom.

"Who sent you the packet?" I ask.

"The brother, who refiled the claim, was also kind enough to include photographs. The before picture of Buck was nice, but the after pictures were a bit on the gruesome side."

"Did they check for a DNA match?"

"They said they didn't have any fresh Buck DNA to match."

"Dental records?"

"None. Evidently Buck hated going to the dentist."

"So you paid off the claim?"

"No."

"Why not?"

"No beneficiary and no executor named for the estate."

"Who was going to get his money?"

"I don't know." Bree pauses. "And here's an odd twist: the policy was purchased when he was one."

"Year old?"

"Yep."

"How did he pay the premiums?"

"He didn't." Bree sits back.

"Who paid them?"

"Don't know. The payments were received in cash once a year until the interest on the policy was used to pay the premiums."

"I would be surprised if Buck even knew the policy existed."

"This is weird."

"Actually, it's not all that odd for parents to take out insurance policies for their kids, especially when they're infants. The policies are cheap, have a cash value, and are actually a great way to save for the kid's college."

Why didn't I think of this? In a couple of years I'll have two kids in college and the only thing I've saved, so far, are my two kidneys.

"So who gets the money?"

"The estate."

"Is there a will?"

"Not that I know of."

Tiffany harrumphs. "This is dumb. Can we get to the part where we find out the guy's not dead?"

Bree tries her best to ignore Tiffany as she says, "And here's where the story takes somewhat of a personal twist."

A pensive, almost embarrassed look comes upon Bree's face. I wait.

"As you know I was a bit distraught over losing the love of my life a few months back, and it took me quite some time to regain my emotional equilibrium. One day I decided it was time to put it all behind me and get right back in the saddle."

"Of a Clydesdale," Tiffany interjects.

Bree ignores her. Thank God.

"I started dating again, but couldn't find the next man of my dreams. I was determined, and decided to take any means possible, so I began internet dating. I started on Match.com, Plenty-of-Fish, eHarmony, but I wasn't getting much in the way of quality. I went to Bumble, J-Date, Tinder, Corporate Couples, Zoosk, Mature Singles Only, Dating DNA, and YouCanDoBetter.com. I must have searched a million guys, not many of whom appealed to me. And one night, I'm up late, scrolling away, and I see a picture of a guy I've seen somewhere before. I'm on NatureLovers.com, and here's this guy sitting in a boat, lifting up a big trout. Why guys think women go for men holding a big, dead fish, I'll never know. The face is familiar, but I just can't place it. The guy's internet name is Big Fish in Small Pond, and he's advertising for the *nature girl of my dreams*. I go to bed that night with his image stuck in my mind.

"And at three-fifteen AM, I awaken and say out loud, 'It's Buck.'"

"What did you do?" I ask.

"Got up, got back on the net, and responded to his ad."

"So what did you do next?" I ask.

"Put a stop on the million-dollar payout."

"Did Buck write back?"

"No."

"No big surprise there," Tiffany remarks.

"You call the skip tracer with the news?"

"Yeah. He laughed at me."

"Let me guess what happens next," I say. "The brother and wife threaten to sue for the claim?"

"Half right. The brother did."

"With a death certificate, coroner's report, and whatever else."

"Yes," Bree says.

"By law, don't you have to pay off on the policy?"

"Yes."

"No," Tiffany screams.

"Why not?"

"Because we have to find this Buck guy."

"He's dead."

"No, he's not. Here's his picture. The only thing dead in it is the fish," Tiffany says. "Daddy says we have to find him."

"'We?'"

"Yes, Mr. Sherlock," Tiffany says. "And we can work on the case together."

Bree leans towards me and says, "Lucky you."

I hate my job.

"What's the name of the skip tracer?"

"I have his card right here." Bree pulls a business card out of her top drawer and hands it to me.

"Oh, no. Not Larry Flemm with two m's."

# CHAPTER 3

A skip tracer is a so-called detective assigned by a credit card or insurance company to find people who run off leaving their debts behind. The deadbeats include credit card con artists, lousy husbands, corporate crooks, bigamists, and guys who are really cheap. On average, 90,000 persons disappear each year in America.

I have to admit, in the depths of my miserable divorce, I considered vanishing myself, but I could never leave Kelly and Care.

Our boy flashes a toothy smile, and puts out his meat hook to shake.

"Larry C. Flemm, and it's Flemm with two m's."

Tiffany feels the grease on his hand as they shake and asks, "What's the 'C' for? Creep?"

"Well, you're a feisty little thing, ain't ya?" Larry says, not letting go of her hand. "And I love a feisty little thing."

I use both hands to physically separate the two.

"How you been, Flemm?"

"Good, Sherlock. How you?"

"I've been better." I wince in pain, as my back hits the back of his cheap wooden office chair.

"Tell me about Buck Crouch," I say.

"He's dead. They found the body in the woods in Nowhere, Wisconsin."

"What about the picture Bree Bisonette found on the internet?"

"Oh, God, Sherlock, you'd believe a picture on an internet dating site? How lame are you?"

"Why couldn't it be him?"

"First, nobody puts a current picture on a dating site. They use one from years past, when they had hair, all their teeth, and didn't yet sprout a beer belly."

"How old is your picture, Mr. Flemm?" Tiffany asks.

"All I have to do is breathe, and the women come runnin'."

"The other way, I bet," Tiffany says.

"Can we go back to the topic of Buck Crouch?"

"It's a bot, Sherlock," Larry says.

"A bot? What's a bot?" I ask.

"An internet bot is a phony picture put up on the dating site to pump up the quality of its members. The other members see the bot, and think they're finding their soul mates."

"I thought that was a troll," I, the tech-unsavvy one, admit.

"No, a troll is a guy who lives under a bridge," Tiffany explains to me. "Where they catch big fish like the one in the picture."

Larry Flemm and I go back a long way. Larry used to be a CPD detective working white-collar crime, which is what used to be called the "Bunco Division." He would sit at his computer for hours at a time and pretend to be searching databases for information on nefarious scams being perpetrated. While the rest of us were out beating the bushes, trying to uncover clues, and question witnesses during humid summers and frigid winters, Larry sat in his nice, cozy cubicle tapping on the keys of his computer. Other non-tech-savvy detectives like myself would ask Larry for assistance, and would invariably receive one of his three stock answers: "Can't, my computer's down." "No can do, I'm on a big case right now." And my favorite, "Sorry, I've had a relapse of fingernail fungus, and doctor's orders are 'No typing for a week.'"

When the police tech powers-that-be ran an undercover sting on sites visited by officers on duty, Larry won, hands down, for most YouTube videos, pay-per-view movies, and porn sites watched. "Congratulations, Larry. You're fired."

"I will admit, this Crouch guy was good," Larry tells us. "Almost everyone who disappears screws up in the first three months, but not Buck. He got away clean and stayed clean. He never left a trace of a trace to be found."

"Maybe because he was dead?" I toss in.

"Even dead men tell tales, Sherlock."

"Who found him?" I ask.

"Geocachers."

"Geo-what?"

"Geocachers." Larry says it as if we're both idiots for not knowing.

"Sounds like a disease one of those environment people could spread," Tiffany says.

For all I know, Tiffany could be right.

"Geocachers are whack-ass computer geeks who get this ridiculous app on their phones that allows them to play this dumb game of hide-and-seek," Larry informs us. "Some idiot goes out and hides a box of junk, then puts the co-ordinates on the internet so other idiots can go out, slosh through mud and muck, and find it."

"What do they do when they find it?"

"Sign the log book or trade their geo-trinket with the trinket in the box, then rebury it for the next idiot to come by."

"Sounds like a swell time to me," I comment.

"Sounds like a scavenger hunt for nature lovers who need to get a life," Tiffany says.

I ask, "So the GPS co-ordinates pinpointed where Buck's body was?"

"No," Larry says, "the body was about twenty feet away. Some lady tripped over what was left of Buck's right foot."

"You should always watch where you walk," I lecture.

"And what shoes you wear." Tiffany adds fashion sense to the conversation.

"Here's what I think happened," Larry says. "Buck can't take his wife, and once you'll meet her, you'll see why. He stashes some cash and, one night, splits. He hightails it to the hinterlands to lay low, and while he's on the way, trips on some twig, falls down a crevice, and either kills himself hitting bottom or breaks so many bones, he has nothing better to do than lay there and die. The animals find him, chew him up good, and then the Wisconsin winter goes to work on him, followed by rain, sleet, bugs, leaves, fungus, decay, and other fun stuff. By the time the coroner gets there, Buck's a mass of once-human mush."

"Yeah, but we still got a picture of him on the dating site," Tiffany says.

"And I'd be more than happy that you and I get together over a couple of drinks at my place and search each other's sites, Miss Tiffany."

"Sure," Tiffany says, "as long as what you're drinking is poison."

"Oh, I love a feisty one, Sherlock."

***

Larry's right on one count. Buck was a master when it came to disappearing. He literally vanished into thin air. There were no sightings, car rental receipts, credit cards used, emails, phone records, or friends contacted, all the usual activities where disappearing folk slip up. Buck probably also knew that if a missing person isn't found in the first couple of days, the odds of finding him go up dramatically, and keep going up with each passing week. Truth be told, if it is not a child who disappears, and it's obviously an adult shirking his financial responsibilities, cops lose interest real quick.

Larry's nice enough to allow me to take home his file for a more careful study. Actually, he *loaned* the file to Tiffany with the caveat that she redeliver it at the time and place of Larry's choosing.

"Oh, sure, Mr. Flemm with two m's," Tiffany assures him. "What's the dress code where I'll drop it off?"

"A halter top would be nice," Larry says with a sparkle in his eyes.

"I can't wait to see you in one," Tiffany replies.

***

We sit in one of Tiffany's health food emporiums. She's eating charred tofu, topped with a radish roux, over a bed of brown rice with a side of sprouts. I'm having a free-range chicken sandwich. I've seen a range where the buffalo roam and a range where cattle feed, but I've never seen a bunch of chickens grazing on a hillside pecking out their lunch.

"What are we going to do now, Mr. Sherlock?"

"The longest journey starts with the first step, Tiffany."

"I thought it started with a first-class airline ticket."

"Well, not on this trip."

"Should we get a better travel agent?"

I show her a copy of the death certificate. "The only real proof of identification is the Cubs tattoo on his upper arm. There are no fingerprints, facial photos, DNA, or blood sample."

"That's a good thing, right?"

"Maybe." I page through the report.

"Height was five-nine, weight undetermined, hair color black. Only one out of the three match."

"How about eye color?"

"Plucked out."

"Not his brows, Mr. Sherlock, his eyes."

"Let's just say his pupils ended up in an eyeball hi-ball cocktail at Critters Bar and Grill."

"That's enough to make you quit drinking."

"The distinguishing characteristic, the tattoo, was determined to be enough to identify the body."

"Matching tattoos were a big thing a few years ago, Mr. Sherlock," Tiffany informs me. "Every couple I knew who got 'em broke up a few months later."

"Problem is, Tiffany, there's no way to recheck any of the findings."

"Why not?"

"They cremated the body."

"Ashes to ashes and dust to the dustpan?"

"So to speak."

"We can't be cooked, Mr. Sherlock. You got to figure something out. A million bucks are on the line."

I page through the remainder of Flemm's file. "I don't know if this is going to be worth it, Tiffany. Your daddy may have to bite the bullet on this one."

"No, Mr. Sherlock, he'll break a tooth."

"We're coming into the game after the final bell has already sounded."

"As long as the money's still on the table, we still have a chance to cancel the reservation."

"Then I guess we better hit the road."

## CHAPTER 4

Believe it or not, this is actually a good time to be traipsing around the forests of the Midwest, searching for clues that don't exist. Why? Because my kids are currently at summer horse camp in the wilds of the Chicago suburbs. They begged me to allow them to spend my allotted vacation time at horse camp. And not only did I have to send the two of them, I had to get their horse up there too. You would think at least one Uber driver would have a horse trailer, but no.

Kelly and Care have been gone for four days, and I have four left before I see them again and get my remaining days of court-ordered vacation, during which I have no clue what I'm going to do to keep them occupied.

"Let's go shopping," Kelly will suggest.

"I don't have any money."

"But I need new clothes. I don't want to walk into my first day of high school looking like some kid right out of middle school."

"You are a kid just out of middle school, Kelly."

"No, Dad, I've been out for months and grown much more mature."

I haven't noticed the change.

Care, my youngest, will suggest sport camps, adventure trips, amusement parks, and safari expeditions, all of which I also can't afford. Best I can do is the Lincoln Park Zoo; it's free.

Tiffany picks me up at 11:15 AM, her version of "first thing Monday morning."

"Where's your Lexus?" I ask, as I climb up into a new, massive, black Land Rover.

"Since we're going into the wilderness, I thought it would be best to drive something a little more appropriate."

Land Rover automobiles were originally designed to navigate through the sand dunes of the Sahara and the swamps of the Amazon. Today, they are a favorite of suburban housewives whose most treacherous road obstacle is a speed bump in a shopping mall parking lot.

"You didn't go out and buy one just for today, Tiffany?"

"No, I called the dealer, told him who I was, and said I wanted to test-drive one. He jumped at the chance."

Yes, the rich are different.

It takes us over two hours to get to the northern edge of Washington County and into the wilds of Wisconsin. The Office of the Sheriff is located in Slinger, a town of 5,000 and home to the Little Switzerland Ski Resort.

"Howdy."

"Hi, I'm Richard Sherlock, and this is my assistant, Tiffany."

"Nice to meet-cha."

Sheriff Cliff Adolph has been on duty in Washington County for over thirty years and proud of every day he's been on the job. There must be fifty framed pictures hanging on his wall with him shaking hands with elected officials, politicians who ran and lost, civic leaders, pastors, and members of every winning oom-pa-pa band in Slinger's annual Oktoberfest Battle of the Beer Bands competition. In the latter category, Sheriff Adolph is the only person in the pictures not wearing lederhosen.

"Yer name's Sherlock and yer a detective?" Cliff asks me.

"Yep."

"I've read all your grandfather's books."

"Actually, there's no relation, but I certainly hope you enjoyed them."

"Where's your English accent?" he asks.

"I left it with Dr. Watson."

"Now what can I do for you folks?" Cliff asks. "Is some game afoot?"

"Would it be possible for us to see where the body of Buck Crouch was found?"

"Sure. You want the bird's-eye view or the up-close-and-personal?"

"Which one would you suggest?" I ask.

"I'd start with the bird's-eye and work my way down."

We take Cliff's SUV up and around the towers that support the chairlift, over what would be the ski slope in the winter months.

We must be on the mogul run because we bounce up the incline like cans of paint in a shaker machine.

"Eighteen hundred feet of elevation at Little Switzerland. We put other Wisconsin ski areas to shame," Cliff proudly announces, which is equal to saying "You're in the best ski area in all of Wisconsin, Iowa, and Kansas combined."

At the top of the slope, Cliff parks at the end of the chair lift. We get out and follow him to the opposite edge of the so-called "mountain."

"Down there." He points.

It must be a thousand feet to the bottom of the rock-lined crevice, which isn't wide and is filled with dense vegetation.

"That's where they found him?" I ask. "All the way down there?"

"I figured the guy was up here taking in too much of God's green earth, wasn't watchin' where he was goin', slipped, and by the time he hit bottom was already dead."

I get a little woozy looking down and don't get too close to the edge. This would not be the place for my back to spasm and me to bend over, lose my balance, and take a header down to certain death.

Cliff continues, "Once he hit bottom, the snow buried him, and after a couple of seasons, there wasn't much left of old Buck to identify."

"This is a little dangerous, isn't it?" I ask.

"In the winter they put up snow fences to keep the skiers out, but the rest of the year there's no other way to get up here," Cliff says. "So why bother?"

"Is there any other way of getting to the spot down there, other than from up here?" I ask.

"Yeah, but only after spring. The snowmelt has got to be gone and the bottom pretty well dried out before you can walk on it. They had to helicopter down to get to the body."

"Did you go?"

"No, I'm afraid to fly."

"Did you consider it a suicide?" I ask.

"That would be great," Tiffany says excitedly. "If he did himself in, we wouldn't have to pay off on the claim."

"What a nice thought, Tiffany."

"You always tell me to find the rainbow behind the dark clouds, Mr. Sherlock."

"There's a lot easier ways of killin' yerself," the sheriff says.

"How about murder?" Being a detective, I have to ask.

"I ruled out homicide," Cliff says.

"Why?"

"Who would want to go to this much work just to kill somebody?" Cliff rhetorically asks. "With the body parts they dug up, there were a ton of broken bones, but no bullet holes, knife wounds, or indented skull. If he'd been iced, we would have seen something in that mass of rotted flesh. Buck Crouch wasn't murdered, he was clumsy."

"Damn," Tiffany says.

Sheriff Cliff Adolph is kind enough to drive us to the bottom and show us where we would have to go to hike into the crevice. One look is all it takes.

"No way I'm ruining a pair of Jimmy Choos to go in there," Tiffany announces.

"I'll draw you a map if ya want," Cliff offers.

"Maybe another day," I tell him.

"Suit yerselfs."

We return to the Sheriff's office, where I go through his file on the case and find nothing more I don't already know. He also shows us the refrigerator Buck was stored in. Thankfully, it's empty except for a case of bottled water. With all the fresh water in Wisconsin, why would he buy bottled water? Yet another waste of the taxpayers' money.

Next stop on our day in the country is at the home of Deloris and Debbie Diggler. A middle-aged sister couple, who share well-endowed pairs of personal peaks.

"How long have you two been geocaching?"

"Couple of years. There's a whole group of us that do it."

"Why?" Tiffany asks.

"Not much to do up here," Deloris admits. "Especially in the summer."

"We make it into a contest, on who's the most clever hiding their cache," Debbie adds.

"One person put his under a waterfall. One, next to a beehive, and one, in a skunk hole. That one drove us crazy."

"The guy who put his in a cow corral got kicked out of the group," Deloris says.

"We put ours on an island in the middle of a lake you had to canoe to."

"We showed them."

I get back to the topic at hand. "When you were looking for somebody else's cache, you stumbled across the body?"

Deloris answers, "Actually it was his shoe I tripped on. It was sticking out of a clump of green slime."

"I noticed it was a pretty nice shoe, but something was

sticking out of it," she continues.

"A shoe tree?" Tiffany asks.

"No, a stick. But as I got closer, it wasn't a stick, but a bone. Closer still, I saw what was left of a foot inside. I kept looking and saw a lot that I didn't want to see."

"Did you lose your lunch?" Tiffany asks.

"No, I called Debbie over."

"And I lost my lunch," she says. "It was totally disgusting."

"You didn't dig him up?"

"Enough to see what we didn't want to see."

"Can you describe him for me?"

"A B C," Debbie says.

I don't get it. "A B C?"

"Already Been Chewed."

"We called the Sheriff, explained what we found, and gave him the exact co-ordinates of the location."

"Then what did you do?"

Debbie answers, "Went and found the cache we came to find."

"What was in it?"

"Half-off coupons for an outdoor store in Milwaukee, a Harley-Davidson key chain, and the log book. We were the first geocachers to find the cache."

"Lucky you."

I contemplate for a few seconds and ask, "Who was the geocacher who buried the stuff?"

"Nature Boy Bob."

"That's his name?"

"No," Deloris says, "that's his handle. Geocachers don't use their real names."

"Can't say I blame them."

"What's your handle?" Tiffany asks.

"The Forty Double D's."

## CHAPTER 5

Tiffany dropped me off at my apartment building a little before four in the afternoon.

"What are you going to tell the guy at the Land Rover dealership?" I ask.

"I'll tell him, 'I wanna think it over and talk to my accountant.' That way, if he starts bothering me, I'll let CPA Chester tell him 'No.'"

"You're so kind, Tiffany."

Before I get out of the monster vehicle, she asks, "What are we going to do tomorrow, Mr. Sherlock?"

"I thought I'd go to the spa, get a massage, mani-pedi, facial, maybe do a little Botox, and derma-abrasion."

"On the case, Mr. Sherlock, on the case."

"I haven't the faintest idea, Tiffany. The death certificate has been issued, we didn't find any opposing evidence, and unless we have something new to add to the investigation, we're pretty much out of luck."

"That's not what I want to hear, Mr. Sherlock."

"Why don't you come up with something?"

"Because you're the detective."

"There's nothing left to detect."

"We're not giving up," Tiffany emphatically announces.

"Why not?"

"It's personal."

"What's personal?"

"I can't tell you."

"Why not?"

"It's personal."

Oh jeesh.

I step down to the truck's runner step, slowly. Next, I hit terra firma, turn slightly to argue with Tiffany, and feel a roadside bomb go off four inches above my butt crack.

"Ouch!"

It feels like a firecracker exploded between my lumbar vertebrae.

"See, Mr. Sherlock? This is your punishment for giving up too early. You go inside and find a way for us to keep our million bucks, and I'm sure you'll feel much better."

"What are you going to do?"

"Go to my spa. I want to get all that nature off me and stop smelling like a Christmas tree."

I trip on a sidewalk crack, catch myself before collapsing, and manage to hobble up the path and into the building. I don't try walking up the three flights of stairs; instead I sit backwards and go up one stair at a time. By the time I reach my front door, I'm an exhausted mass of humid sweat. I get the key in the lock, twist, turn the knob, open the door, and crawl inside on my hands and knees.

Once inside, I hear a strange sound, look up, and get my second major shock of the day.

"What are you doing here?"

Kelly and Care are seated on the couch watching TV.

"Wilting," Kelly says.

"What's the matter with the a/c, Dad? It's like a sweat lodge in here," Care says.

"My skin's losing valuable moisture," Kelly tells me. "If it dries out, I could get zits. I don't want to show up for the first day of high school looking like I'm wearing a face full of red Skittles."

I get to a kneeling position, but the pain is so horrendous, I can't speak.

"Are you praying, Dad?" Care asks.

"Hopefully to the god of air conditioning," Kelly adds.

"What are you two doing here? You're supposed to be at horse camp." I barely manage to get out.

"Oh Dad, that camp was lame," Kelly says.

"It was one nose-to-butt ride after another," Care fills in.

"Nose to butt?"

"One horse behind another horse with its nose up its butt."

"It was boring, so we left."

"How'd you get here?"

"Uber."

"Why didn't you go to your mother's house?"

"She's not home."

"She's at camp too," Care informs me.

"She went to a nose-to-butt camp?" I ask.

"No, a spiritual awakening camp. Mom's trying to get in touch with her inner self."

I wonder if there's a bad back camp out there I could attend.

"Dad, could you please get the a/c working?" Kelly requests. "I could die if I don't moisturize soon."

I crawl on my butt over to the window unit and have to hold one switch down, the other up, while I pull out the plug and quickly plug it back in. For some reason this turns the unit back on.

The room cools down.

"Dad," Care says, "all this cold air's making me hungry. What's for dinner?"

Will parenting ever end?

I call the horse camp and inform them my daughters have left the camp, they're with me, and not to send out a nose-to-butt search party.

"Gee," the woman on the phone tells me, "we didn't even know they were missing."

I wonder where her nose is.

After pizza and about fourteen Advil, I can sit without a lot of pain, but any adagio dancing would be a serious mistake. The girls watch TV while I man the computer.

In Google's realm, Buck Crouch doesn't exist. I try every combination and misspelling of his name, and he still doesn't rate on Google. I go to the Tribune and Sun Times obit pages and find nothing. I try the Milwaukee Journal, the Slinger Weekly Sentinel, and the Wisconsin Pennysaver, and come up empty. I try the listings of Chicago-area funerals, cremations, and weekly burials, and get bupkis.

I'm just about ready to log off when I get a hit on an obscure website. *Die Hard Cub Fans* with the subhead: *People want their ashes scattered in Wrigley Field.*

I read and find the information unbelievable on a number of counts.

I call Tiffany.

"I found something. Did you?" I ask.

"Of course not. I knew you would, so why would I waste my time?"

Some assistant I've got.

I tell her what time to pick me up tomorrow. Actually, I tell her to pick me up an hour before we really have to leave, after considering she exists on *Tiffany time.*

"Dad," Kelly asks me before bed, "what fun things do you have planned for us to do tomorrow?"

"None."

"You don't expect us to hang around here all day?"

"I have to work to make money to pay for the horse camp you're no longer attending."

"Can't you do that later?"

"No, I'm on a case."

"We can help."

"No, you can't."

"Why not?"

"Because this is a very slow case, very boring, kind of like walking around nose to butt."

"Heck, we can handle that. We'll go with you."

"No, thanks."

"It's the least we can do to help out," Kelly says. "Where are we going?"

"A celebration of life."

"Oh, great," Kelly says. "I love parties."

# CHAPTER 6

Tiffany shows up exactly one hour after I told her to arrive, which is actually the time I wanted her to be here.

"Well hello, little dudettes."

"Tiffany!"

Why do teenage girls always have to screech and scream?

"Why are you so sad?" Care, the more observant of my two, asks.

Tiffany, who's dressed in a black dress, black shoes, black purse, and black hat with a black gauze veil over her face, says, "I'm not sad. What would I ever have to be sad about?"

"You're all in black."

"I thought that would be the couture of choice for today."

"You said we were going to a party today, Dad," Kelly says, giving me the eye. "What is it, some kind of happy funeral?"

"Kinda."

We pile into Tiffany's Lexus and drive over to what was once my house. I find the key, not well hidden under the doormat, let the girls in, and tell them, "Hurry up, or we're going to miss the celebration."

I return to sit in the car and wait with Tiffany.

"Why don't you go in and help them, Mr. Sherlock?"

"I'm not allowed in what used to be my house."

"Used-to-be's don't count anymore, Mr. Sherlock."

"You hear that in a Neil Diamond song?"

"No, I just made it up."

The girls come out of the house twenty minutes later, looking cute in summer dresses.

"Dad, I don't have anything to wear," Kelly complains.

"If that was true, Kelly, you'd be sitting in your underwear."

Tiffany takes the expressway. We exit at Addison, head toward the lake, and turn left on Sheffield.

"There's not too many churches around here, Mr. Sherlock."

"I'll bet there's been more prayers said in there than any church in Chicago." I point to the backside of Wrigley Field.

"You sure you know where we're going?"

"That's the place, right there."

"Murphy's Bleachers?"

Located not too far from the left-field entrance to the park, Murphy's Bleachers is a Chicago bar known to be one of the rowdiest places on earth before, after, and during a Cub game.

"I got dressed up in funeral clothes to go to Murphy's Bleachers?" Tiffany laments. "What's next, wearing Dior to the Lincoln Park Lagoon?"

Tiffany parks in a handicapped spot, hangs the placard on the rearview mirror, and the four of us exit the car.

Wrigleyville is quiet, which means the Cubs must be out of town. There are only a few tables occupied on Murphy's outdoor front patio.

"With kids, you have to sit out here and order food," a behemoth guy in an XXL Cub jersey tells us as we enter.

"What's going on inside?" Kelly asks the man.

"Ash-hole day."

There's a reason why they call them *Diehard Cub Fans.*

For over 108 years the Cubs went without winning a World Series. The futility of the team may not have been responsible for many immediate deaths, but I'm sure it contributed so much heartache and disappointment, it probably sped up the process for a lot of Cub fans. Some of whom didn't want their devotion to end because they died, so they would will their ashes be spread over the Wrigley Field infield. Whether any ashes ever got spread is pure conjecture, but the number of requests were so great that, over twenty years ago, the club had to issue the ultimatum of NO ASHES, NO WAY, to anyone considering such action. I wonder now, since the Cubs have broken the Curse of the Billy Goat and won the World Series, if the requests will increase, but for a totally different reason.

As a poor replacement for personal ash spreading, one day a year a celebration takes place where Diehard families gather together with urns of remains to pay homage to their loved ones' devotion to their favorite team. Today is that day.

"You guys order," I tell my crew. "I'm going inside to check out the services."

"I'm going with you," Tiffany says.

"We'll get a couple of brewskis and just chill," Kelly tells me.

Inside there are about thirty urns lined up on the bar, each with a photo of the deceased wearing a Cubs hat, jersey, or full uniform. Family members of the dead are packed in tighter than a nose-to-butt horse ride. They mill about with beers or cocktails in hand, happily or unhappily chatting up or weeping alongside other Cub fans.

I tell Tiffany, "You start on the left. I'll start on the right. Try to find the guy who looks like the guy holding up the fish."

"I bet I'll smell him first."

"And if you do find him, remember we're operating incognito today, Tiffany."

"Ten-four, Mr. Sherlock."

Behind the bar, black crepe paper has been hung on much of the Cub paraphernalia. It looks like fandom with a Satanic bent.

I work my way from the outside, and about halfway in, I find my dead guy. It's Buck, leaning up against his urn. In the photo, he's close in age to his fishing picture, dressed in a full Cub uniform, holding a Louisville Slugger, with a chaw of tobacco bulging out from his left cheek. Chewing tobacco is much more cancerous than smoking tobacco, if you didn't know.

"Is that him, Mr. Sherlock?" Tiffany comes up behind me and asks.

"Yes."

"How do you know? He's not holding a fish."

"You can see the tattoo on his arm and his name's at the bottom of the picture, Tiffany."

"When it comes to detecting, Mr. Sherlock, you are the best."

We move forward to get a closer look and I hear, "You knew my brother Buck?"

I turn to the voice and see a guy who looks like a small-size Grizzly Adams. Bushy dark hair, beard down to his chest, well-worn Levis, enough dirt under his fingernails to plant corn, and bad teeth. The guy could eat corn through a picket fence.

"Indirectly," I answer.

"I only wish he could have lived to see the last out in game seven." The man looks to the sky as if he's channeling God. "I'm Cato, Buck's younger brother."

"Richard."

The crowd is loud; we have to pretty much scream to be heard.

"I can feel your pain," Tiffany says.

Behind Cato is a diminutive little woman of Asian origin, a massive plus-sized woman I wouldn't want to meet in a dark alley, and a medium-sized African-American woman who would win the looks contest of the three, but not many other competitions. The latter two are forty-something, the first, early thirties, or maybe even late twenties.

"Buck died a couple of seasons too soon?" I ask.

"Went off a cliff," Cato says.

"Suicide?" Tiffany asks.

"No," the big woman states emphatically. "He was up there trying to find his inner self."

I wonder if he was at the same camp as my ex-wife.

"It seems to me," Tiffany says, "it would be pretty easy to find yourself. All you need is a mirror."

"I believe she's referring to the emotional aspect of the term." I turn to the big woman. "Hi, I'm Richard."

She puts out her meat-hook hand to shake. "Blanche, Buck's wife."

The Black woman behind Cato immediately puts out her hand to shake, and when I extricate myself from Blanche, I move on to her paw.

"Travianna. I'm Buck's other wife."

"No one's speaking to you," Blanche snaps at her.

"I'm just as much Buck's wife as you're Buck's wife."

"Knock it off, would you two?" Cato admonishes the pair, screaming louder than the crowd around us. "We're at a funeral, remember?"

"Which one of you was numero uno?" Tiffany asks the women.

"Me," Blanche says.

"But I was his favorite," Travianna says.

"No, you weren't."

"Of course I was." Travianna raises her voice. "He obviously didn't like you, so he went out and found me."

"When he was taking out the trash."

"So he divorced you?" Tiffany asks Blanche.

"No, of course not. We were together until forever ended."

"So were we," Travianna says.

This is confusing.

"Enough," Cato orders, then waits for quiet, and asks me, "How did you know my older brother?"

"We never really met him," Tiffany pipes up. "We're just trying to find out if he's really dead."

I look at Tiffany with shock written in capital letters across my forehead.

"What?" Cato bellows out.

"Yeah, we saw him on a dating site not too long ago," Tiffany continues.

"That's impossible," both wives say in unison.

"Who the hell are you?" Cato asks.

"Tiffany Richmond. I'd shake hands, but yours seems to have been in places I wouldn't want to visit."

"Richmond, as in Richmond Insurance?" Cato asks.

"How'd you guess?" Tiffany says.

"The crooks that won't pay us our money?" Blanche is livid.

"You came here to check up on his death?" Travianna adds.

"Well, we certainly wouldn't come here for the food," Tiffany explains. "Everything on the menu is a cholesterol cluster bomb."

"You don't believe he's dead?" Cato continues his question tirade.

"I certainly hope not," Tiffany says.

"You want proof, little lady? Hold out your hand."

Tiffany puts forward her black-gloved right hand.

Cato grabs the urn, pops the top, reaches in for a handful, and deposits the *remains* on Tiffany's palm. "That enough proof for you?"

I step between the two. "I'm sorry, we're here merely to do a follow-up on the death of your brother."

"You want to do a follow-up, buddy?" Cato yells at me. "Then follow up with the million bucks."

This is not going well. Time to exit stage left.

"It was very nice to meet all of you. I assure you the claim is in process and I'm so sorry for your loss."

I take Tiffany by the arm and pull her away from the Crouch family or families, out of the building to the patio outside, where Kelly and Care are munching down on burgers and mounds of French fries.

"Tiffany, what were you doing in there? I told you we were going in incognito."

"I thought in-cog-neato was Italian for something really cool inside a cog."

31

Oh jeesh.

Before she sits down at the table, Tiffany asks, opening her palm, "What should I do with this?"

I look down on the ashes. "Next time you're at a Cub game, wait till no one's watching, and toss it on the infield."

## CHAPTER 7

"**P**ay them the money, Tiffany."

"No."

"You don't have a choice."

"Yes, I do."

"You had what's left of dearly departed Buck in the palm of your hand. What more do you need?"

"We're not giving up, Mr. Sherlock. Those could be bogus ashes."

"That's the spirit, Tiffany," Kelly says from the back seat of the Lexus.

"Never say die," Care adds with an oddly fitting choice of words.

"See? Your children agree with me, Mr. Sherlock."

I try to turn toward her, but my back won't let me. "There's something else going on here. What is it, Tiffany?"

"Why would you say that, Mr. Sherlock?"

"Because you're about as good keeping secrets as Wikileaks."

"Wiki-who?"

"Is that in Hawaii, Dad?" Care asks.

"Are you taking us to Hawaii?" Kelly adds. "It's about time."

"No, no, and no." I pause. "Own up, Tiffany. What's going on?"

Tiffany taps a perfect fingernail against her perfect front teeth.

"Daddy's put me on communion."

"Communion?"

"He said I have to start earning my keep—"

"You mean commission?"

"Whatever. He's going to pay me a percentage of the money I save the company by my investigations."

"Your investigations?"

"Well, so to speak." Tiffany pauses and gets animated. "So we have to solve this case, Mr. Sherlock. You don't want to see me in the poorhouse, do you?"

"Tiffany, have you ever even seen a poorhouse?"

"Ah, duh, yeah. I take the elevator past the lower floors of my building every day."

"How much are you getting?"

"Ten percent."

"So, we break this case and you make a hundred grand?"

"If that's ten percent of a million, yeah."

"Wow, that's a lot of money," Care says.

"You have to help her, Dad," Kelly adds.

"What do I get out of the deal?"

"You already get paid, Mr. Sherlock."

"Not much."

"This is not the time to get greedy, Dad."

"We'll help, Tiffany. You can count on us," Kelly says.

This is all hard to believe.

"So, Tiffany, your trust fund has been cut off, and you got to work for a living?" I ask.

"Oh, no. Even Daddy can't touch my trust fund. What's at stake is my mad money. Like the money I'll need for a new car soon. I can't be seen riding around in this old thing forever."

Her Lexus is less than a year old.

"Tell you what, you can borrow my Toyota anytime you want."

"Oh my God, Mr. Sherlock. I wouldn't ride in that thing even after I was cremated."

We continue the ridiculous argument until she pulls the Lexus up in front of my building.

"Dudettes, you stay with me," she tells my girls.

"Where are you taking them?" I ask.

"First, home, where I can get out of these disgustingly depressing clothes, then to my spa, dinner, and a movie."

"Yes!" My two scream in tandem.

"How about me? Do I get to go?"

"You have work to do, Mr. Sherlock. Somebody has to get to the bottom of this case."

"So you can make your first communion?"

"Exactly."

Why bother arguing? I get out of the car. "Make sure the movie isn't R- rated."

"Oh, Dad, you are so uncool," Kelly says.

"Dad, be sure the air conditioning is on when we get back," Care says.

"Your wish is my command," I say facetiously.

"That's what I like to hear, Mr. Sherlock."

The Lexus speeds away. I make my way, very slowly, into the building, and even more slowly up the stairs and into the apartment. The girls could have saved themselves some time and taken their sauna here, because the place is as hot as a Thanksgiving Day oven.

I take more Advils, get the a/c going, sit down at my computer, and go to work. In the next six hours, this is what I discover:

Dr. Landis Keenshaw is the name of the Washington County Medical Examiner. He is the doc who studied and tried to autopsy the remains of Buck Crouch.

Buck's house was purchased before he was married to either of his wives, and the title remains in his name. The property is free and clear. I wish I had a house that was free and clear. Actually, I wish I merely owned a house, preferably with central air. Buck had a credit score of 790, drove a Ford Taurus, and paid his taxes on time, filing individually each year.

There is no record or records I can find of Buck marrying Blanche or Travianna. Ditto for Buck's divorces.

Buck was employed by the Chicago Underwear Company of Skokie, Illinois. For close to eighteen years, he was an on-the-road sox salesman, and the Salesman of the Year eleven of his eighteen years.

Buck bowled on Tuesday nights with a 157 average, for the Uptown Bowl Movements. He had never been arrested, gone to college, served in the military, or received a moving violation.

Oddly enough, I could find no medical records for Buck. He either hated doctors, practiced healthy voodoo, or sold his soul to the devil in exchange for perfect health. Right now, I'd gladly sell my soul for healthy lumbar vertebrae and a new air conditioner. Where is Beelzebub when you want to make a deal?

The APB on Buck didn't go out until days after his disappearance. Maybe they thought he was out selling socks, but since he didn't take his car, it seemed unlikely. Maybe he did go up the mountain, discovered his true self, but didn't like what he found and jumped off the side. Or maybe he liked what he found, jumped for joy, but landed a thousand feet down instead of on his feet. This way, he would have at least died happy.

Overall, from what I am able to find out, Buck seems like a

pretty good guy, except that he had two wives, abandoned both, and didn't pay his credit card bill before stealing away in the night. Hey, nobody's perfect.

In the hours of my search, what does jump out at me is the fact that nothing jumps out at me. In these cases there's always something screwy or wacky, or that comes out of left field, no Cub consideration intended. I run all I know through my head ten or twenty times and come to the conclusion I am getting absolutely nowhere on this case.

I call Bree Bisonette, pronounced Biz-o-nay, to go over the paperwork with her once again. The first request for the claim was made after his disappearance but before the discovery of the body, and rejected for lack of a death certificate. The last claim had all the bells, whistles, and body identification attached. There is still no will as far as Bree knows, which means the estate will go to the wife/wives or his brother, who is the next closest living relative.

I ask Bree if the fisherman who was looking for his nature girl ever got back to her.

"No, I mostly get creeps who ask me if I 'prefer bikini panties to a thong?' Or 'Would a pet boa constrictor bother me?'"

"You got to kiss a lot of frogs before you find your prince, Bree."

"Then I wish somebody would invent a lip condom."

That's not a bad idea.

"That woman call you yet?" she asks.

"What woman?"

"Said her name was Jupiter. She called about the Crouch case."

"What did she want?"

"You."

"Me?"

"She said she saw you today."

"She did?"

"At a Cub fan funeral, said she wants to meet you."

"Really?"

"It's bad enough I can't get a date, Sherlock, but being your dating service is as demeaning as fixing up OJ Simpson."

"It's a tough job, Bree, but somebody has to do it."

"I gave her your number. Was that okay?"

"Sure."

I haven't had a date since the flip phone was introduced.

"You find anything we can use to reject the claim, Sherlock?"

"No. It looks like Mr. Richmond will have to ante up for this one."

"Mr. Richmond's not going to like that. You want to be the one to tell him?"

"Can't."

"Why not?"

"He refuses to take my calls."

"I know the feeling," Bree says, but she's not talking business.

I thank her for her time, don't mention Tiffany's new "communion" payment plan, and tell her I'll keep her posted.

"By the way, Sherlock, know any wealthy single men looking to date a middle-aged corporate woman?"

The only guy I can think of is my 400-pound computer genius buddy Herman, or as Tiffany refers to him, Herman the Vermin. But I doubt Bree and Herman would make a good match, too much class for too much ass.

"No, but I'll keep an eye out for you."

## CHAPTER 8

Tiffany and my girls arrive back at the apartment a little after noon the next day.

"Did you crack the case yet, Dad?"

"No."

"Did you find out anything new?" Care adds.

"No."

"Why not?"

"I'm not sure if there's anything new to find out. The guy's dead, remember?"

"We have to do something, Mr. Sherlock," Tiffany tells me. "Quitters never finish because they quit before finishing."

Poetic.

"Okay then, fire up the Lexus. We have a doctor's appointment this morning."

"This is not the time to be taking time off for a hangnail, Mr. Sherlock. I got a hundred grand on the line."

I wish I did.

\*\*\*

In a number of scarcely populated rural counties in the Midwest, it is economically unfeasible to employ a full-time coroner. Instead, the doctors in the area take turns on a rotating basis. They pronounce the end, sign death certificates, visit crime scenes, and do any required autopsies.

Dr. Landis Keenshaw is one of these physicians. On this day, his waiting room is packed with teenage boys. Kelly is in heaven.

"Mr. Sherlock, he'll see you now," the receptionist calls out.

"Dad, I'll stay here," Kelly says.

Tiffany, Care, and I are escorted into the doctor's small office.

"I apologize if we're interrupting your schedule of patients today, Doctor."

"Don't fret an instant," the cordial country doctor, who looks like he stepped out of a Norman Rockwell painting, tells us. "School's about to start and the boys need an examination to be able to play football. I've been grabbing privates and listening to coughs all morning."

Hearing this, I pray Care doesn't ask any questions.

"What does the cough tell you?" Tiffany asks.

"If they're healthy enough to perform," the doc tells her.

"I might try that next time around," Tiffany says. "Nothing's worse than getting on the field and not being able to get in the game."

I should have expanded my prayer reach.

Before anyone says another word, I ask, "Doctor, why didn't you perform an autopsy on Buck Crouch?"

"There wasn't much to work with," he says. "A body left out in the four seasons decays at a much faster rate than the urban corpse, shall we say. His remains froze and thawed multiple times, washing away the fluids. Add in the dirt, leaves, and what the animals gnawed on, and there wasn't a lot left to work with."

"Broken bones?"

"Lots. I didn't bother to count."

"How about his teeth?"

"A number were broken or missing. I didn't believe there was enough to make a mold."

"His eyes?"

"Eyes are one of the first organs to decay due to the amount of fluids within."

Care enters the conversation. "Why do people's eyes stay open after they die?" She asks what I consider a very good question.

"Because they want to see who killed them, or who's standing around waiting to get their money," Tiffany answers.

"Ah, no," Dr. Landis says. "Because once deceased, the muscle in the eyelid has no power to close itself."

"Good answer," Care says.

"Doctor, there's really only one question I have to ask," I say.

"Please do."

"With all the decay, animal snacks, and ravages of the four seasons, how was the Cubs tattoo on his arm able to survive?"

"A very good question," Dr. Landis says. "One I asked myself." He removes his wire-rimmed glasses, thinks a bit before he speaks. "First of all, that section of his upper arm was positioned under the torso of his body when he came to his last landing spot. Being partially covered is one explanation, but the more prevalent reason was that the ink under the skin worked as a preservative. Considering how cave drawings last for centuries, I surmise it worked on the same principle."

"Then should some of the DNA still exist?"

"Possibly, but DNA can be compromised, both while living and after death."

"I thought DNA was DNA, Doc."

"It is, but what we put into our bodies and what happens to our bodies can change the make-up of our cellular structure. Consider a person who has smoked for forty years. His original DNA doesn't have a chance after being inundated by the toxins from the thousands of cigarettes he's smoked."

"Listen to the doctor, Care. That's why you never start smoking."

"In cases where a desecrated body is found, DNA is unable to be used as identification."

"Thank you, Doctor."

We pick up Kelly in the waiting room where she's holding court with three or four boys.

The high school years are going to be a challenge.

\*\*\*

We're in the Lexus, speeding towards the Wisconsin/Illinois border.

"Did you learn anything that can help our case, Mr. Sherlock?" Tiffany asks.

"No."

"Maybe you're not asking the right questions."

"I didn't hear you asking any, Tiffany, except the one about coughing."

"I didn't want to get in the way of your choo-choo train of thoughts."

"Your cordiality never ceases to amaze me."

"I amaze lots of people, Mr. Sherlock."

The *Welcome to Illinois* sign flies by.

"You want to know what I learned, Tiffany? I learned there was no blood evidence, no DNA, or autopsy. Dr. Keenshaw used height, hair color, and a preserved tattoo to identify the body. And since it was good enough for him, it's good enough in the eyes of the law, and plenty good enough for heirs to get the money from his life insurance policy, which they deserve."

"Bad attitude, Mr. Sherlock, we already knew all that."

"You should be trying to learn something new every day, Dad." Kelly tosses back at me what I tell her each morning before dropping her off at school.

Nothing's worse than when your kids use your own words against you.

"Dad, can we make a stop on the way home?" Care asks.

"Care, I told you to use the bathroom before we left."

"Not that. I want to stop and see how Miss Buttonwillow is doing?"

"Who?"

"Miss Buttonwillow, our horse."

"I thought your horse's name was Spanky?"

"We changed her name to Buttonwillow."

"Actually, we changed it to Mare-a-lee We Ride before we changed it again to Buttonwillow."

Horse has had more names than a phone book.

"Good call, girls," Tiffany says. "A girl horse named Spanky is a little creepy."

"Can we stop, Dad?"

"Sure, and why don't I drop you off so you can enjoy the rest of the money I've already spent for you to attend the horse camp you both couldn't wait to go to?"

"No, Dad, bad idea," Kelly says.

"Why?"

"Because we're busy helping Tiffany work on the case."

"And thank God they are, Mr. Sherlock, since you're hardly tearing up the playing field with all you've done so far."

\*\*\*

The Trip and Trot Horse Camp and Stable is located about ten miles northwest of Libertyville, Illinois. The owners of the establishment must have been going for an authentic western, rustic look because every structure seems to be ready to collapse from the next strong wind.

Tiffany pulls up between the outdoor rink and the barn.

"Okay, go find your horse if that's what you want to do."

My girls pile out of the back seat, and when they do, the car is engulfed with an air so unpleasant, it sticks to your skin like acid rain.

"Ick! What's that smell?" Tiffany hollers as she adjusts the car's a/c to full throttle.

"Future fertilizer would be a good guess, Tiffany."

"Oh my God, it's one hundred times worse than nature. I'm going to need emergency aromatherapy before it damages my nostrils."

My cell phone rings. I don't recognize the number on the screen, but I answer anyway. "Hello."

A woman's voice asks, "Is this Richard Sherlock?"

"Yes."

"You don't know me, but I was at Murphy's the day of the Cub Fan Funeral."

"Your name?"

"Jupiter."

"Who is it, Mr. Sherlock?" Tiffany asks, obviously able to breathe again and be her nosy self.

"Excuse me one second." I put my hand over the cell phone speaker. "It's personal, Tiffany."

"I don't care. You talk in my car, you have to tell me who it is."

I pull the catch for the door, swing it open, letting the putrid air return in force, and Tiffany immediately wilts like a daisy in the desert.

"That's not fair."

She doesn't follow me out of the car as I walk upwind.

I'm back on the call. "What can I do for you, Jupiter?"

"I'd like to meet you." She pauses. "I got your number from a lady at Richmond Insurance."

"Why do you want to meet?"

"I'd like to talk with you."

"About?"

"Us."

"When?"

"Tonight."

"Where?"

"There's a little place, 3300 north on Damen, called the Four Treys."

"I know the place."

"Seven?"

"Fine with me," I tell her. "One more question: is Jupiter

your first or last name?"

"It's my only name."

As I hang up the phone, Kelly and Care come running up.

"We can't find Buttonwillow."

"She's probably out doing the nose-to-butt thing."

"Can we wait for her to come back so we can say 'hello'?"

"No, we have to get back into the city."

"Why?"

"'Cause your dad's got a date.

\*\*\*

Tiffany drops us off at our apartment and hurries off to the Purity of Life Institute for an hour in the Michael Jackson Memorial hyperbaric oxygen chamber and a "bottom-up cleanse," as she refers to the additional procedure she scheduled.

I wish her the best.

I get the apartment a/c cranked up and order a pizza while the girls sit in front of a blaring TV and play with their cell phones.

Before I leave for the Four Treys, I repeat the rules: "Don't leave. Don't buzz anybody into the building. And never open the front door for anyone."

"Yeah, right, Dad."

\*\*\*

Four Treys is an old, family-owned tavern that has seen its neighborhood change more times than a runway model during Fashion Week. The place is old, dark, comfortable, dart- and dog-friendly. I walk into Treys a few minutes before seven and find two empty seats at the bar. One I sit on. The other I will attempt to reserve. I order a light beer.

I have an oddball memory that allows me to see a particular scene and never forget it. This, for a cop, can be a blessing and a curse. Great for remembering clues, but I'd give anything to erase the image of a triple mafia hit I saw of three victims of two shotguns in a two-chair barbershop. Try to get that picture out of your head.

I recreate in my head the scene at Murphy's: There's the

urns on the bar, the black bunting on the Cubs stuff, and a whole lot of diehard Cub fans, both alive and dead. I get an image of the crowd, but am unable to see anyone who could be named Jupiter, or was orb-like in appearance.

Ten minutes later, I might as well be having a Woodstock flashback, even though the closest I ever got to Woodstock was renting the movie. The woman is about five foot, slight, wearing a frilly summer dress with enough tie-dyed patterns to dizzy Dizzy Gillespie. Her jet-black hair is down to her waist, braided Pocahontas style. Her ears are pin-cushion pierced and her fingers laden with so many rings, she'd be deadly in a bar fight.

She walks right up to me without hesitation, puts out her hand to shake, and says, "Richard Sherlock, I'm Jupiter."

I stand. "Nice to meet you."

"You remember me now?"

"No." And I have no idea how I couldn't. The woman sticks out like a swollen thumb at a marble-shooting tournament.

"Have a seat. Would you like a drink?"

"I'll have a Potawatomi Pale Ale."

"What's that?"

"Craft beer Indian style."

"What kind?"

"*How* Indian, not *Dothead*," she explains, raising her right hand upward.

"Have you always been into Native American spiritual suds?"

"Yeah, ever since I found it's got eleven percent alcohol to help the spirits along."

We get as comfortable as you can get on bar stools, and after her Potawatomi Pale arrives, we clink bottles.

"So, do you call unknown men out of crowds often?" I ask, trying to be cute.

"I knew who you were."

"How?" I try not to sound too Potawatomi-ish.

"I heard you speaking with Cato Crouch."

"You know Cato?'

"Indirectly."

"Through his wife?"

"Which one?"

"You pick."

"The Black one isn't bad, but Big Bad Blanche, that chick's

whacked." She takes a long swig and says, "I overheard you say you were the investigator from the insurance company."

"You overhear anything else that tickled your chakra?"

"That young babe you were there with is a little on the whacked side herself."

If Jupiter only knew how spacy Tiffany actually is.

"I want to hire you, Mr. Sherlock."

"To do what?" My mind races with possibilities, all of which are major male ego boosters.

"Investigate."

So much for my prowess as dating material.

"But I don't have any money," she adds. "I could pay you with positive spiritual vibes."

Which is a lot more than I'll get from Tiffany's communion money.

"What do you want me to do?" I ask.

"Find Buck."

"I did. He was in the urn on the bar."

"No, he wasn't. Buck's not dead. He's out there somewhere and I want you to find him."

I try not to look too shocked.

"Why?"

"I'm still in love with him."

It usually takes me three or four dates with a woman before she tells me, "I've decided to go back with my old boyfriend." But to be told she's going back to a guy who's already dead puts me into a whole new class of *failed-rebound boyfriend.*

"You sure this isn't some spiritual thing where you're looking to hook up with Buck in the netherworld?"

"No, he's out there, alive and kicking. I can feel it."

"How can you be so sure?"

"I've been gifted with a spiritual sensitivity that allows me to see into the unseen, ethereal universe with incredible accuracy."

"That must make you fun at parties."

"I was conceived in the Summer of Love, raised in a commune, and given, by heredity, psychic powers of observation."

"That's impressive, but I don't know if that's enough to overrule ashes in an urn, Jupiter."

"He disappeared, didn't he? And you certainly can't blame

45

him for that; you met Blanche, his first wife."

Jupiter has a point.

"And he emptied out his bank account, left like a thief in the morning, and disappeared without being noticed by anyone."

"Then he tripped on a mountain, fell a thousand feet, and died a horrible death."

"Nope, I don't buy it. My third eye tells me different."

"Jupiter, what's your connection to Buck?"

"Soul mates."

I should have guessed.

"I was his muse, guiding light, friend, confidant, spiritual advisor, and pickle ball partner."

"That all?"

"Plus, we were really good in the sack together."

"Were you ever married to Buck?"

"We didn't need some flimsy paper marriage certificate. We had the moon and the stars traveling in concurrent orbits, which sealed our bond like gin and tonic, fire and brimstone, and peanut butter and jelly."

"How long were you and Buck an item?"

"Off and on for eighteen years."

Eighteen years? I do some quick figuring in my head.

"But didn't Buck marry two other women during that time?"

"I didn't say it was a relationship without its bumps."

"Jupiter, maybe you're merely having a difficult time letting Buck go. Grief can be a funny thing."

"Nope. He's alive. I know it. And I want you to find him."

"Why me?"

"You got good vibes. I can feel them."

"Really? How do they feel?"

"Soft and squishy."

# CHAPTER 9

I can't sleep.
It could be because I'm on the couch sweating, I drank a Potawatomi Pale Ale, or because my back is going through one conniption fit after another, but the reality is I can't sleep because I'm wondering if Jupiter could be right.

If Buck is still alive, the claim will be dismissed, Bree will be a Richmond hero, Tiffany gets her hundred grand, Jupiter's chakra gets spiritual kudos, and there will be a very strange homecoming with two wives and one girlfriend in attendance. But there are a few hurdles I have to get over, and with my bad back, they won't be easy. These include an urn full of ashes, a stamped death certificate, an unknown geocacher, and the answers to the questions why a human being would want a Cubs tattoo on their upper arm, and if it wasn't Buck, whose body was it?

And if I do figure it all out, what good will it do me? Nothing.

I hate my job.

I get up off the couch, lie on the floor with my feet up on the couch cushions, and think.

People who disappear will go to great lengths to disappear. Most choose water as their cover of choice. They have an empty boat wash ashore, leave clothes on the beach, tack a suicide note on the Tallahatchie Bridge, vanish from a cruise ship, or post a selfie on Facebook of themselves on the shore facing away from approaching alligators in the background.

People who disappear get caught because they return to their roots in some way, shape, or form. They miss their wives, need money, their cell phone gets tapped, or their email gets discovered. It's not easy to *leave it all behind*, especially if you have a family, and that family isn't as careful as you thought they'd be. And it's even harder to dispose of your old personality. You have to lie constantly, can't fly, rent a car, or get insurance. To start over, you need a new birth certificate, social security card, driver's license, credit history, and resume for employment. Most of these you can purchase on the internet with few questions asked, but it's not easy becoming a whole new person. It is estimated that ninety per cent of the disappearing folk get caught, emerge from the shadows, or return to their former selves because they found themselves worse off as someone new than as the jerk they were before.

If Buck did pull it off, where could he be? And where would I start looking? Skip tracer Larry Flemm with two m's had no luck finding him, and he's supposedly an expert. And if I do find the guy, I get a ride in Tiffany's new top-of-the-line Lexus. Whoopee.

I would love to put this all to bed, alongside myself, but there is one aspect that's bugging me. Who gets the million dollars?

***

"Where are you taking us today, Dad?" Kelly asks, as she munches on her toast.

"Who said I was taking you anywhere?" I return, answering her question with a question, which is a verbal tactic I personally hate when reversed.

"Your child's vacation responsibility, as a father, is to entertain us."

"May I remind you, Kelly, you have many fun activities waiting for you at the Trip and Trot Summer Horse Camp."

"Dad, we've been there and done that."

Care comes in and joins the conversation. "Dad, whatever fun things you had planned for next week, can we just move them up to this week?"

"You assume I had plans for next week?"

"Yes."

"First rule of life: Assume nothing."

"Dad, this isn't fair. We need to be entertained."

"Call Tiffany. Maybe she has plans," I suggest.

"Tiffany won't be up. She needs her beauty sleep."

"And that's my problem?"

"Dad, we can't hang around here all day. What are we going to do?" Kelly asks, exasperated.

"Vacuum, clean the bathrooms, dust, do the laundry; there's lots to occupy your time."

"Dad, we're on vacation."

"You two made the choice of leaving the Trip and Trot, and now you have to deal with it. Welcome to real life, ladies."

The sisters sulk off to watch TV and play with their phones.

Two seconds before I'm leaving the kids to fend for themselves, the a/c unit starts to sputter, puffs out some smoke, and exhales like a defective Whoopie Cushion. If I leave them in this hothouse apartment, they could bake like a slow-cooked roast.

"Get dressed, get in the car, let's go."

"Are we going to Six Flags?" Care asks.

"No."

"Are we going shopping?" Kelly asks.

"You go shopping all the time."

"I know, and I can't wait to go back."

"No. We're not going shopping."

"Then where are we going, Dad?"

"To offer our condolences."

\*\*\*

Realtors say, "Buy the worst house on the best street." Buck must have listened because he achieved the goal, except the part about the best street.

His house is a small, two-bedroom claptrap on a dead-end street off Lawrence Avenue, on the edge of the city in a neighborhood of aging ranch houses that were architectural travesties when they were built. The only thing missing in Buck's front yard is a decaying 1960's Ford pickup truck with four flat tires. No wonder nobody saw Buck leave. Who would ever want to get close to this dump?

"Who lives here?" Care asks from the back of my Toyota.

"The wife of the guy who's already dead."

"Why are we here?" Kelly asks.

"To grieve."

The temperature has already hit the nineties, and the girls jump out of the car before it becomes an oven. I tell them to be careful of the loose floorboards as we step onto the porch, where I also notice an oddly placed vertical white line painted down the front door.

Knock, knock.

"Who's there?"

"It's Richard Sherlock. We met at Murphy's Bleachers."

Another female voice: "Who?"

"The guy from Richmond Insurance."

A verbal duet returns. "You got our money?"

The front door swings open.

On the left side of another white line drawn down the middle of the room stands Big Blanche, and on the right side, Black Travianna. Both are surrounded by a forest full of animals, some complete, some partial. Moose, three deer, antelope, and what I believe is a gazelle, ducks, geese, fox, and armadillo twins. And this is just what's mounted and stuffed in the front room. Buck's house is a dead animal dump. There's a beaver, ram, mountain lion, and the head of an elk mounted on the dining room wall.

"No bear?" I ask.

"He missed."

"I've often wondered: if you shot another hunter, would you get to stuff him too?" I ask.

"Only if he shot at you first."

There is also a glass case of hunting rifles, which are thankfully locked up.

And to make the design of the home really come together, the remaining décor of the house is a testament to art being in the eye of the beholder. At first it reminds me of the walls of Care and Kelly's kindergarten classrooms on Parents' Night. Every conceivable inch of space in Buck's house is filled with art so hideous and un-artful, a six-year-old's finger painting would be a welcome relief. This stuff makes *The Original Carlo* look like a Renoir.

I can feel the soothing cold air inside.

"Can we come in? It's a bit warm out here."

"Yeah," Blanche says, opening the door wider, "but that's my cold air you're breathing."

"I pay half the electric bill," Travianna says.

"These are my kids, Kelly and Care."

"Nice to meet you," they say in unison.

I point to the chalk drawn on the floor. "What's that?"

"Our Mason-Dickson Line," Blanche says.

"House is just as much mine as it is hers," Travianna explains.

"You share everything here?"

"Yeah, and it ain't easy," Travianna answers.

"It seems you had a lot of practice at it, since you did share a husband."

"You got our money?" Big Blanche bellows.

"I'm working on it," I assure them.

"Work harder."

I peer around the house and see middle-of-the-floor chalk lines in every room. "How many bathrooms in this house?" I ask.

"One."

"I hope the dividing line runs right through the toilet."

"Where's our million bucks?" Travianna cries out.

"Funny you should ask," I say. "One of the aspects of the case, not yet known, is who gets the money once it is disbursed."

"Me."

"Me, too," Travianna adds. "I'm just as much a wife as you are."

"Let me guess," I say to wife number two. "You moved in here to stake your claim on your portion of the estate?"

"Damn right I did."

Death doth maketh strange bedfellows.

"What does Buck's will specify?"

"Beats me," Travianna says.

"Is there one?"

"We don't know."

"Is there an executor?"

"Cato's doing that," Blanche says.

"You draw straws?"

"No, we had a vote. Guess who won."

Out of nowhere, Care asks the two, "How many TV's do you have?"

"One."

"I bet that's a problem," Kelly comments.

"Especially when I'm CNN and she's Fox News," Travianna explains.

"Do you really think Buck's dead?" I ask.

"Of course he's dead." Blanche points to the urn on the fireplace mantle.

"He couldn't live without us," Travianna adds.

"He couldn't live without me," Blanche corrects her fellow wife.

"He sure didn't seem to be having a problem with that when he was with me," Travianna argues.

"Look," Blanche says, "all we want is our money so we can get past all this, and she can move out of my house."

"Our house."

"I'm sorry for your loss," I tell them.

"Yeah, right," Blanche says.

Kelly and Care wander around the deceased forest friends.

"Before Buck left was there any discussion, warning, or suspicion he was leaving?" I ask.

"He was acting a little weirder than usual, but nope, he never said a word," Travianna tells me.

"Were you surprised?"

"I thought he was with her and she thought he was with me," Blanche says.

"Why do you think he left?" I ask,

"Her."

"No, her."

"Besides Cato, does he have any other living relatives?"

"Don't think so," Blanche says. "I never met his mother and his old man was nuts."

"How did he get along with his brother?"

"Buck used to say they were Cain and Unable," Travianna quotes.

"Unable?"

"Buck called him 'Unable' because he was unable to hold a job."

I say as I look around the room, "I see he was quite the outdoorsman."

"Buck hated being indoors. Every chance he got he was fishing, hiking, hunting, exploring; he loved being out in God's country."

"He take you with him?"

"Once. That was enough for me," Blanche admits. "I don't do well without a toilet."

"Buck hated civilization," Travianna adds. "Not me, though."

"When do we get our money?" Blanche asks again.

"These things take time," I tell them. "Patience is a virtue."

"I hate patience," Blanche says.

"So do we," Kelly adds.

"By the way, you wouldn't happen to have Cato's address?"

"I don't," Blanche says. "Ask her."

Thankfully, I don't have to repeat the question.

"I'll get it," Travianna says, disappearing into a bedroom.

I stand admiring—actually dis-admiring—the festooned walls, and see a pattern to the pathetic paintings and awful artwork.

"Quite a display," I comment.

"Yeah, real museum pieces."

Travianna returns and hands me a slip of paper with an address.

"Thanks." I motion to my kids *We're outta here*, and head for the front door.

"And you tell that jerk Cato, he tries to screw with us, he'll end up like Buck's animals," Blanche says as we head out.

I'm not sure what that entails, and don't really want to know.

We get back to find my Toyota on broil. The steering wheel is so hot I have to put on gloves to touch it. I must look cute wearing winter mittens in ninety-degree heat.

"Roll down the windows. Once we get moving, it won't be so bad."

"Dad, I think you have serious air conditioning issues," Kelly tells me.

"Let me tell you, air conditioning pales in comparison to the rest of my issues."

My cell phone rings.

It's Tiffany.

I can't answer because I have no fingers. I hand the phone to Kelly. "Here, you talk to her."

"Hello."

I hear through the phone's speaker, "Where are you, Mr. Sherlock? I've been calling for four minutes."

"Hi, Tiffany. It's Kelly."

"Good morning, little dudette."

Morning? It's twenty minutes after noon.

"Where are you people?" Tiffany asks.

"We're leaving this house with dead animals, where two people had to share one TV. It was horrible," Kelly tells her.

"You shouldn't be at a zoo doing TV surveys, you should be out working on the case," Tiffany replies.

"Ask her what she's done on the case today," I interrupt.

"Tiffany, I have a question," Kelly says putting the phone to her ear so Care and I can't hear. "When can we go shopping?" Kelly hesitates before adding, "With your money?"

"No, tell her we want to work on the case," Care orders from the back seat.

There is a pause while Kelly listens.

"Dad, Tiffany wants to know if you discovered a way to save her the million bucks."

"I discovered she should get her daddy to pay up and we can all forget this absurdity."

Kelly repeats, listens, and says to me, "Tiffany says that's a bad attitude."

"Well, I don't have a better one."

"Dad, Tiffany wants to know where we're going now."

"Tell her my two young daughters and I are going to check out what's new in the world of underwear."

"Tiffany says 'that's really creepy.'"

***

The Chicago Underwear Company is in Skokie, a misnomer in my book.

I'm in the office of Benny Ficus, the Director of Sales, while my girls are on the edge of the office cubicles, looking up at the display of the numerous undergarments on the wall. They take particular interest in the different types of men's briefs currently available.

"Why isn't this the Skokie Underwear Company?" I ask Benny.

"Don't know, never asked."

"Buck Crouch used to work here, correct?"

"For years. Guy could sell socks like nobody's business."

"But that was his business."

"Well, yeah."

"Do you miss him?"

"Not really."

"Buck was one of your top guys, right?"

"Truth be told, I was getting ready to fire him."

This is an interesting revelation.

"Why?"

"I'm not supposed to say."

"Why not?"

"Personnel Department said he could sue us."

"He's dead."

"You sure?" Benny Ficus asks before answering my question.

"Well, most people think so," I say. "Tell you what, I promise our conversation will be off the record."

"Well, Buck had a few discrepancies in his reporting methods," he tells me.

"Faking his sales or commission figures?"

"Worse than that. His expense account was an exercise in creative writing. The guy had more ways of cheating than a horny, philandering husband."

"He was pretty good at that too, if you didn't know," I tell him. "How long was it going on?"

"Years."

"And nobody noticed?"

"When a guy's selling that many socks, ya kind of look the other way. At least that's what the past three sales managers did before me."

"But you were going to blow the whistle?"

"It was really getting out of hand, or our pocket, in this case."

"Did Buck suspect he was on the way out?"

"Couldn't tell ya."

"Did you like him?"

"Everybody liked Buck because it's hard to dislike Buck. He was everybody's best buddy when he was here, but when I think back, Buck actually wasn't around much."

"Where was he?" I'm thinking he was busy servicing two wives.

"Buck loved being on the road. Sometimes we'd go weeks without seeing him. He phoned it in most of the time."

"How did he cheat on his expenses?"

"Mostly he'd get a cash advance, then fill in the form listing a lot more expenses, and we'd include those with the next upfront money he'd request."

"All cash?"

"On the barrelhead." Benny continues. "We tried to get him to use a company credit card, but he refused. They didn't push it since he was our number one guy. That Buck could sell socks."

"How well did you know him?" I ask.

"Not well. I knew he was a big Cubs fan, liked to fish, hunt, gamble, and had an eye for the ladies, but he wasn't the guy you'd invite over for dinner with the wives."

If you did, you'd have to put out an extra chair.

"Why are you asking all these questions?" Benny asks.

"I'm just trying to tie up some loose ends before the insurance company pays out on his life insurance." I pause, getting a new thought. "By the way, did Buck have a 401(k) or profit-sharing account with the company?"

"He did, but he cashed it in right before he left on his last sales trip."

"Thanks for your time."

"Let me ask you something," Benny says. "Boxers or briefs?"

"A little personal, isn't it?"

"Not around here."

I pick up the kids on the way out.

"Dad, why do some of the men's underwear have a pouch and others don't?" Care asks, pointing to items on the display.

"That's not a pouch," Kelly answers. "That's a package. God, don't you know anything?"

One of these days, I've got to sit down and have a long talk with my girls.

## CHAPTER 10

If Buck's house was a testimonial to dead animals and bad art, Cato's place is a tribute to the Airstream of old. Cato and wife live in a singlewide, parked in a trailer park in Batavia, a burb of Chicago. If it seems a bit worse for wear on the outside, inside its wear is much worse. If home is where the heart is, this one needs a transplant.

"You bring my money?" Cato's way of saying "Hello."

"Not yet. I thought I'd stop by so we could chat."

"About my money?"

"So to speak."

We enter the home as a group, which is difficult at best.

"Are you an investigator or a babysitter?" he asks.

"Today, both."

"Okay," Cato says, "let's talk about my money. When do I get it?"

"We're still in a pending investigation."

"What's to investigate?" Cato says. "Buck's dead. We have the death certificate, his ashes, and the report from the coroner. What more do we need, a signed statement from his guardian angel?"

"You have to believe me, Mr. Crouch, I'm on your side. For some reason, Richmond is putting me through hoops on this one." I'm not lying, just kinda lying.

"Why?"

"Well, his disappearance is a bit unsettling. Why do you think your brother just up and split?"

"You met his so-called wives, didn't you?"

"You think it was a spur-of-the-moment decision on his part?"

"I don't know and I don't care. What difference does it make?"

The only thing that holds Cato's ire back is his younger, Asian wife Estalita coming into the front area, offering Kelly and Care treats from a tray. I can't help but notice the rock on her married finger. Must have been a cubic zirconium sale on the Home Shopping Network.

"These are Filipino candies," Estalita says.

The girls don't hesitate to dig in.

"And what about a will?" I ask. "Richmond likes to know

where to send the money."

"Don't send it. I'll be more than happy to drop by and pick it up." The vein in his neck has swollen up like an Asian carp.

Cato should really work on controlling his temper or he'll end up having a stroke and not be able to enjoy the fruits of his brother's sock sales.

"Listen, insurance gumshoe, if I don't get my money pretty soon, I'm letting my lawyer loose, reporting you to the Illinois Insurance Board, and telling my story to one of those TV news investigative teams. I'll bring the Richmond Insurance Company to its knees. I'll get their name so muddied, the terminally ill wouldn't consider buying one of their crummy policies."

"But we have this picture of him on the internet—"

Cato gets a very odd expression on his face, points a finger at me, and says, "Forget that. It's a bunch of crap. It wasn't him."

Odd he remembers the photo.

"I'm telling you right now, don't cross Cato Crouch." Cato's so worked up his beard is bristling.

"I can hear you, Cato. I can hear you." I say one of my most hated phrases; it's even worse than "Oh, wow, that's totally awesome."

"Consider yourself warned."

Time to make an exit before Cato goes Ted Bundy on us.

"Girls, thank the nice lady for the treats."

"Thank you," they say in unison and take a couple of the snacks for the road.

"You're welcome," Estalita returns.

I hurry the girls out of the house and get into the car, which could double as a sauna on wheels. I put on the mittens, start the car, and we're off.

"Boy, I bet that guy is a load of laughs at his local Neo-Nazi meeting."

"Now where are we going, Dad, shopping?" Kelly asks.

"No."

"Malls are air-conditioned."

"Forget it, Kelly. Call Tiffany and ask her where she's taking us for dinner."

\*\*\*

Twenty years ago, Lula's was a four-table restaurant in heavily Hispanic Logan Square only cops and locals knew about. Today, it's a hip, gourmet-Mexican millennial hangout in a restored neighborhood few Hispanics or I can afford. The only reason Tiffany would ever venture this far from downtown is to be as hip as the hipsters she hip-hops and hangs with.

"I've been thinking a lot about this case, Mr. Sherlock."

This is frightening.

"And I think we're going about it all wrong." She sips on a margarita in a glass the size of a rain barrel.

"We?"

"While everybody else is proving he's dead," Tiffany says, "we should prove he's alive."

I might as well let this play out. "How so, Tiffany?"

"I read this story once where this guy faked his own death."

"Really? What was the name of the book?"

"Actually, it was a TV show on the Reality Channel," she admits. "This guy scams all this money, then pretends to jump into a river with piranhas that eat him totally up, and the only thing left is his leather jacket and his American Express card."

"Wow," Care says, "that is like totally gross."

"Not to the fish," I comment.

"That guy got caught, Mr. Sherlock."

"When the guy was seen running around naked in the jungle?" I ask.

"No, they caught him playing video poker on a riverboat in Iowa somewhere."

"I didn't know they had riverboats in Iowa, Tiffany."

"I wasn't sure they had rivers in Iowa until I saw the TV show," she admits.

"Tiffany, whether Buck Crouch disappeared or not, isn't the issue. It's the body with the matching Cubs tattoo, the report from the coroner, and the ashes in the urn that substantiate his death."

Tiffany gives me one of her *hard* looks. I'm sure she doesn't know what *substantiate* means.

The waitress comes over to take our order. Kelly gets a burrito, Care enchiladas, Tiffany a taco salad; adventuresome eaters all. I order something I can't pronounce.

"If they take us to court, using a reality TV show as the basis for your case could prove problematic."

"Then maybe we should work the suicide angle?"

"Why would Buck commit suicide? He was probably thrilled to get away."

"Mr. Sherlock, I'm getting the feeling that you're not on our side of the fence in this case."

"Yeah, Dad."

"Every logical argument I bring up, you shoot down like a lead balloon," Tiffany reasons.

"Lead balloons don't fly, Tiffany."

"Neither do pigs, Mr. Sherlock, but that doesn't stop people from using them for target practice."

Best to let that comment pass.

"It would be next to impossible to prove a suicide without a note," I tell her.

"So let's write one."

My cell phone rings. I see who is calling. "I got to take this."

"Who is it?" Tiffany asks.

I don't answer Tiffany. I stand, hear Care say, "Dad's got a girlfriend," and exit as quick as a Thoroughbred out of the gate.

"Hello, Jupiter."

"I've got one word for you, Sherlock."

"Just one?"

"Montana."

"Montana?"

"Yes, Montana."

"That's two words, Jupiter."

"Buck loves Montana. He goes there every chance he gets. Fishing, hunting, skiing, hiking, the Big Sky sky—he loves it."

"You're adding on words quite rapidly, Jupiter."

"Because that's where Buck is. I can feel it."

"And what does it feel like?"

"Like I'm right." She pauses and adds, "You got to get on this, Sherlock."

"Montana's a pretty big place, isn't it?" I ask.

"Huge."

"So where would you suggest I start my search?"

"I'm not sure."

"Well, tell you what," I say. "Why don't you hook up your ethereal feelings and Buck's inner vibes to a GPS system, and when you narrow it down to a time and place, give me a call."

"I will, Sherlock, and until I MapQuest this thing, don't be giving those no-good Crouch people any of Buck's money."

"Unfortunately, it's not my money to give out."

I return to the table. Three plates look like they came from a Taco Bell, while mine looks like a mash-up from a deranged South American foodie.

"Dad's got a girlfriend," Care starts the chant. "Dad's got a girlfriend."

"Who is she, Mr. Sherlock?"

"None of your business, Tiffany."

"You should tell me, Mr. Sherlock."

"Yeah, Dad, tell her," Kelly adds.

"Why should I?"

"Because when it comes to women, Mr. Sherlock, you need help."

"Who says?"

"Everybody," the three answer.

## CHAPTER 11

The apartment is as cold as a Whirlpool crisper drawer. Something must have gone wacko on the air conditioner, and it's been pumping cold air all day. My electric bill's going to rival the national debt.

"It's freezing in here, Dad. Turn up the heat."

I unplug the a/c.

The girls wrap up in blankets and sit in front of the TV on the couch that will be my bed soon.

"Dad," Care says, "why don't we put all the clues on *The Original Carlo* and figure out the case?"

*The Original Carlo* is an especially bad piece of art I bought years ago for eight dollars, frame and all. It doubles as a bulletin board for pinning up index card clues in some form of logical order, to help me make sense of mostly nonsense. And even after a number of cases, the painting still has fewer holes than most of the cases I have to work on.

"What's to pin up? We don't have any clues or even a crime for that matter, Care."

"Yeah, but it's fun to do."

My cell phone rings. Two calls in one night, that's a lot for someone who doesn't have many friends.

"Hello."

"If I have to go, you have to go."

"Go where?"

"Court."

"Why?"

"Oh, let me tell you," Bree Bisonette, pronounced "Biz-o-nay," says.

This should be good.

"I finally get a response on One Percent Singles dot com. I'm thrilled. His profile picture is great: 47, lots of hair, no gut, in a three-piece suit, divorced, no kids, loves to travel. Perfect. We meet at the Palm for lunch and he looks even better in person. He quit his job in the tech biz and is now in law school. He tells me he's had to pick up some oddball jobs in the interim, but he's about to take the bar and is sure it will be worth all the time and effort he's put in. He's open, cordial, conversational, the perfect gentleman. I'm in heaven, Sherlock."

"Congratulations, Bree."

"We get through lunch, we're having coffee, the check comes, and he reaches for it, but I beat him to it. 'Let me,' I tell him."

"'Oh, no. I can't let you do that,'" he says.

"'Your turn next time,' I tell him with a big smile on my face.

"We get up from the table and I'm about to give him a little good-bye kiss when he pulls out of his pocket an envelope. He says, 'This has really been fun, but before you go, I want you to have this.'" Bree pauses. "I'm figuring he's giving me his phone number."

Bree pauses again, this time a longer pause than the previous one.

"It's a summons to appear in court," Bree blurts out. "He was a process server!"

"You're kidding?"

"Not only did I get served, but I paid for lunch!"

I don't say it, but I'm thinking, "This guy's pretty darn clever."

"What case?"

"Buck Crouch."

"Who's suing?" I ask.

"Buck's brother, Cato."

Cato might have been a jerk, but so far he's a man of his word.

"Can't say he didn't warn us."

"You knew about this, Sherlock?"

"Well, he did make the threat when we visited the other day."

"Why didn't you warn me?"

"It was on my to-do list, Bree. Honest."

"I don't want to go to court."

"So don't. Pay him what you owe him, and let's put this case to bed."

"Can't."

"Why not?"

"Because when I told Mr. Richmond about the lawsuit, he dug his heels in even deeper. Evidently, someone has convinced him that Buck isn't dead, merely disappeared, and is bound to show up playing video poker on a riverboat on the Iowa River."

Gee, I wonder where that came from.

"Mr. Richmond has ordered me to hold off on any payment until there is total, unmitigated, absolute proof that Buck's as dead as a doornail."

Why are doornails always dead?

"As they say in legal circles, Sherlock, I'll see you in court."

She gives me the details. Before we part, I say, "One last question, Bree."

"What?"

"Do you think you'll see the process server guy again?"

"I'm thinking it over. He was really hot."

\*\*\*

The cold air in the apartment is causing my back to stiffen up like leftovers in the freezer. I hobble into the hall closet, pull out my Oriental Oscillator, and carry it back to the front room.

"What's that thing?" Care asks.

"Hopefully relief. My back's killing me."

"What's it going to do, roll you into a spring roll?" Kelly says as I find a spot on the floor and sit down.

"Dad, I'll be more than happy to walk barefoot on your back," Care, the more medically inclined of the two, says.

"No, thanks. I've been stepped on enough lately."

The Oriental Oscillator resembles a large abacus with four strands of rolling rubber balls; while you're soothing your sore vertebrae, you can also solve math problems. I place the contraption behind me, lie down, and push myself to and fro on the rolling rubber.

"You look like you're on a conveyor belt that's hiccupping, Dad," Care tells me.

Actually, my back's feeling a little better.

"Dad, are you going to be well enough to take us to the mall tomorrow?" asks Kelly, who is obviously unconcerned with my current pain and suffering.

"Hopefully, but no."

"What does that mean?"

"No mall."

"But I need new clothes for school."

"Ask your mother," I tell her, rocking back and forth.

"What are we going to do tomorrow, Dad?" Care asks.

"I have to go to court."

"Why's Mom taking you to court this time?" Care asks.

Before I have a chance to answer Care, Kelly says, "Oh, good. I'll get her to add a bigger clothing budget to whatever she's suing you for. I'll wear something crummy and the judge will be convinced just looking at poor, little me."

"And I'll take pictures of you dressed like Little Homeless Hannah and post them on Facebook, Kelly."

"That's not funny, Dad."

\*\*\*

I get the girls seated in the back row, point at the bailiff, and tell them, "Don't say anything or he'll throw you in jail." To make my point even clearer, I tell Kelly, "And you'll have to wear one of those orange and black striped jumpsuits."

Kelly's mouth clamps shut tighter than a clam.

My back is feeling a little looser, but I walk slowly to the front of the courtroom to meet Bree and Richmond's in-house counsel, Dewey Diddier, Esq.

Dewey is in his usual thousand-dollar suit and Bree's dressed as if she stepped out of an Ann Taylor website.

"What's our strategy?" I ask.

"I don't have one yet," Dewey says, "but don't worry. I'll come up with something."

Gee, great strategy.

Dewey's usual modus operandi in a case is to start telling lies, and keep telling lies until everyone's so confused over which lie he told, they don't know where to start contradicting. He was hired by Richmond not so much for his legal expertise, but on the notion that *It takes one to know one* when it comes to being crooked in a courtroom.

Bree says, "We should use the internet dating photo as proof that Buck's alive and kicking."

Before Dewey can yea or nay Bree's suggestion, Cato Crouch and his lawyer walk up the center aisle to the prosecution's table on our left.

"Oh, no," Dewey says with fear in his eyes.

"What's the matter?" I ask.

"It's Seedy Arnold Sheedy."

"Who?"

"The plaintiff's lawyer," Dewey says. "This guy's worse than me. He tells lies I'd be proud of."

A titanic battle of the Courtroom Corrupt Club is about to begin.

"All rise, court is in session, the Honorable J Philpot Pennington presiding."

The aged judge enters, sits, gavels, and looks down at his first case of the day—us—and says, "This day can only get better."

"Hearing on Cato Crouch vs. the Richmond Insurance Company," the bailiff reads.

"Attorneys, approach the bench," the judge surprises all.

Arnold and Dewey rush to get up, and push each other like Black Friday shoppers at Walmart to get to the bench first.

"Listen, you two," the judge makes no effort to control his voice, "the first one who tries anything funny will be out of this courtroom faster than a convicted murderer released on a technicality. If I hear one lie or one ridiculous falsehood, the other side is going to win by default, no matter what the law may be. Understand?"

"Yes, Judge."

"Yes, Your Honor."

On the way back to their respective seats, Seedy Sheedy snarls and Dewey Diddier returns the compliment.

"All right, Mr. Seedy, I mean Sheedy," Judge J says, "what's this all about?"

All five-foot-four and one hundred twenty-six pounds of Arnold stands and begins, "As the attorney for Mr. Cato Crouch, the now named executor of the estate of Leonard 'Buck' Crouch, I come to inform the court that the Richmond Insurance Company is refusing to pay a million-dollar claim on the death of said Buck Crouch. All requested supporting materials, including the death certificate, coroner's results, and sheriff's report, have been verified and sent, yet Richmond continues to refuse payment."

J Philpot looks over at Dewey. "Why?"

"We don't think he's dead, Your Honor."

All of a sudden, out of a Jewel shopping bag, Cato pulls out Buck's urn and slams it on the table. The top pops off and a little of Buck puffs out onto the wood table.

"If this don't prove it, I don't know what could," Cato says over the admonitions of Seedy Sheedy, his lawyer.

"Where do you think you are?" Judge J yells at Cato. "Wrigley Field?"

"No, they don't let you do that at Wrigley," I want to say, but don't.

Judge J Philpot looks back over at Dewey. "So why do you think he's not dead?"

"Well, first off, there are unresolved questions and issues concerning the abrupt disappearance of the man. Second, there is no DNA or blood evidence. And third and foremost, we have a picture of the deceased alive and fishing from an internet post, well after his body went missing and was subsequently found."

"Why no DNA?"

"Body had lain in a Wisconsin forest for over a year and was cremated because there wasn't enough left to autopsy," Sheedy explains.

Cato holds the urn up for the judge to see. "This is all that's left of my dear brother."

"Quiet."

"Therefore, we rebut all findings, Your Honor, on the basis of incomplete and inclusive evidence," Dewey says, rising to his feet.

Seedy Sheedy argues, "We have a signed death certificate, Your Honor."

The two lawyers shout at each other for a few minutes, doing a lot more screaming than convincing.

During the fight, the Judge looks over at me.

"That you, Sherlock?"

"Yes, Judge. How have you been?"

"Okay. What have you been doing since they kicked you off the police force?"

"Unfortunately, this."

The two attorneys continue to snipe at each other.

The Judge says to the lawyers, "You two sit down. Sherlock, get up here. I could use a voice of reason amongst this din of dishonesty."

I approach the bench.

"Tell me about this internet sighting."

"Well, Judge, a picture of the dead man was found on a dating site a few weeks back."

"What did it say?"

"The guy was seeking *the nature girl of his dreams.*"

"You have it with you?"

I quickly retrieve Bree's cell phone, which already has the page pulled up, and bring it to the Judge. "This is him."

Judge Pennington takes a long look at the photo. "Nice fish," he says.

"We can explain that," Seedy Sheedy calls out.

"How?"

"It's not Buck, it's me," Cato yells out. "But please don't tell my wife."

The Judge takes a second look. "No, it's not."

"Yes, it is, Your Honor," Sheedy tells the judge.

Cato rushes to the bench. "Look, it's me without my beard, long hair, and twenty pounds."

"My imagination's not that good," Judge J P P says.

"It's me, not my brother," Cato restates his claim.

Nobody's buying it. Dewey's probably thinking what a great lie this is.

"We're twins," Cato tells the Judge.

"Twins?"

"Identical."

"Who's older?" the Judge asks.

"Buck, by seven minutes."

I didn't see this coming.

"Please don't tell my wife," Cato pleads. "It was a momentary moment of weakness on my part."

"How long were you looking for a nature girl?" Judge J asks.

"Let's just say it was longer than your normal moment of weakness."

The Judge hands back the phone, which I in turn hand back to Bree.

"Everybody sit down," the Judge orders. "And put the urn away." He waits until we are all seated before speaking again. "Due to the presence of the death certificate and the coroner's report, I conclude that Richmond has no reason to refuse payment, and I order the claim to be paid in full by the next Monday of this month."

The gavel comes down and we're out of luck.

# CHAPTER 12

"What? What do you mean we lost? What about my new car?" Tiffany ranks her priorities.

"We didn't have a snowball's chance on a Chicago summer sidewalk of winning," I tell her. "All you need to prove a death is a death certificate, Tiffany."

"It could be a phony. I see those things all the time."

"You do?"

"I saw one on TV once."

"Once?"

"Twice. I saw a rerun of the same show," she says. "Mr. Sherlock, we have to do something to stop my money from going to the wrong people."

I might as well try to reason with the unreasonable one.

"Even Bree Bisonette knows we don't have a leg to stand on in this case, Tiffany."

"Who'd want to stand on one of Bree Biz-o-net's bad pins, Mr. Sherlock?"

"Tiffany, listen. Just pay him the damn money."

"No, I can't hear you." Tiffany puts her hands over her ears and loudly chants, "La, la, la, la. I can't hear you," over and over.

While this is going on, Care and Kelly plead, "You have to help her, Dad."

"What do you want me to do?"

"Find a hole in the case, like you always do."

I can't take Tiffany's chant any longer. I pull her hands from her ears and she shuts up.

"All right, all right. I got one and only one idea of what to do next."

"Well, it's about time, Mr. Sherlock."

\*\*\*

I'm sure I'm the only one who notices the tacky signs beginning three blocks from the house, but I'm just as shocked as the others in the car when we see Buck's barren front yard filled with tables, clothing racks, furniture, appliances, books, stuffed animals, and more useless junk than you'd see at a secondhand store's Going Out of Business Sale.

We climb out of Tiffany's cool Lexus into the hot Chicago humidity and join other bargain hunters in the search for diamonds in the rough or very rough diamonds.

"What's going on, Dad?"

"One man's trash is another man's treasure," I tell Care.

"What are you doing here?" Blanche, who carries a thick wad of bills in one of her meat-hook hands, says as we approach.

"We wanted to know how the stuffed animal carcasses were moving."

"Not as well as the guns. Boy, they went real fast," Blanche says.

Kelly asks, "Dad, can we get one of the armadillos?"

"No."

Care, Kelly, and Tiffany spread out to search for bargains. I stay with Blanche.

"Where's Travianna?"

"She had to go out of town for a few days."

"And you suddenly decided to have a sale?"

"Timing's everything in life," Blanche says to me, then looks over at a customer fondling a Jim Beam Bourbon collectable bottle. "You break it, you buy it, buddy."

"Missed you this morning," I tell her.

"Missed me where?"

"At court."

"I didn't have to go to court. I got my tickets fixed," Blanche explains.

"With Cato. He's suing to get Buck's money."

"He didn't mention any lawsuit when he came over to borrow Buck's ashes the other night."

"Maybe it slipped his mind," I suggest. "Maybe he's decided to go it alone getting Buck's million bucks?"

"Brother-in-law Buck wouldn't do something like that."

"You sure?"

"That wouldn't be very nice."

"Only for you and the rest of his wives."

I feel a tugging at my sleeve.

"Dad, this is really cool. Can we buy this?" Care asks, holding up a square piece of so-called art from a very deranged artist. It is an awful Dali-style painted canvas with all kinds of keys haphazardly glued to it.

"No, put it back."

Blanche goes into salesman mode. "That's an original Crouch. He called it his *Keys to his Kingdom Piece du Resistance.*"

"Please, Dad? It's only five dollars."

"No."

"Why not?"

"Because, Care, I have a strong resistance to spending any money on junk."

Care sulks off.

Back to Blanche. "Cato might be doing an end run around you to get Buck's money."

"He wouldn't do that."

"Kinda like what you're doing, selling Buck's stuff without telling Travianna."

"Who said I was doing that?"

"I did."

"Don't worry, she'll get her share."

"Yeah, right." I pause to let it all sink in, and say, "You sure you can trust Cato?"

Blanche doesn't answer.

I leave her to ponder, drift away, and as she takes money from a customer buying a dead duck, something strikes me funny.

"Hey, Care," I say, approaching the girls as they peruse more useless items.

I see Tiffany has put on a pair of latex hospital gloves. "Performing surgery soon, Tiffany?"

"You don't know whose germy hands have been on this stuff, Mr. Sherlock."

"Something to be thankful for, Tiffany." I look over at my youngest. "Care, go get that key thing you found."

"Super!"

Care is back in a flash with the horrendous piece of artwork. I take it from her, stare at the keys on the front, and turn it over. On the back is scrolled poorly *Hereth, the keys to my kingdom, to whatever I looseth, mayeth be yours on earth,* signed Buck Crouch.

I hand the thing back to Care, pull two dollars out of my wallet. "Here. Go offer Blanche two bucks."

"But the price says five."

"Show her the money, she'll take it."

Care runs off.

"Since Care got to buy something, Dad, I should get something too," Kelly says.

"Fine, what do you want?"

"A Fendi purse with matching shoes."

Tiffany smiles at me. "Excellent choice."

I pull out my wallet, hand her two bucks, and say, "Hope this covers it."

Care comes running back with her purchase. "How'd you know she'd take the money, Dad?"

"Your father: What a shopper!"

We get back in Tiffany's Lexus. Feeling the a/c go on and hit my sweaty body is like diving into an oasis in the Sahara.

"Well, that sure was exciting, Mr. Sherlock, but do you want to tell me what that was all about?"

"Tiffany, when outnumbered, it is best to divide before you attempt to conquer."

"What does that mean?"

"Google it."

Tiffany pulls out of the spot, turns the car around, and we're off. "Where to, Mr. Sherlock?"

"Get back on Lawrence Avenue." I turn to my youngest. "Care, let me see what you bought."

Care hands it to me. I immediately begin to pry off one of the keys.

"Dad, what are you doing? You're going to ruin it," Care says excitedly.

"No matter what I do to it, I don't believe I can make it any worse than it already is."

I have the one key in my hand. It's thin, smaller than the rest. I scrape off some of the paint and see a number engraved. "Stop at the first bank you see, Tiffany."

"You want to use the ATM?"

"This mean you're taking us shopping, Dad?" Kelly asks.

"No."

"Why are we doing this?" Tiffany asks.

"People usually bank close to where they live."

Of course, this comment makes no sense to any of these three, but it's true. People almost always bank at the bank closest to where they live. Even with branch banking, customers usually return to the same bank location time and time again.

The first bank we stop at is a Chase. The girls follow me inside to an open teller window.

"Excuse me," I say to the girl on the other side of the glass, "my name is Cato Crouch and my brother Buck recently passed away. I found his safe deposit box key, but I don't know which bank he had the box at."

The woman looks at me quite funny, as do my three women, who must think I'm losing it.

I continue, "I know I will need a letter from the estate to gain access, but at this time, all I'm trying to find out is if this is the bank with the safe deposit box where this key fits." I push the key through the tray to her. "Could you look it up for me, please?"

The woman doesn't really know what to do. She says something to the lady next to her, who shrugs her shoulders in a *Why not* fashion. She then taps on her computer, waits, searches, and says, "Nope, not at this bank."

At the seventh bank we visit, we hit pay dirt.

"Thank you very much," I tell the teller. "We'll return with the proper paperwork at a later date." She slides the key back to me. I smile and leave the window.

"We can't leave now, Mr. Sherlock. Let's get in there and see what's in the box." Tiffany pulls me back.

"Yeah, Dad, finders keepers."

"No."

"Why not? We found the key," Tiffany says.

"We?"

"And I bought it," Care says.

"With my money."

"Come on, Dad," Kelly says. "Maybe there'll be enough in there for me to get the Fendi purse you promised me."

"Sorry, folks. No can do."

"If we can't get into the box, what good is it going to do us?"

"Probably nothing, which is the amount I usually have in the bank."

# CHAPTER 13

"**I**'ve got absolute, irrefutable, positive proof Buck's dead."

"Who is this?"

"Travianna, Buck's wife."

This isn't the way I thought I'd start my day.

"What's the proof?" I ask.

"I'll show you when you get here," she says, "but only if you bring along the Richmond chick with her checkbook."

"That's not really the way it all works, but if you have something of merit, there's no doubt it will help your cause," I tell her.

"Get here as soon as you can. I want my money."

"Do Blanche and Cato know?"

"I really couldn't say."

"Well," I inform her, "you might want to invite all to the party because the more the merrier."

"You just make sure you bring that dingy Richmond chick with you, ready to write me a check."

"Don't worry, Tiffany's not one to miss a party."

It's not quite 9 AM and if my two haven't gotten up yet, I'm sure Tiffany will be an hour or two behind them. I decide to make the most of my time. First, I use the Oriental Oscillator and loosen my back up. I slept on the floor last night to keep my back flat and only had to get up twice, once to re-jigger the a/c unit, and the second time for the usual reason.

After twenty minutes of lumbar rolling, I get on the computer to search, far and wide, for anything on Cato Crouch. I didn't find much, but I did find the birth record. And much to my continued amazement, it is true: Buck and Cato are twins, two peas from one pod. Of course, if they were more like Chang and Eng, this would be a pretty simple matter, but from what I've seen and heard so far, the two brothers weren't that close, or very similar. Clean shaven/bearded, slob/neatnik, one has one wife while the other had two with a girlfriend on the side, and all four women couldn't be more dissimilar. Cato didn't impress me as the salesman type, while Buck was a super sock salesman. Buck was good with money, while Cato is in debt up to his earlobes. Buck worked eighteen years selling socks, Cato seems to have a problem staying employed past a year. Buck and Cato might have shared the same womb at the same time, but birds of a feather didn't fly out together.

The more you delve into people's lives, the more disconcerting things seem to become. The power of Google at your fingertips is pretty amazing, but it can also easily slant your perception. How do you know what you read is true? Anyone could post anything on the net with no one doing the checking. People read and immediately believe. There are so many ways of screwing up the truth. Outright lies, false facts, personal recollections can differ like night and day, and certain styles of writing can easily be read differently by whoever is doing the reading. Most of all, people are just too lazy to discover the actual truth. Nothing has promoted laziness better than Google. I read a story once about a history teacher who posted a Wikipedia story filled with falsehoods and mistakes concerning a Civil War battle that happened to be covered at length in the textbook for his class. He gave his students a test on the battle and afterwards it was easy to see who read which version. Wikipedia won the battle.

I do discover Cato's abode is a rental. He and Estalita have been together for a year with no kids. She's from Manila in the Philippines, is twenty years his junior, and arrived in the States a year or so ago, quite a quick courtship before heading straight to the altar. Cato is a member of the America First organization, the NRA, and the BPOE. Cato being an Elk and having an elk's head on his brother's wall seems a bit hypocritical; so much for preservation. From what I've read and the time I've spent with Cato, I'd have to place him in the category of *People I'd least want to hang with*. There's so much about the guy I just don't like.

Care and Kelly stumble out of the bedroom a little before ten. I whip up pancakes using chocolate chips to add smiley faces. They each drench the cakes with syrup, making a mockery of *Breakfast is the most important meal of the day.*

"Get Tiffany on the phone. Tell her to get over here ASAP."

They each run for their phones. Whose speed dial is quicker?

"Why, Dad?"

"Tell her one of Buck's wives says she has proof that he's as dead as disco."

\*\*\*

"What proof does she have, Mr. Sherlock?"

"I don't know."

"Why not?"

"Travianna wouldn't tell me."

"Did you ask?"

"No, Tiffany, I didn't."

"Why not?"

"I love surprises."

"That's a bad answer, Dad," Kelly comments.

"Mr. Sherlock, could this be something that could ruin my communion on the case?"

"I wouldn't be a bit surprised."

"Wow, now that's a bad answer," Tiffany says, driving onto Buck's street.

We're not the first to arrive at Buck's house. There's a car in the driveway with Cato and wife exiting.

"You don't happen to have any more of that candy with you, do you?" Care asks Estalita.

"No, sorry."

"You know what this is about?" Cato asks me as we head for the front door.

"She said she had proof of Buck's demise."

"I've already given you proof. What's missing is you giving me my money."

I knock. Blanche opens the door. She currently sports a very distinctive bruise around her right eye. Travianna obviously wasn't afraid of moving up a couple of weight classes for her last fight.

From inside the house, we hear, "Come on in. You can stand on my side of the house."

The house looks naked; only one opossum remains from the dead menagerie. What a shame.

Once inside, Travianna asks Tiffany, "You bring your checkbook?"

"I don't have a checkbook," Tiffany replies. "Checkbooks are for the little people."

Kelly adds, "I don't have a checkbook either."

Travianna then asks Cato, "Who invited you?"

"I called him," Blanche says. "I told him it was pot luck, but evidently he didn't whip anything up."

Six of us stand on Travianna's side of the room. Blanche is on her side of the line. The majority of the bad artwork, which filled the walls like a summer rash is gone. All that remains are the nail holes and chips in the plaster, making the wall look like it has acne.

"All right, what's this all about?" Cato says.

"It seems during the recent illegal apprehension and selling of Buck's worldly possessions, I have found proof that my loving husband is undeniably deceased."

"What?" Cato asks.

Travianna pauses for maximum effect. She takes out a folded sheet of paper, holds it up for all to see, and says, "This is difficult for me to read, so bear with me as I struggle through."

This should be good.

Travianna unfolds the paper slowly. The peanut gallery waits with baited and bad breath. "To all it may concern, I Buck Crouch, being of sound mind and body, has decided he can't go on any longer. Unable to give my entire heart to my one true love, the lovely Travianna, I'm going to end it all and wait for her in heaven. I hereby bequeatheth all my worldly possessions, including my Richmond Life Insurance policy to her, Travianna Mapp. I know I take the coward's way out, but I see no other means to the end, except to end it all. Sincerely Leonard Crouch, aka Buck."

Bequeatheth?

Travianna stops to wipe a phony tear from her eye. "There's nothing that says more about a person's death than his own suicide note."

"So, you believe this proves Buck committed suicide?" I ask.

"Absolutely."

"Let me see that thing," Cato says and takes the typewritten note from Travianna.

Blanche crosses the line of demarcation to read over Cato's shoulder.

"So he did himself in?" Tiffany asks me.

"Evidently, according to wife number two," I tell her.

"Yippee!" Tiffany yells and goes into a dance of joy rivaling a bad contestant on *Dancing with the Stars*. "New Lexus, here it comes!"

We all watch in bemused horror.

"What the hell's rich dingbat going bonkers about?" Travianna asks. "How can you be happy at the death of the love of my life?"

"He committed suicide," Tiffany screams. "I love it."

"Why?" Blanche asks.

"Buck's policy doesn't pay off for suicides," Tiffany explains. "We always put a line in that says you got to crap out in the usual ways."

Everyone stares at whirling dervish Tiffany, who's obviously been possessed by a happy Satan on Devil's Night. She twirls around like Linda Blair's head in *The Exorcist*.

"She's right," I concur. "Ya can't kill yourself to get the money."

"What?" Travianna screams. "Nobody ever told me that."

Blanche quickly reaches forward and whips the suicide note out of Cato's hand, crumples it up, stuffs it in her mouth, and starts chewing.

"No! Get it out of there," Tiffany screams, seeing the chomping jaws.

Blanche masticates like a hungry coyote, chewing as fast as she can, but chokes on her mid-day snack. She must be running short on saliva because she hightails it out of the room and heads for the kitchen. Tiffany takes chase, but Cato grabs her by her twenty-inch waist and holds her back.

"Get back here! That's evidence!" Tiffany screams.

"Wait," Cato says. "It's not polite to disturb someone who's eating."

"Let me go. That's my new Lexus she's chewing up." Tiffany breaks free.

By the time I get into the kitchen, Blanche is chugging from a half-pint of Old Crow, swishing it around in her mouth to get enough juice for her to take a big swallow, and get the massive spit wad into her massive tummy.

Tiffany makes a leap onto Blanche's backside and pulls out her manicured claws to pry Blanche's lips apart. Cato leaps on Tiffany. They're grappling like the Housewives of Beverly Hills fighting over the last Prada purse at Saks.

Blanche flips left and right, and shakes Tiffany off like a gnat. Cato goes down with Tiffany. Blanche gets one more swig of Old Crow into her before she makes the big swallow in front of all assembled with a gulp that can be heard halfway down the block. Satisfied, she gets half a smile on her face, is about to burp, but her success is short-lived. Blanche's entire body contorts like the Elephant Man's samba move and starts to jerk like a death-row inmate after an electric chair shock during a Flex Alert.

Blanche's face turns bright red, her ears almost purple, her eyes bulge out like a constipated bullfrog's. She tries to suck in air, but all passageways are blocked. Her entire body convulses like a hip-hop rapper on discount opioids.

"She can't breathe!" Estalita calls out.

"She doesn't deserve to breathe," Travianna counters.

"Help, Mr. Sherlock, that's my new Lexus in there."

I circle around Blanche, get my arms around her, which is no small feat due to her refrigerator-sized girth. I do my best to measure the spot between her diaphragm and rib cage, grip my hands tightly, and pull back with a plus-sized, heavy-duty yank that would make Dr. Heimlich proud.

It doesn't work. Blanche slings me around like the last kid in a playground whip, but I hold on for dear life. Once I get my feet back on the ground, I sink my gripped hands into her excess, hard-to-lose belly fat, jerk upward with all my might, and do my best to reverse her flow of air up the chute, through the trachea, past the teeth, and out the mouth.

"BURRP."

She sounds like Krakatoa, east of Java, erupting.

A boozy, papier-mâché substance shoots from Blanche's mouth like a torpedo from a U-Boat.

SPLAT.

The gunk hits the floor with such a resounding wet thud, all circling the spectacle leap away to protect their shoes.

"Barf-a-roni" and "Eeeeeuuuuu, upchuck" are the comments from my kids.

Tiffany, with hope in her eyes, is the only one to come close enough to inspect the validity of the stomach-juiced-with-Old-Crow suicide note. But before she can make an evaluation, a boot comes down on the wad of wet gunk as if it were a pile of fresh doggie doo-doo and re-splatters it into the crevices of his knock-off Eddie Bauer hiking boot.

Cato smiles at his perfect landing. "Whoops."

"You can't do that," Tiffany screams. "That suicide note was evidence."

"What suicide note?" Cato asks.

"Yeah, I don't see no suicide note," Blanche says and adds, "That's what's left of the Egg McMuffin I had for breakfast."

Tiffany looks to the second wife. "But you just read us Buck's suicide note."

"No, that was me rehearsing my latest gangsta-rap song," Travianna explains.

"But, Mr. Sherlock—"

"It's our word against theirs, Tiffany."

"That's not fair!"

Well, this has certainly been out-of-the-ordinary exciting, but the festivities are now over. The assembled stand and stare blankly at each other, not really knowing what to say or do next.

Cato fills the void. "Now when do we get our money?"

"Soon," I say.

"The judge said Monday," Cato replies.

"For all I know, the check's already in the mail."

"I want my money," Cato says.

"As a rule," I tell him, "in cases such as these, the claim is paid according to the directions of the will." This isn't really true, but these folks wouldn't know any better.

"There ain't no will."

"Are you sure? Have you looked everywhere?"

"Yes."

"How about Buck's safe deposit box?" I ask.

"What safe deposit box?" Cato asks.

"The one I found."

"Where is it?" Blanche asks.

"In a bank."

"Which one?"

"The one I found."

"Let's go," Travianna says.

"Can't."

"Why not?"

"You'll need a notarized letter of authorization from the lawyer for execution of the estate." This is also horse-pucky, but these people are so greedy they'll believe and do anything to get Buck's bucks.

What wheels there may be in the brains in front of me are moving as fast as they can, which won't break any speed records.

"When you get the letter, let me know, and we can all go on a treasure hunt."

I quickly grab my girls and hurry out of the house. Tiffany follows, but stops before exiting to say, "We're going to make you take a lie detector test and the truth will prevalent."

I think she means "prevail," but with Tiffany you can never be too sure.

Back in the Lexus, Care asks, "Can we go get something to eat? I'm hungry."

Care's always hungry.

"Then can we go shopping?" Kelly follows up.

"It's up to Tiffany," I say.

Tiffany is lost in thought. She finally turns to me and says, "I hate driving this old thing, Mr. Sherlock."

My Toyota is old enough to be her Lexus' great-great-great-grandparent.

"I'm telling you, Tiffany, you're going to end up biting the bullet on this one. Pay them their money and end this charade."

"If that's what you think I should do, what was all that stuff you did in there?" she asks.

"I was just buying a little more time to watch greed be forced to run an obstacle course."

## CHAPTER 14

Seedy Arnold Sheedy calls late in the afternoon.
"You really find a box or is that cheap-ass insurance company of yours stalling?"
"To be honest," I tell him, "which I'm sure you're not used to hearing, both."
"Tomorrow, Sherlock?"
"Maybe."
"What does that mean?"
"There's something we want before we go safe-deposit-box-diving."
"What?"
"If there is a will, I want a full reading, where all concerned can hear."
"Why?"
"Because if you didn't know, there's more people in the audience than you realize."
"Who?"
"Throw a will-reading party and you'll find out."
Seedy Arnold Sheedy ends our conversation with a word I'm positive he detests: "Deal."
As if by incredible coincidence, kismet, or cosmic occurrence, my phone rings just moments after I hang up with Arnold.
"Buck's alive."
"Are you sure?"
"Yes."
"Your planets line up to let you know?"
"Better than that."
This should be good.
Jupiter says, "I got pictures."
"Meet me at the Treys in an hour."
I text Tiffany and tell her, "Whatever you're doing with the girls, keep doing it."
I seldom text because I despise texting.
Texting is a communications invention designed for people who don't want to talk to people they have to talk to. It works like this: if you want to relay a message, but don't want to further the conversation on the matter, you text the least amount of characters, which simplifies the message to its least

degree. For example: "I'm sick. Can't help you move your furniture tonight." Or "Sorry, can't afford to pay you back, ever." Or, and this is a big favorite of mine, "I'm breaking up with you. Have a nice life." If the person being texted wants to respond, they will invariably text back, and all you have to do is ignore it, then block all future texts from their number.

Texting can be an unfair and rude practice. It unfairly eliminates any additional dialog, emotion, revelation, and important information, which may lead to a better, more fulfilling understanding of the conversation or situation. It cuts everything off at the knees. No *Who, What, When, Where, and Why*. One hundred-forty characters, hit Send, and you're done. Texting is also bad because so many idiots text while driving, which has proven to result in almost certain dismemberment and death. We have a hard and fast rule in the Sherlock house that no texts should ever come between us. My kids hate the rule.

Today, Tiffany doesn't text me back. And I certainly hope she doesn't show my text to the girls, which would make me a hypocrite and lousy father.

***

Jupiter's dressed for a Haight-Ashbury love-in. She's got enough beads dangling down on her to separate the kitchen from the den in a cheap apartment. She orders a Potawatomi Pilsner. I get a Coors Light.

"Okay, Jupiter, what do you got?"

She pulls a leather satchel off her back, opens it, takes the only manila folder inside it out, and places it on the bar. "If these don't prove Buck's alive and well, I don't know what else could."

There's a stack of 8 x 10 photos, each a shot from the same vantage point, and grainy as a decomposed silent movie still.

"Professional photographer?"

"They were taken by one of those security cameras."

"Where?"

"Bozeman."

"Bozeman, what?"

"Bozeman, it's in Montana. Buck loved the place. It's the Gateway to Yellowstone."

"And these were taken at the turnstile when you enter the park?"

"No, they were taken at Heeb's."

"Heeb's? What's a Heeb's?"

"Grocery store."

"There's a grocery store named Heeb's? I bet it doesn't get a lot of the Rosh Hashanah business."

"I don't think they have Jewish people in Montana, and if they do, they're very quiet."

I begin to page through the photographs. There isn't a clear picture in the bunch because the angle of the shot only shows the person from the top of their head down, and there isn't a guy in any of the shots who's not wearing a baseball cap.

"Which one's Buck?"

"All of 'em."

Besides the hat, each of the men photographed wear boot-cuff jeans, a plaid Pendleton shirt, a big belt buckle, and hiking boots.

"How can you tell? I can't make out one face."

"I've seen Buck in every one of those outfits," Jupiter says. "It's got to be him."

"I have a suspicion that every guy in Montana has a closetful of these outfits."

"Then it's the boots," Jupiter says.

"The hiking boots?"

"Buck loved to wear his Salomon GTX boots."

"So?"

"That proves it's him."

"No, it doesn't. You can't tell all the boots are the same."

"I can."

"No, you can't."

"Those boots are all top of the line and very few guys can afford those boots."

"You're saying nobody else in Montana wears Salomon boots except Buck?"

"Well, not many."

"I'm not sure if we could put these photos into the Collected Proof category, Jupiter."

She downs the rest of her Potawatomi Pilsner with one swig.

"You don't believe me, do you?" she asks.

"No."

"I know Buck's alive, Sherlock. I've never been so sure of anything in my life."

"I'm sorry to break this to you, Jupiter, but I'm pretty sure Buck's deader than Jerry Garcia."

"Using the name of a Grateful Dead man is cancer to my chakra."

I order her another Potawatomi Pilsner to help ease her pain.

"Did Buck have a will?" I ask.

"I doubt it," she says. "Why do you ask?"

"I might have found one," I inform her, after the brewski arrives.

"Where?"

"In his safe deposit box."

"Buck had a safe deposit box?" she asks, which makes me wonder if I'm asking the wrong person the right questions.

"I'll find out tomorrow," I say. "And if he did, you might want to be there for the reading."

"Why? The will's no good because Buck's still alive."

"Because there's a million dollars on the line."

"A million dollars?"

"Life insurance policy."

"Buck?" Jupiter says incredulously. "Buck would never buy insurance."

"Well, there's a policy in his name, and if there is a will, and you're in it, and if Richmond ever gets around to disbursing it, you might want to get in line for your share before the money disappears faster than Buck leaving his two wives."

Jupiter gives me an odd look, as if she can't figure out what road to take.

"Jupiter, if he doesn't come back, it wouldn't hurt to settle for door number two."

# CHAPTER 15

Due to Tiffany operating on Tiffany time, we're the last to arrive at the bank.

"We're here to get into a safe deposit box," I tell the teller lady.

She gives me an odd look and points to the door around the back of the teller windows.

"You people stay here, I'll be right back," I tell my posse.

"Oh no, Mr. Sherlock, I'm going with you."

"Us too, Dad."

"I'm not sure you're allowed."

"If there's one place I'm always welcome, it's in a bank, Mr. Sherlock."

The three follow me around the teller area and a woman meets us halfway.

"Are you the guy with the key?" she asks.

I hold it up for her to see.

"'Bout time you got here."

I look over at Tiffany to transfer the blame.

"We're coming too," Tiffany says.

"We can't take any more," the banker lady says. "Only two people can go into the vault at one time."

"Is Seedy Sheedy here?" I catch my own mistake. "I mean Arnold Sheedy?"

"Yes, he's waiting impatiently," she tells me and looks at the rest of my group. "You'll have to wait with the others."

"Darn," Care says. "We love a good treasure hunt."

We all go through an electronic door and then are split into two groups. I watch as the girls and Tiffany are ushered to one of the small rooms where people can peruse their safe deposit boxes in private. As the door opens, I see Big Blanche, Travianna, Cato, and Cato's wife packed into the room like commuters on a Tokyo subway car during rush hour. I wait until Tiffany, Kelly, and Care are squeezed in with the others before going left to enter the vault where Seedy Sheedy awaits.

"Nice of you to show up, Sherlock."

"I thought it'd be fun to be fashionably late and add to the suspense."

I hand the key to the vault attendant, who looks like he's been in this vault way, way too long. The older-than-dirt, pasty-faced man walks slowly to the far wall, where the smallest boxes are installed. Buck's, of course, is on the top, and the guy has to get a stepstool out to reach. Molasses moves faster than this fellow. He inserts his key, then mine, turns both, and pulls the long, thin box out of the wall. He steps down and hands it to Arnold, who opens it.

At first glance, it's as empty as my savings account.

"I'm glad I'm getting paid by the hour for this waste of my time," Arnold says, and drops the box at his feet in disgust.

"Wish I was," I confess.

I pick up the box, peer inside, tip the box opening downward, give it a good shake, and see a small envelope slide my way. On the front side of the sealed envelope are the words: *Last Will and Testament.*

"Bingo."

Arnold slips his thumb under the back flap and starts to rip it open, but I stop him. "Wait. Don't forget our deal."

"Deal? What deal?" Seedy Sheedy's selective memory kicks in.

"You don't open it until all the players are on the field, remember?"

"Do you have that in writing?"

"Listen, Arnold, you don't want to open it now anyway. The family members will tear you to shreds to find out how much they're getting."

"Good point, Sherlock. See you tomorrow."

Sheedy hustles out of the vault quicker than a hare bidding adieu to a mountain lion. I wait until the clerk returns the box to its rightful spot, relocks it into the wall, and hands me the key, all of which seems to take a month of Sundays to complete. "Thanks."

"Excuse me," the man says. "Is the war over?"

"Yes," I tell him, "it's finally over."

"What did they do with Hitler?"

I exit the vault, go to the door of the viewing room where the greed group awaits, and twist the knob to open.

The people inside tumble out of the room like frat brothers from a phone booth, and spill onto the floor in front of me like circus clowns out of a Mini Cooper. Luckily, Kelly and Care are on top of the pile.

Once all the arms and legs are untangled and most are back

on their feet, I'm peppered with questions.

"Was there a will?"

"Yes."

"What'd it say?"

"I don't know."

"Where is it?"

"Sheedy's got it."

"What's he doing with it?"

"Probably reading it."

"Why isn't he reading it to us?"

"He will, pun intended," I answer, attempting to add some needed levity to the conversation.

"When?"

"Tomorrow."

"What else was in the box?" Blanche asks. "Any cash?"

"Besides the will, it was as empty as Buck's promise of fidelity."

As we exit, each family member is equally as angry and disappointed as a jilted bride at the altar.

Back in Tiffany's car, Kelly is first to comment. "Wow, Dad, I thought the nose-to-butt thing was gross until we got shoved in the room with those smelly people."

"That Blanche lady took up half the room," Care adds.

"I'm taking the girls to get exfoliated immediately," Tiffany tells me. "We could have all suffered permanent pigment damage."

"Not too much, just a little off the top, okay?"

I have Tiffany drop me off at my apartment before the three go have a layer of skin sandpapered off. What fun.

Once inside, I get a bad feeling. And once the air conditioner goes on and the place cools down, the feeling stays with me.

There's something wrong. I don't know what, but something is definitely wrong.

Where's the rest of the money?

Before Buck died, he emptied his 401(k) and took whatever money he'd been saving by cheating on his expense account. This has to be a pretty hefty pack of cash. So, where is it?

There was nothing on the body, no wallet, keys, papers, or money clip. Except for the will, there has not been one additional piece of paper found: no bank statement, financial form, checking or savings account, forwarding address, Get out of Jail Free card, or Starbucks coupon. Nobody leaves a trail this clean, then falls off a mountain with nothing to show for it.

I can't stop thinking Jupiter may be right. Buck's alive. He disappeared clean as a whistle, never to be found again. Maybe it wasn't his body the Diggler sisters found. There could be other diehard, tattooed Cub fans that fall off a cliff, get buried under leaves and brush, and end up lunch for a pack of hungry coyotes; you just don't hear about them very often. The body wasn't autopsied, and there was no matching blood, facial recognition, or matching fingernail color. Something's not right. I can smell malfeasance in the air.

Nothing would make me happier than to put the entire megillah behind me and forget the whole thing, but the whole scenario is driving me crazy. I hate the feeling, it's the worst feeling a detective can have, with the exception of his back going out and lying on the ground writhing in absolute pain and suffering. On second thought, relief from my aching back would make me much happier than finding the answer to the riddle of Buck Crouch.

I sit on the couch. I hold a legal pad on my lap and a pen in my right hand. I'm going to write down every aspect of the case, no matter how trivial. I'll write down every question that needs an answer, and every answer that needs a question.

In the next three hours, the only time I get up is to answer the phone. It's Tiffany telling me she's taking the girls to Ambria for dinner.

"Can I go too?"

"No, Mr. Sherlock, you have to find a way to help me earn my commission."

"That's not fair."

"Nobody said it had to be fair, Mr. Sherlock."

Again my words come back to haunt me.

"We'll meet you at Sheedy's office tomorrow for the reading of the will."

"Why would you want to be there, Tiffany?"

"Because maybe Buck will leave his money to someone else, and I'd hate to miss the looks on the faces of his wives and brother when that happens."

"That's mean, Tiffany."

"Yeah, but it sure would be fun."

She's spot on with that one.

I speak to Care first, then Kelly, telling each, "Be good, I love you, and sleep tight."

Kelly says before we hang up, "Dad, I love you too."

Isn't that sweet. "Thank you, Kelly."

"And would you take me shopping tomorrow?"

"No."

"But I need new clothes for school."

"No."

At midnight, I look down upon the legal pad and see not one written word. There are some very interesting yet disturbing squiggles made during my absences of thought. I crumple them up and discard them before calling it a night.

I still feel rotten inside, and on the outside my back is stiffening up like a corpse entering rigor mortis.

## CHAPTER 16

A rnold Sheedy's law offices are located on the fourteenth floor of the Oriental Building on Randolph Street. The building, across the street from the Daley Center and a block from City Hall, is the spot where the cheapest lawyers rent the cheapest office space. The ride up in the ancient elevator is scarier than the American Eagle rollercoaster at Six Flags.

Seedy Sheedy shares with three other lawyers a conference room that looks like it gets too much use. The table is coffee-stained by every Starbucks combination imaginable, the chairs have more split seams than an escaped fat farm detainee on a burger binge, and the *Coolie in the Rice Paddy* wallpaper I suspect was personally hung by the Mings before their dynasty took root.

The head chair at the table is empty, but to its sides, Blanche and Travianna have staked their claims on the best seats. Cato and Estalita are next to Blanche. Jupiter, wearing a Pink Floyd *Dark Side of the Moon* tee-shirt and a pair of bell-bottoms so flowered that she'd sprout if she was planted in good soil, sits as far away from the others as possible. Tiffany, Kelly, and Care are at the back of the room. There is enough tension in the air to rival the contested divorce mediation of a poorly arranged marriage.

"Where's the snacks, Dad?" is Care's whispered greeting to me.

Good lawyers always provide food for their clients in these situations, which explains the absence of food.

"We're dying of hunger," Kelly fills me in. "The only thing to eat at Tiffany's were bean sprouts."

I don't have the time to answer because Tiffany pulls me aside to ask, "Who's Ms. Flower Power, Mr. Sherlock?"

"You'll find out in a minute."

"You got my money?" Cato calls from across the room.

"That's why we're here, to find out who gets what," I tell him.

"Who's she?" Travianna points to Jupiter.

"I'm the asteroid in your orbit," Jupiter informs her.

"I've had those," Blanche says. "Some mornings I could barely get off the toilet."

Arnold Sheedy comes into the room carrying one thin

manila folder. "Hope you enjoyed the wait," he says before sitting down at the head of the table.

I motion for Tiffany and the girls to sit, and do the same.

Arnold takes the envelope from the folder, removes its one page, and holds it up for all to see.

"This is the last will and testament of Leonard 'Buck' Crouch."

The greed-infused assembled lean forward to hear every word and hopefully their names in first positions.

Arnold puts the one page in front of him and reads: "I Leonard Crouch, resident of the State of Illinois, in the County of Cook, in the good old USA, hereby say that I am of sound mind, body, and in especially good spirits. If I have anything left when I die, whenever that day may come, I would like what money I didn't get around to wasting passed down to my offspring; my closest living relatives, if they're still talking to me; and any current wife, who made the mistake of marrying me. I hope this will and testament never has to go into use, even though it won't bother me since I'll be dead. Sincerely, Leonard Crouch, who everybody calls 'Buck.'"

Arnold looks up to see a huge smile on Cato's face, Blanche licking her lips as if dessert is about to be served, Travianna's smile lines pronounced, and Jupiter with an amazed face, as if she's currently on a groovy acid trip.

"Ring that bingo bell," Cato screams out. "When do I get my money, Sherlock?"

"Any day now, I'm sure."

Arnold concludes, "The will is notarized and dated June 4, 1987."

"When?" I can't believe what I just heard.

"1987."

"Buck would have been eighteen in 1987."

"Yeah," Arnold says, "that kind of threw me too."

"He did it as a joke," I conclude.

"This is even better than I thought," Cato says. "And it's perfectly legal. Yahoo!"

"Yeah," Arnold says, "I'd have to say so."

"The money and house are mine," Cato says. "I want you two bimbos out of there this afternoon."

"What you talkin' about?" Travianna asks.

"I'm his only living relative," Cato says.

"I'm his wife," Blanche says.

"Me, too," Travianna adds herself to the list.

"Prove it," Cato tells them.

Both hold up their left hands' adorned ring fingers.

"Buck never married either of you," Cato says. "You got no license, didn't have a church service, and never visited a Justice of the Peace. He gave you both a cheap Cracker Jack prize ring, a couple of broken promises, and an inordinate amount of communal grief." Cato points at Blanche. "He used you to keep house and cook," and he says to Travianna, "and you for booty calls."

Blanche and Travianna are up and out of their seats, screaming at Cato. They claim in no particular order: "He loved me." "We were soul mates." "Till death do us part." "We were two hearts beating as one." "Actually, three."

Cato answers, "You two are about as married to Buck as I am to a real job."

While all this is going on, I'm thinking: What kid at eighteen writes a will? And writes a will so incredibly stupid?

"Insurance money is mine, little lady," Cato says to Tiffany. "I got the law behind me now."

"I don't see anyone behind you except your wife and Seedy Sheedy," Tiffany tells him.

The screaming continues. "You can't just throw us out on the street," Blanche yells at Cato.

"Her," he motions to Travianna, "I can throw out. You," he says to Blanche, "I'll need a crane."

"There's such a thing as a common-law wife, you know." Travianna brings up a so-so point.

"Illinois doesn't recognize common-law marriages."

"Buck told me they do," Blanche wallows back.

"Buck lied," Cato says. "Gee, big surprise there."

I feel a tug on my sleeve.

"Sherlock."

Jupiter pulls me down toward her and whispers, "I want you to stop looking for Buck."

"Why? Did you just get a cosmic vision of him in heaven?"

"No, but if he wants to be dead that badly, maybe it's time to let him rest in peace."

This is unexpected. "Why?"

"Buck has a son."

"A what?"

"A son, offspring, a sprout from his seed."

"Who?"

"His name's Moonjava, but he likes to be called Draconian."

"How do you know he's Buck's kid?"

"I'm his mother. I was on the bottom during his conception."

Oh jeesh.

This won't merely be a fly in Cato's ointment, but more like a fissure in his mountain of new money.

"Not now," I tell Jupiter. "This is not the time to enter a new chapter and footnote into Buck's history book."

"But the money?"

"Trust me, I know Mr. Richmond, and it's going to take a lot more than a dumb will to pry a million dollars out of his cold, almost dead hands."

Cato is screaming at the wives and the wives are screaming at Cato.

"We had a lovely ceremony. Elvis was our best man. We both wore white," Blanche bellows a boldfaced lie.

"Just because we didn't have a piece of paper, doesn't mean we weren't married," Travianna says.

Amid the chaos, my daughters come to my side. Care does the talking. "Dad, if we don't get a donut into us soon, we're going to pass out."

"Enough!" Seedy Sheedy screams louder than all the others. "Everybody shut up and sit down."

The combatants comply with his request.

"As the lawyer for the estate, all I can say is I need a break in the action to figure this out. The case is hereby on hold until further notice."

"You can't do that," Cato says. "I'll sue."

"You're going to sue your own lawyer?" Arnold asks. "You're the one who got me appointed executor."

"I'm getting Buck's money. I don't care what I got to do," Cato tells all.

"We ain't leavin' our house, Cato," Blanche tells her assumed brother-in-law. "And if I catch you hangin' around, you'll be hearing from my lawyers, Smith and Wesson."

The only one who doesn't say a word is Cato's wife Estalita, who sits through the whole rigmarole as if she has no knowledge of the English language. Lucky her.

Enough of this peculiar brilliance. "Come on, we're leaving," I tell my supporters.

"We need food, Dad. We need food."

The moment we're out of the room and at the elevator bank, I tell Tiffany to go ahead with the girls. Jupiter and I wait for the next elevator, not wanting to take the chance of us all dying in the same death trap if it crashes.

After we shake, rattle, and roll to a stop, Jupiter and I stand in the lobby of the Oriental Building.

"You want to start at the beginning?"

"You want blow by blow of our roll in the hay?"

"Did Buck know?"

"I was just about ready to tell him."

"Why'd you wait so long?"

"Buck hated kids."

"So do a lot of dads."

"I didn't really need him until now," Jupiter says.

"Wouldn't he have noticed something a little different about you when you were on the nest?"

"I already told you, our relationship wasn't real smooth. 'On and off again' would be an understatement."

"How off and how on?"

"It started with a 'Want to come up for a nightcap joint?' and then we had intermittent returns to the scene of the crime, so to speak." She pauses. "Until the last year or so when we hooked up over the internet."

"Isn't social media wonderful?" I comment.

This is certainly new information, but I'm not sure how it will affect the Richmond claim or Tiffany's new car.

"I want you to work for me, Sherlock, to prove paternity."

"It's hardly my forté, and you don't have any money, Jupiter."

"Oh, come on. It's gonna be groovy."

\*\*\*

Kelly and Care are devouring bear claws like hungry bear cubs. I'm eating kreplach soup, and Tiffany's munching on an organic kosher pickle. I couldn't think of a better spot than

Manny's Deli to satisfy the different food cravings of our group.

"That was really fun in there, Mr. Sherlock. Now that we have more time to work on the case, what are you going to do next?"

"Tiffany, you're still under court order to pay out the money in a couple of days."

"We are?"

"Yes."

"But the shady, seedy Sheedy put a hold on everything."

"That only concerns who gets what money, not the money going into the estate."

"Then what's going to happen next?" Care, my more inquisitive daughter, asks.

"Blanche and Travianna have to prove they're Buck's legal wives, Arnold has to prove Buck's will is authentic, and Jupiter has a lot to prove." I find it best not to mention the new addition to the clan at this point in time.

"Who's going to get the money, Dad?"

"I don't know and I don't care," I tell Care. "What bothers me, though, is why would an eighteen-year-old kid with a million-dollar life insurance policy write a joke-filled will instead of naming a beneficiary?"

"I think Buck's still alive," Kelly says, licking sugar glaze off her fingertips.

"Why?"

"A Cubs tattoo on his arm just doesn't seem to be enough of an identification."

"Excellent point," Tiffany lauds Kelly's thought process.

"He couldn't get on an airplane by showing that to the TSA guy," Kelly says.

"Exactly," Tiffany adds. "We should go back to proving he's still kicking, Mr. Sherlock."

There's that "We" again.

"If only we had a picture or something," Tiffany says.

I make a mental note to myself never to let Jupiter and Tiffany shop at Heeb's together.

"It wouldn't help, Tiffany. They already have a death certificate."

"Well, then, maybe we should get our own certificate saying he's not dead."

"Yeah, Dad," Care adds.

"There's no such thing," I regretfully inform them.

"Create one."

"You have to climb out of the box, Mr. Sherlock."

"Yes, Dad, if at first you don't succeed, try, try again," Kelly says.

"Fine," I say to the girls, "I'll take you back to the horse camp this afternoon and you can try to master nose-to-butt trail riding again."

"No, Dad. Bad idea."

My cell phone rings.

Jupiter didn't wait long to call.

"I want you to come over and meet Draconian."

"Why?"

"So you can see the resemblance."

"I've never seen Buck, so what resemblance could I see, Jupiter?"

"You have to believe me, my kid's Buck's kid."

"It's not that I don't believe you, Jupiter—"

"Just meet my son. You'll see why I'm doing this."

"Jupiter."

"Please."

"No, I can't, especially not today."

"Tonight's better. Draconian only comes out at night."

"I'm sorry, no can do, Jupiter."

Our food is put on the table.

"I got to go, Jupiter."

"I'll call after the sun goes down."

My veggie omelet looks great, Care and Kelly both have French toast, and Tiffany has a fruit plate covered in granola and soymilk. Manny's has come a long way from bagels, blitzes, and kosher pastrami.

I'm just about ready to dig in when my phone rings again. Am I ever going to get a moment's peace? I don't recognize the number.

"Hello."

"Is the Tiffy-babe with you, Sherlock?"

The voice sounds somewhat familiar. "Who is this?"

"It's Larry Flemm with two m's."

"I'm right in the middle of lunch, Larry. You're ruining it."

"I got something you'll want to see."

"What?"

"Bring your little Tiffany lady over and I'll show you."

"I show you mine and you show me yours? That's tacky, Larry."

"It'll be worth it to you."

"I don't think so, Larry."

"You can take this one to the bank, Sherlock, because that's what Buck did."

"What are you talking about?"

"Bring Tiffy over and find out."

*** 

"This place is creepy," Kelly says as we approach the office. "Who works here?"

"A guy who fits right in," Tiffany says.

"Just stay in the back and don't touch anything, girls."

We go in the door. Larry, waiting inside like a snake ready to strike, sees his prey and slithers forward.

"My little kitten caboodle has come back," Larry announces. "Tiffy darling, I got something big you're gonna love."

"A little nothing would be nice."

Larry ushers Tiffany into his office and we follow like servants behind the royal couple.

"Who are the rug rats, Sherlock?"

"Girls, this is Larry Flemm."

"That's Flemm with two m's."

"Hello, Mr. Flemm with two m's."

For once my pair follow orders and don't shake hands.

"This better be good, Larry," I tell him.

"Oh, it is."

I wait.

"Did you find Buck?"

"Better than that."

"What?"

"Four thousand dollars better," Larry says.

"'Four thousand dollars?"

"It's my reward."

"For what, being obnoxious?"

"No. Clearing his credit."

I'm not sure what Larry's talking about.

"Four grand," Larry says with the smile of a Cheshire cat. "I get a third of the balance, plus expenses." He leans across his desk towards Tiffany, "And I can't think of a better place to spend it than spend it on you, Tiffy-Tussly-Pooh."

"Knock it off, Larry, and tell us what the heck's going on."

Larry folds his hands like a schoolboy, smiles again, and says, "Two days ago a guy walks into a bank in Lewiston, Montana, plops down sixteen grand in cash, and pays off the credit card of one Leonard 'Buck' Crouch."

"What?"

"He must have known I was hot on his tail."

"Were you?"

"No, but I must have got him to think I was."

"Buck's alive?" Tiffany shouts. "That's fantastic."

"Don't get your hopes up, Tiffany. Just because the money got paid, doesn't mean Buck was the one shelling it out." I turn to Larry. "Proof?"

"What do I need proof for? I got the money."

"Why would he pay off his debt now?" I ask.

"Because," Larry says, "now, he's free and clear. He's tied up the last loose string. He's got no other debts, no one needs to find him, and if he doesn't care about what he left behind, nobody will ever come looking for him again."

Buck has filled in the last piece of his disappearing puzzle. He pulled off the impossible. Game's over and he's free to go his merry way.

Larry rises, hikes his pants under his belly overhang, and says to Tiffany, "Now, how about we talk about us hookin' up, my little love bundle?"

"How about we don't," Tiffany answers, "and say we didn't."

## CHAPTER 17

Buck is better off dead than alive to everyone in this mess except Tiffany. Why did I get put on her team? I want to be traded.

To end a bad day and a worse week, I cook a lousy dinner, and the girls complain about every bite. We settle into a night of watching the undead get their heads blown off in some ridiculous TV binge-watching experience, all over the din of the a/c unit, which now burps every three or four minutes. A little after nine, the buzzer rings.

"Somebody's at the door, Dad," Kelly informs me, without moving an inch off the couch.

"Gee, how'd you guess?" I say, getting up slowly and going to the little speaker on the wall in the kitchen.

I depress the button and speak. "I don't buy anything from anyone who comes to my door or calls me on the phone, so you might as well leave."

"Sherlock, let us in."

"Who is this?"

"Jupiter."

"What are you doing here?"

"He hath risen and we need to talk to you."

I hit the button, hear the door open, and think: *What did I do to deserve all this?*

"Who is it, Dad?"

"A blast from the past and I'm not sure what else."

Jupiter has changed into a Monkees' *I'm a Believer* tee shirt, although her *Dark Side of the Moon* tee would have been much more appropriate because behind her is a walking advertisement for the Goth lifestyle. His skin is vampire white, black stringy hair hangs down in relaxed Medusa curls, eyes are circled with black eyeliner, lips reddened by blood-red lipstick, and his clothes are pure black from the tips of his toes to the nape of his neck. His fingernails shine blacker than his pair of spit-shined storm trooper boots.

"This is Moonjava," Jupiter introduces her son.

"Call me Draconian," he enunciates with a Bela Legosi twinge.

"Nice to meet you. Can I call you Drac?"

"No."

One step into the living room and my girls bolt upright at the sight of a hippie, Goth, and me in the same frame.

"Draconian, meet Kelly and Care."

"Yo."

The girls recoil as if the cobra jumped out of its basket.

"Sherlock, can we talk privately?"

I let the three young'ns get acquainted and pull Jupiter into the back of the kitchen, where we won't be heard.

"You have to help me."

"Jupiter, I can't work for you."

"Why not?"

"Because I'm already on the case for Richmond."

"That's not a reason."

"Then give me some time and I'll come up with a better one."

"Sherlock, what do we need to prove paternity?"

There's another "we" I don't need to hear.

"Is Buck's name on the birth certificate?" I ask.

"Ah, not really."

"What do you mean 'not really'?"

"I told you, Buck and I were on the outs when Moonjava was born."

"So you left the Father's Name line blank?"

"I thought I could fill it in later."

"Dumb move."

"Well, how was I supposed to know he was going to be worth a million bucks some day? I thought we were just planets passing in the night."

"One-night stands are a little hard to prove in a court of law, especially when the dad has been ruled dead."

"How about this?" Jupiter says.

"What?"

"DNA, Sherlock, DNA."

"There isn't any."

"Everybody's got DNA."

"Not if he's left outside to be gnawed by wild animals, then cooked to a crisp."

Jupiter isn't thrilled with this news.

I'm reaching the end of my very short rope. "Does the kid even know who his dad is?"

Kelly comes into the kitchen and we quiet immediately.

"Dad, Draconian asked if we have any absinthe."

"Tell him the Jewel was all out of absinthe this week. See if he likes lemonade."

"He's scary, Dad, really scary."

"Go back," I tell Kelly. "Don't leave your sister alone."

"Sherlock, I need the money to get my kid out of Goth Gulch," Jupiter tells me. "He's quit school, won't work, stays awake all night, and he worships Sekhmet."

"Who?"

"The Egyptian goddess of death and destruction."

"I bet that's an interesting church service."

"You have to help me, please."

I hear a horrified yelp and run right back into the living room to see Kelly and Care crammed to one side of the couch, cowering in fear as Draconian sits on the other side.

"How are you? Your mom tells me you're into music," I say to get his attention.

"I'm in a band."

"Which one?"

"Scumbag Death Cult."

"Party band?"

"We do covers of Christian Death, Alien Sex Fiend, and Merciful Nuns."

"I bet you really kill with those," I tell him.

Why any musician would want to be in a cover band has always amazed me, but there's so many of them. The Lead Zeppelins, Kneel Diamonds in the Rough, Leonard Skinners. I wonder if one of these tribute bands was so good, there would someday be a tribute band to the tribute band?

Draconian gets this weird look on his already weird look, slides off the couch, moves to a wide spot of the floor, lies down on his back, and assumes his rendition of the Corpse yoga pose. We all watch him lie there barely breathing.

"What's he doing?" Kelly asks, in awe of the somewhat human spectacle.

"Full moon tonight," Jupiter explains. "You know the way the moon controls the ocean tides? I think the same thing happens to the fluids inside Draconian's brain."

"If he starts leaking, Dad," Kelly tells me, "you have to clean it up."

"See what I'm talking about, Sherlock?" Jupiter says to me.

"He needs help."

"Maybe it's just a phase he's going through."

"Yeah, the dark side of the moon phase," Jupiter says. "I got to get him a shrink, but I can't afford one."

"I don't know what I could do to help, Jupiter."

"We prove Draconian's Buck's kid, and he'll get in on the payout."

"How?"

"DNA."

"There isn't any."

"Oh, come on, there has to be an old pair of Buck's Jockey shorts laying around."

"If Buck didn't get rid of whatever was his, Blanche sold it at her garage sale."

"There has to be a way, Sherlock. A guy just doesn't get up and leave his spit and shinola behind."

"You're too late. The judge isn't going to overrule a signed, notarized death certificate without the victim showing up for a guest appearance." I pause to let it sink in, then add, "The money is going to be transferred on Monday. It's a done deal."

Jupiter gives me a look of total desperation. "That's why I wanted Buck back, to tell him he had a son, and his son needs help."

"I'm sorry."

"Please."

"You could go before the court and tell them your story, but rebutting an urn full of the guy's ashes might be a little difficult."

"There has to be a way, Sherlock," Jupiter says. "There has to be a way. If Cato gets his hands on that money, he'll be out of the country quicker than a Vietnam-era draft dodger."

"There's nothing I can do," I tell her.

"Some doctor has to have some record of a blood test or something."

"There isn't."

"Then what do you suggest I do?" Jupiter asks.

"Put it all behind you and move on with your life."

"And leave that million bucks on the table for that slimeball Cato and the wacko wives to waste on cheap beer and Cheetos while my son needs help? I don't think so."

"I don't know what to tell you, Jupiter."

"Well, I'm not giving up."

I feel sorry for Jupiter as she gets down next to the boy, slaps him gently across his face a few times, being careful not to ruin his makeup. "Come on, Draconian, time to go."

It takes her quite a few slaps to raise the kid from the netherworld.

Draconian finally does a Dracula rising out of the coffin move, gets to his feet, and says, "See you people on the dark side."

"Thanks for stopping by. Next time, come again when your blood's running smoothly or during a quarter moon," I tell the boy. "We'll play charades."

"Yo."

Our guests exit.

"Dad," Kelly says, "if that's your new girlfriend, and you end up marrying her, there's no way I'm living in the same house with Deathly Draconian."

## CHAPTER 18

I'm in the middle of doing my back exercises on Saturday morning when the phone rings.

"You keep this up, Sherlock, and the legal fees are going to be higher than the million dollars we're supposed to pay out." Someone's got up on the draconian side of the bed.

"I didn't do anything."

Bree Bisonette, pronounced "Biz-o-nay," continues, "Then it must have been that pea-brained, poor excuse for an offspring, Tiffany, who got Mr. Richmond so riled up."

"What did she do?"

"Convinced him Buck Crouch is alive and kicking. And he's ordering me to get back into court and stop the flow of our money."

"The money has to go out on Monday," I remind her.

"Dewey Diddier pulled some strings to get Judge Pennington to hear our latest plea."

"What plea?" I ask.

"We don't have one yet. So come up with one and be in court Monday morning."

"We can't keep going on like this, Bree."

"That's what Mr. Richmond told me once." Bree sniffles before hanging up.

Kelly and Care emerge from the bedroom after ten.

"What do you two have planned for today?" I ask the girls.

"Nothing, Dad. You're in charge of planning," Care answers.

"I could see doing a little shopping," Kelly tells me.

"Not gonna to happen."

The girls land on the couch and turn on the TV.

"What do you want for breakfast?" I ask.

"Fruit Loops."

"No."

"Lucky Charms."

"No."

"Donuts."

"Scrambled eggs it is."

I do feel badly about having to be so matter-of-fact with Jupiter. I'm sure I would do anything humanly possible to get Kelly or Care out of some mind-bending satanic cult, but what can I do here? Without Buck's name on the birth record, DNA from each, or a marriage certificate, Jupiter's going to have a heck of a time convincing anyone that Buck and Draconian are father and son, especially on the day of the dead. I mean dance. Her sudden change in direction, flipping from "Buck's alive" to "all we got to do is prove paternity," to me doesn't add up to a strong belief that her word is her bond.

Sure, there are more holes in the case than a tavern's dartboard, but so far there isn't one bit of substantial proof of Buck being alive. Judge J Philpot is going to hear what we have to say and blow a judicial gasket.

Oddly enough, we don't hear a peep out of Tiffany all day; for the girls, a disappointment, for me, a welcome relief.

"Tiffany's probably got some fancy party for rich people to attend, where we wouldn't be welcomed unless we were serving the canapés," I explain to Care and Kelly.

We do our weekly chores: laundry, bathroom sparkle, vacuuming, and kitchen scrub in the morning, and follow up in the early afternoon with our outside stops: market, drug store, and cleaners. What fun. In the afternoon we take in a movie, PG rated, and order a pizza for dinner. All in all, a pretty good day.

Sunday morning, I try to convince my two to attend a church service with no luck. A little before noon, somebody lies on the door buzzer and doesn't let up.

"Don't answer it," Care yells. "It could be the Goth guy."

"Quick, hide!" Kelly says, scrambling to find a hiding place.

"Can't be him," I reply. "He doesn't come out during the day."

I make my way to the kitchen to answer the buzzer. "Who is it?"

"It's me. Hurry up and open the door, I'm melting."

I recognize the scream, but the girls don't.

"Who is it, Dad?"

"The Wicked Witch of the West."

"If she's a friend of Draconian, don't let her in."

I hit the open button.

A couple minutes later, Tiffany enters the apartment, fanning herself with her Fendi purse. "Why can't you live in a building with an air-conditioned lobby, Mr. Sherlock?"

"Because you don't pay me enough."

"Tiffany!" The girls run out from their hiding places.

"Hello, little dudettes."

"We thought you were a member of the Scumbag Death Cult."

"Sounds like an ugly Facebook Friends group."

Tiffany heads for the window a/c unit, spreads herself in front of it, and hogs all the cool air.

"Just drop by for a breath of our fresh air, Tiffany?" I ask.

"Look what I got, Mr. Sherlock," a cooler Tiffany says, turning toward us.

We watch as she opens her purse and pulls out a bad copy of a bad photo.

"Meet Buck."

Tiffany unfolds the paper to reveal an 8 x 10 copy of a photo, and it's the same baseball cap, jeans, belt buckle, plaid shirt, and boots as the Heeb's picture. I can't believe my eyes.

"That's him paying off his credit card."

"Where'd you get this?"

"Every inch of every bank in America is photographed 24/7 and there's a photo of each transaction made."

"How did you know that?" I ask her.

"*Law and Order* episode."

I have to hand it to her, she's right.

"That's Buck Crouch?" Kelly asks.

"In the flesh."

"You're kidding?"

"No, my little dudette, I'm not kidding. He's alive."

I make the mistake of thinking out loud. "It's exactly the same as the other one."

"What other one?" Tiffany asks.

"The one from Heeb's."

"What's Heeb's?"

"Grocery store."

"There's a grocery store named Heeb's?" Tiffany asks. "Is it located inside a temple?"

"It's in Montana." I pause. "There's a picture of the same guy going into a grocery store in Bozeman, Montana."

"You saw other pictures of Buck and you didn't tell me, Mr. Sherlock?" Tiffany raises her voice. "Why not?"

"Yeah, Dad, why didn't you tell her?" Kelly adds fuel to the fire in Tiffany's eyes.

"Or tell us?" Care adds. "We're family."

"Because I didn't believe it."

"Why not?"

"Because I couldn't see his face."

"You didn't know what his face looked like."

"Dad, we are so disappointed in you," Care says.

"You should get grounded," Kelly adds.

I sit, trying to make sense of the photo.

"This is what we're taking to the judge tomorrow, Mr. Sherlock, to stop the cash from flowing."

I stare at the picture. I can't see his face. "Tiffany. This is hardly a presidential portrait."

"But if we tell him the story, the judge will give us a pardon," Tiffany suggests.

"A pardon?"

"Yeah, pardon our payment, and I can get my communion commission."

"And what happens if the judge rejects it?"

"Then we'll have to try something else."

"Tomorrow's the day you have to pay out the money."

"Well, then you better come up with a B Plan, Mr. Sherlock, because I've already decided on the color of my new Lexus."

"Let me guess: the color of money with gold trim and a platinum finish?"

# CHAPTER 19

Judge J Philpot Pennington peers over his cheater glasses at the assembled and says, "Oh, this better be good."

The gang's all here. Dewey Diddier, Seedy Sheedy, Cato, three wives, Tiffany, Kelly, Care, Bree Bisonette, pronounced Biz-o-nay, and way in the back, Jupiter and Moonjava/Draconian, who has added a black cape, cowl, and Ray-Ban sunglasses in addition to other dark duds, to ward off the rays of the sun.

"Okay, who wants to go first?" the Judge says.

Seedy Sheedy beats Dewey to the punch. "The money is due today. Tell these no-good sandbaggers to pay up and pay up now."

"Judge," Dewey interrupts, "we have indisputable evidence that Leonard 'Buck' Crouch is alive and living in Montana."

"No way," Buck's wives yell out in tandem. They must have decided to join forces in their battle for Buck's house.

"He personally entered a bank last week and paid off the past due amount of his credit cards," Diddier says. "A dead man doesn't do something like that, Your Honor."

"If he's up there, then who's in here?" Cato calls out, lifting Buck's urn to the sky.

"Would you put that thing away," the Judge orders Cato.

Blanche rushes over and whips the urn out of Cato's hands. "You've had him long enough. Buck's going home with us."

"Buck was also spotted at Heeb's grocery store in Bozeman, Montana," Dewey adds.

"There's a grocery store named Heeb's?" the Judge asks.

"Yes, and we have proof that Buck's a regular shopper."

Sheedy gets back into the fight. "May I also remind the court that we have this." He holds up a copy of the death certificate. "Signed, sealed, and delivered."

Tiffany, who is seated with us in the middle of the courtroom, jumps up and says, "We have also launched a special covert investigation to find Buck Crouch."

"Sit down, young lady," the Judge says. "You have not been recognized to speak in front of this court."

"But I'm already starting to get responses that will prove Buck's alive," Tiffany argues.

What is Tiffany talking about?

"Sit down, Miss, or I will order the bailiff to sit you down."

Not to be left out, Blanche and Travianna state their case. "Judge, buggered brother-in-law Cato is trying to take our house away from us. You got to stop him."

"Quiet!"

The gavel comes down so hard, it almost cracks the top of the bench.

"The next person who speaks without being recognized will be forcefully ejected from my courtroom."

The courtroom pauses for air.

I look back to see Draconian has slept through it all. I wish I could sleep that soundly.

Judge J Philpot peers down at Dewey. "If you have proof, let's see it."

Dewey places the bank's security camera's shot in front of him. "This was Buck at the bank."

"Okay."

Dewey adds the Heeb's pictures to the pile. "And this is the same man in the grocery store."

Sheedy boosts himself up to see. Cato and the wives stand to get a better look.

"And here's the receipt from the bank. It's Buck, no doubt about it," Dewey Diddier announces.

"Did you bring a *before* picture of Buck, so I can see what he did look like?"

Dewey pulls out the picture of Buck in his Cubs shirt, holding the Louisville Slugger, and hands it to the Judge.

The Judge peruses the photos side by side. "You can't see his face in any of these." The Judge holds the Heeb's pictures up for all to see.

"That ain't Buck," Blanche says.

Cato says, "Buck isn't bow-legged."

Sheedy yells out, "I don't see any matching tattoos."

"Quiet."

Judge Pennington stares down at Dewey. "You call this proof?"

"Yes, Your Honor."

"I don't."

Dewey is in trouble and he knows it.

"Judge, you have to give us more time. The fact that the

credit card was paid off should be enough for you to at least consider Buck's still breathing."

"No, it isn't."

"And the fact that Richmond is still in the midst of investigating the very suspicious disappearance," Dewey adds.

Tiffany jumps up out of her seat to wave. "I'm on that, Judge."

"Quiet."

"Dead men don't tell tales, Judge, or pay off past due credit cards."

"Sorry, not buying it."

"And, Your Honor, we have a witness who has personally seen Buck and can identify him beyond a shadow of a doubt."

"A witness?"

"Yes, an eyewitness."

There are fibs, white lies, stretchings of the truth, statistics, little lies, medium lies, lies that don't hurt anyone, cover-up lies, politician's promises, and then there are violations of the truth so flagrant and absurd they totally blow past all rules of propriety, reality, and sanity.

Dewey Diddier has resorted to the last on the list.

"Where is this witness?" the Judge asks.

"Montana."

"What is he doing in Montana?"

"Fishing."

"And why didn't you bring him along today?"

"The fish are biting."

Judge J Philpot Pennington removes his glasses, checks out the confederacy of dunces before him, and says, "You got twenty-four hours."

Seedy Sheedy explodes, "You can't do that."

Cato yells out, "I want my money."

Tiffany whoops it up, joined by Kelly and Care, who whoop it up with her just for the heck of it.

Instead of trying to quell the rabble, the Judge sees the hippie and the sleeping man in black in the rear of the courtroom. Jupiter holds her hand up, as if she has a question for the teacher.

"Yes, Miss?" the Judge asks.

"Judge, can I say something?"

"Who are you?"

"Buck's girlfriend."

Her answer brings the crowd's arguing, celebrating, and pointless whooping down to a mumbling, dull roar.

"Girlfriend?"

"Why are you here?" the Judge asks.

"I thought I'd better speak before I held my peace forever."

There's a phrase Blanche and Travianna wished they'd heard.

"Who's that next to you?"

"My boy." Jupiter shakes Moon/Drac and gets him to his feet.

"And why is he here?"

Jupiter scans the room with her eyes and says, "I'd like everyone to meet Moonjava, although he likes to be called Draconian. He's Buck's son."

This new revelation fills the room like tear gas tossed into an illegal assembly. People are choking on the news, but no one is more surprised than Draconian, who looks like he just saw a ghost, even though he usually looks like he just saw a ghost.

"Would you please repeat that, Miss?" the Judge says.

"Buck's got one more heir, our son."

"No way."

"He never mentioned anyone to me."

"Buck hated kids."

"I thought he was a child of the devil," Kelly says.

Cato follows up the random comments with "I want proof."

The two so-called wives sit wondering why it wasn't one of them. Arnold is in a state of awe. Bree Bisonette is speechless.

The final comment is spoken by the offspring himself.

"I got a daddy?"

*** 

I don't say a word until we are out of earshot of the others and alone in the elevator on the way down.

"You don't lie to a judge, Tiffany. It's called perjury, it's a felony, and people go to jail for it." I raise my voice.

Tiffany doesn't respond.

"I can't believe you did that." I'm hotter than a branding iron.

More silence.

"What do you have to say for yourself, Tiffany?" I wait. "Tell me."

"You told me never to talk in an elevator."

My words come back to haunt me.

The elevator doors open in the lobby. We step out.

"I didn't lie," Tiffany says.

"What special covert investigation?"

"The one I started," she responds with verve in her voice equal to mine. "Just because you wouldn't do anything, Mr. Sherlock, doesn't mean I was going to go down with the yacht. I took the balls of the horny bull and put 'em in my court."

"What did you do?"

"A lot more than you, Mr. Sherlock." Tiffany is defiant.

"Whatever you did, Tiffany," Kelly says, "can I help?"

"Sure, and when we win, you can be the first to ride in my new Lexus."

"Cool."

"Me too?" Care chimes in.

"What did you do, Tiffany? Tell me."

"I baited up the worm and now all I got to do is wait for Buck to take it hook, wine, and stinker."

Is there any wonder why I hate my job?

Jupiter sees us and approaches. Draconian lags behind her like the Grim Reaper. Care and Kelly leap behind me for protection.

"I figured out how we can prove Draconian is Buck's son," Jupiter tells me.

This should be good. "How?"

"We get Cato's DNA," Jupiter explains. "They're identical twins, they'll have the same DNA."

"And you think Cato will submit to such a test?"

"Sure, why not?"

"Money." My turn to explain. "If there's no other heirs and Cato eliminates the two wives, he gets the whole enchilada."

"He's not Hispanic, Mr. Sherlock," Tiffany jumps into the conversation. "And there's gonna be no money handed out because we're going to prove Buck's still alive."

"Who are you?" Jupiter asks Tiffany.

"I represent the Richmond Insurance Company. Who are you and who's that with you?"

"I'm Jupiter and this is my son Draconian."

"Wow," Tiffany says, "he looks like death warmed over."

"Thanks," Draconian acknowledges the compliment.

Bree Bisonette and Dewey Diddier see the group and they come over.

"Well, I bought us more time," Dewey says. "You got to get off the stick and find this guy, Sherlock."

"Who, Buck or your eyewitness?"

"Either one."

"Where am I supposed to find the eyewitness?" I ask the attorney.

"I don't know, that's your job."

"That was nothing but a bold, bare-faced lie you told the judge," I tell Dewey.

"I told you I'd come up with a plan."

"You can't do that."

"I already did, so deal with it."

Bree comes nose to sculptured nose with Tiffany. "I would appreciate you refraining from telling your father your juvenile opinion on cases you know nothing about, Little Miss Tiffy."

"You're just mad because Daddy dumped your ass."

"Am not."

"Are so."

Jupiter continues, "I'll get the DNA, Sherlock. I'll find a snot rag or a toenail clipping, get it analyzed, and match it with Draconian's."

"It won't do you any good unless Buck allows the evidence to go into testimony, which he won't do in a million years."

We're standing in front of a bank of elevators. People are waiting, getting on and off cars, while we're carrying on like the Battling Bickersons.

"Sherlock, I've given you a perfect opportunity to show your true capabilities to the company," Dewey tells me. "You should be more appreciative."

"You told a lie and I got to make it real? Who do you think I am, Penn or Teller?"

"It's a courtroom, everybody lies."

Everybody except Draconian is talking at the same time. Plus, people are telling us to "Get out of the way." "Save it for the courtroom." "Settle the case before somebody gets hurt."

What stops the madness is Tiffany's phone starts beeping like a possessed microwave.

"Mr. Sherlock," Tiffany says, manhandling her erupting phone, "we got to go. The fish are starting to bite."

***

"A hundred and ninety-two and counting, Mr. Sherlock."

Tiffany sits behind the massive computer console in her condo's office; talk about wasted space. Pictures of men flash on the screen faster than mug shots from Interpol.

"How did you ever come up with this idea, Tiffany?" Kelly asks.

"I know men," she answers. "And every man has a weakness, which is women, especially women who look like me. So, knowing Buck's a horn dog with two wives and one girlfriend, and who trolls the internet for more women, all I had to do is sign up on a few Montana dating sites and let him find me."

"Dad, when I'm sixteen, can I try this?" Kelly asks.

"No."

Tiffany continues to scroll through man after man.

"This guy says, 'he wants a woman who needs a whole lot of lovin'," Care reads off the screen.

"Delete," I command.

"'Little Lady, I'll take you to the moon.'"

"What does that mean, Dad?"

"It means delete it now."

"This one says, 'Closer to the bone, the sweeter the meat. And I like a prime filet.'"

"Delete that one twice."

"Dudettes, take my advice," Tiffany tells my girls. "Don't kiss any frogs who obviously have warts." Interesting pearls of wisdom from one who can afford a lot more than pearls.

"How are you going to know it's Buck if he does reply, Tiffany?"

"He'll have his fish with him."

"You think he'll use the same picture?"

"They always use the same picture in the second round," Tiffany says. "Men are dumb. Instead of putting on a better picture, to up the level of sexual intrigue, they put on the same stupid picture as before."

I need a break from our personal digital Dear Abby of

dating. My back starts to hurt. Gee, ya think it could be stress?

I wander around the spacious condo I'll never be able to afford, and end up in a comfortable chair facing one of the picture windows of the unit.

I sink into the comfy leather cushions. It feels great sitting in Tiffany's sky-hugging condo with the temperature set at a perfect 70 degrees, looking out on the lakefront stretching all the way to Wisconsin. Where did I go wrong in life?

"I know he's alive, Mr. Sherlock. For just once, just hang with me," Tiffany says, ruining my quiet time.

I don't tell her "yes" and I don't tell her "no." If I did pick one, she wouldn't listen to me but would do whatever she was going to do anyway.

I stare outside. What a view. I try to think things through. It isn't easy.

"Mr. Sherlock, are you listening to me?"

"What did you say?"

"Are you listening to me?"

"Evidently not."

"You're worse than my daddy when I ask for more money," she says and walks away.

My return to quiet is welcomed.

Maybe I should give Buck being alive another go. This morning when I got up off the couch, before I felt my first stabbing lumbar pain of the day, I thought of something that's been bothering me alongside my back pain. I rise from the chair and go into one of the three other bedrooms in the unit, shut the door, and make a phone call.

"Hi, this is Richard Sherlock. We met the other day."

"Oh, yeah, hi. How you doing?"

"Is this Deloris or Debbie?"

"Deloris."

"There's something I forgot to ask you."

"Fire away."

"On the day you tripped over what was left of the dead man's foot, do you remember what kind of shoe he was wearing?"

"Why would you want to know that?"

"I don't know. I just like to know whatever I don't know."

"Well, I'm not sure, since so much of the material had been eaten away, but they were either Nikes or Nike knock-offs."

"Tennis shoes?"

"Cross-trainers."

I'm amazed at her conclusion. "Really. How can you be so exact?"

"The swoosh."

"You're incredibly observant."

"No, I'm a shoe freak. I got like sixty pairs."

"How about his socks?"

"He wasn't wearing socks."

## CHAPTER 20

Kelly and Care want to stay with Tiffany and peruse the hopeful men who are drawn to Tiffany like kids to McDonald's.

I go home. I need a mental break and multiple rolls on the Oriental Oscillator, since my back is doing conniptions again. While sliding around my front room, I come up with a couple more unanswered questions. I write them down.

First call I make this Tuesday morning is to Dr. Landis Keenshaw.

"Richard Sherlock, Doctor, remember me?"

"Yes, how are you?"

"A couple questions if I may?"

"Certainly."

"What was the exact height and weight of the body that was found? And second, weren't there any fingerprints?"

"Wait one second."

I hear papers shuffling.

"The body was exactly five-foot nine inches, one hundred thirty-seven pounds."

"Fingerprints?"

"None. Fingers are first to get eaten away by animals, kinda like the appetizer before the main course."

"Thank you, Doctor."

The next call I make is to Police Chief Cliff Adolph.

"How are you, Chief?"

"Good. What can I do for you?"

"When you originally examined the body assumed to be Buck Crouch, was he wearing pants?"

"Yes."

"Any boxers or briefs underneath?"

"That's a weird question."

"Weird questions are a big part of my life, Chief."

"You know," he says," not that I can remember."

"One more question—"

"Make it a normal one."

"Is there any way someone could have carried the body into the ravine instead of throwing it off the cliff?"

"Nothing's impossible, but I would never attempt it."

"Thanks, Chief."

"You're welcome."

I'm about to make the third and last phone call on my list when my phone rings.

"Hello."

"You the one who stole Buck?"

"Who is this?"

"Travianna Mapp," she says. "Somebody broke into the house last night and stole Buck."

"The urn?"

"Yep. Was it you?"

"Sorry, I've never been into urn thievery. Did they take anything else?"

"Yeah, Blanche's bong."

"You call the police?"

"No."

"Why not?"

"Blanche's bong."

"I used to be a police detective," I inform her. "Want me to come over and investigate?"

"Sure, why not?"

I do my exercises as best as I'm able, take a shower, eat, and by that time it's after ten, so I call my kids. I get Care on the phone.

"Tiffany's got like over four hundred responses so far. The guys are on her like ugly on an ape, Dad."

"Buck, smiling with his fish, show up yet?"

"Not yet."

"Is Tiffany awake?"

"No."

"Let me talk to Kelly."

"She's not here."

"Where is she?"

"She left to go to the store to get us some donuts. We didn't want to do another morning of bean sprout smoothies."

Can't say I blame them. "Care, I got a few stops to make, then I'll take the El downtown and pick you two up."

"Don't hurry, Dad. Tiffany's place is much cooler than yours."

"In the temperature or atmosphere sense of the word?"

"Both."

I get over to Buck's prior residence a little after eleven.

Travianna and Blanche are waiting.

"You sure you didn't steal Buck?" Blanche asks as I enter.

"Positive."

"How about my bong?"

"No." I enter the house. The lines down the middle of the room have been erased; evidently, the civil war's over.

"How'd they break in?"

"Back door," Travianna answers.

"They jimmy the lock?"

"Naw, it's busted."

Travianna finishes the explanation, "We're not fixing anything until we find out if we're gonna keep the house."

"Where was the urn when it got stolen?"

"On the mantle."

I walk over to the fireplace mantle and see a little of Buck's remains still remain.

"By the way," I ask Blanche, "how tall was Buck?"

"Exactly this tall," Blanche says, holding her flat hand at the base of her chin.

"Did he wear boxers, briefs, or like to hang loose?"

"Briefs. He got 'em free; why wouldn't he?"

"How well do you know Cato's wife?" I continue questioning.

"Not well," Blanche says.

"I don't even think crumb-bum Cato knows her that well," Travianna adds. "She's one of those mail-order brides."

"Really." I wonder what the postage was?

"He hadn't even met her until he went over there."

"To the Philippines," Blanche finishes the explanation.

I'm reminded of my hacker buddy Herman, who went over to Russia and brought back little Ludmila to be his wife. That worked out well.

"Cato ever have a career at anything?" I change the line of questioning.

"No, he's a bum."

"All he likes to do is mooch other people's money."

"Buck bailed him out more times than a fisherman in a leaky boat."

I pretend to search the place for clues to the robbery as we talk. I doubt if I'm very convincing.

"Can I see what's left of Buck's stuff?" I ask.

While we're walking towards the bedroom, I ask Travianna, "Where did you and Buck live?"

"Bucktown."

"He pay the rent?"

"Most of it."

In the bedroom, Blanche opens a drawer in the dresser. "Voila."

Old Cub ticket stubs, unlucky lottery tickets, receipts from National Parks, and a whole lot of socks are inside in no particular order except disorder.

"He never kept much here, since he was on the road all the time."

Can't say I blame the guy. "Why didn't he want his picture taken?"

"Buck was weird about that. Said he always came out with red eye," Blanche says.

"I think it was something to do with his parents," Travianna says.

"Like what?"

"I don't know. He didn't like his dad and he never mentioned his mother," Blanche says.

"And who would ever want to be seen and remembered with that idiot Cato?" Travianna adds.

I give up on finding anything but junk in the junk drawer. I take a quick look into the closet. One side is pretty much empty, due to the garage sale, no doubt. The other side is stocked with Blanche's duds. Many of the items hanging still have the price tags.

"You think you can help us keep the house?" Blanche asks.

"I know some real good slimy lawyers you could use."

"Will they work on a lawyer-now/pay-later plan?"

"You'd have to ask them." I wander out of the bedroom. The wives follow me like lonely sheep.

"Maybe Cato will be satisfied with getting the million and leave you two alone in the house," I wonder out loud.

"I doubt it."

"Whatever you do," I tell them, "don't move out. Make him evict you."

"We'll never see a dime, will we, Sherlock?"

"Ya never know. Stranger things have happened."

"Yeah, but it took the Cubs one hundred eight years,"

Blanche says. "We don't got that kind of time."

I'm done with my robbery investigation. Well, almost.

I see a cardboard banker's box on the floor in the front room positioned under the receiving end of the mail slot. The box is filled to the brim with unopened envelopes, flyers, weekly shoppers, and the rest pure junk.

"Buck's mail?"

"Yeah, we heard it was against the law to throw it away," Blanche says.

"Mind if I take a look?"

"Knock yourself out."

As I lean down to reach into the treasure trove of junk mail, Travianna asks, "Is the money going to be paid out today?"

"That's what the judge ordered."

"Unless you come up with the eyewitness."

"Correct."

"How's that going?"

"I got three experts on it right now." This answer falls into the *White Lie* category.

"Mind if I take this with me?" I ask concerning the box of mail.

"Go ahead, but if you find any checks or really good coupons, they belong to me," Blanche says.

"And me," Travianna adds.

I leave the two wives, get out to my car, stop, put the box in the trunk, turn around, go back to the front door, and knock.

"By the way," I ask the two, "would you have any idea of which shoes Buck wore the day he split?"

"His Salomon Quest 4D II GTX."

"He loved those boots."

***

On my way back from Buck's old house, I look on every street for what used to be as normal as a Starbucks on every other corner. What used to be so easy to find, the phone booth, has quickly become an urban relic. I stop at a neighborhood library instead.

"Do you have a phone book?"

"A what?" the research desk lady answers.

"A phone book. You know, the thick thing with names and

addresses in it."

"Why don't you just use your cell phone and Google?"

"Old habits are hard to break."

I eventually find Jupiter's number and use the reverse directory to get her address. I arrive at her apartment in twenty minutes. She lives on the edge of Evanston, just north of Howard, in an illegal unit behind a one-story ranch that would never be built on a prairie. I rap very gently, not wanting to disturb a slumbering Draconian.

"What are you doing here?" Jupiter asks.

"Why did you steal Buck's ashes?"

"Moi?"

"Yes, moi."

"I didn't steal them."

"Okay, why did you borrow Buck's ashes?"

Jupiter opens the door and lets me into her place.

The only thing that separates this place from a hippie crash pad is the absence of a couple of Jimi Hendrix black-light posters. There's pot plants under grow lights in the kitchen, an old guitar on the wall, beads hanging, and a fancy framed roach clip collection. The front room is packed, not with furniture, but with boxes and boxes of rocks.

"What's all this?"

"Crystals. I buy in bulk, cut 'em, polish 'em up, and sell them at festivals and to New Age stores."

"You make a living doing this?"

"This and selling pot. The customer base is pretty much the same."

"That why you borrowed Blanche's bong too?"

"Mine leaks."

We stand in the middle of her rock quarry. "Is Draconian here?"

"He's asleep."

"Before court, did he know about his father?"

"He knew he had one."

"I figured that. Did you tell him before yesterday about Buck?"

"I probably should have."

"So he wasn't thrilled with the news?"

"Let's just say it's not something he wanted to chat up."

"You sure Buck didn't know?"

"I probably should have told him, too."

I look around the room, searching for the urn. "Where's Buck's ashes, Jupiter?"

"They're not here. I put them to good use."

"Fertilizing the marijuana plants?"

"No, being analyzed for their DNA."

"You can't analyze ashes, Jupiter."

"No, but if there are unburned bone fragments, those can be analyzed. I looked it up on the internet."

"Just because it's on the internet doesn't mean it's true."

"Sherlock, you're such a stick in the mud."

"It won't work."

"Look, at this point I'll do anything to help my son. I've tried to raise him in the ways of peace, love and groovy, but instead he's become an angry, depressed kid who thinks daily about his own death. Do you have any idea how hard that is to live with?" Jupiter sits on a rock crate and puts her head in her hands. "Did I screw up raising him? Yeah, big time. I believed his lifestyle would groove with mine, but it didn't happen." Jupiter looks up at me. "Sherlock, this might be my last chance to get some help for the boy before he does something drastic."

"Isn't there some program or social service you can find to help him?"

"They either won't take him or he won't go. And he certainly won't listen to me."

"I know the feeling."

I'm sorry for Jupiter, but I have to be honest with her. "You're grasping at straws here. You're almost out of time. If Cato gets his hands on that million dollars, I got a feeling he'll be the next one to disappear."

***

I must be in a retro mood today because I decide to make one more stop before I pick up Kelly and Care.

It doesn't take me long to find exactly what I'm looking for at the Cook County Hall of Records.

Estalita's maiden name is Duarte.

## CHAPTER 21

" **S**ix hundred three, so far."
"A couple of the guys look pretty hot, Dad."
"I'm going to pretend I didn't hear you say that, Kelly."
All three girls are seated behind the computer.
"No Buck?"
"A patient is a virtue, Mr. Sherlock."
"Here's one who says he'll 'ring your bingo bell,'" Care reads off the screen.
"Delete."
I see in the kitchen the girls convinced Tiffany to have pizza for lunch.
"I have to tell you, Tiffany, your Plan B may be in vain."
"I'm not pregnant, Mr. Sherlock."
"No, your Plan B as in Buck."
"Why? He'll take the bait, no doubt in my mind."
"I heard from Bree Bisonette."
"What did she want, one of my guys to date?" Tiffany snarkily asks. "Maybe I'll give her the one who wants to 'shake my windows and rattle my walls.'"
"No, she received a certified letter from Seedy Sheedy stating that if the check isn't received by tomorrow close of business, they will sue for daily damages, starting at one hundred K, per day."
"They can do that?"
"Sure, and with the judge on their side, he'll rule in Cato's favor."
"Maybe we should get a new judge."
"It doesn't work that way."
"A check for a million bucks, only an officer of the company can sign one of those." Tiffany informs me of a fact I'm surprised she'd know anything about.
"Bree can sign it."
"Talk about adding insult to insurance," Tiffany says. "Putting a million dollars in her hands is like throwing a swine at the pearly gates."
"Sorry to be the bearer of bad news, Tiffany, but you're going to have to pay up. You're out of time."
"You're telling me I won't be able to get my communion?"
"Yeah, you'll have to spend a year of shame behind the

wheel of last year's Lexus 460."

"Look!" Care screams out.

"That's him!" Kelly follows.

"I'd know that fish anywhere," Tiffany says.

I hightail it to their side of the computer and see Buck and his fish. "It is him."

This is hard to believe.

Care reads off the screen. "We'll be as natural as nature, pure as the driven snow, spring flowers sprouting their beauty." Care looks to us. "Buck sounds much better than the guy who says he wants to 'flip your pancake.'"

"I told you he's alive, Mr. Sherlock."

"But you're too late."

"Call Brat Biz-o-not and tell her not to cut that check."

"She has to."

"No. I'll tell Daddy to let me handle it."

"You'll lose another hundred grand," I tell her. "And when the insurance commission finds out about this, they'll string the whole company up by its bottom line."

"I don't care."

Tiffany runs around the room getting her stuff together.

"This could be Cato fooling around on his wife again, Tiffany," I argue. "We haven't proven anything."

"I don't care." Tiffany runs back behind the computer and orders Kelly, "Hit Reply and write this: *I love a man with a fish that big. Can't wait to meet you. How about lunch tomorrow? Signed Your little nature girl.*"

"Yeah, that'll reel him in," Care says as Kelly types.

Kelly hits Send.

"Call Bree and tell her not to do anything until I get there."

"No. You have to pay off the claim, Tiffany. Even your father won't let you put the entire firm in jeopardy."

"Fine, I'll get the check myself and deliver it personally. Will that make you happy, Mr. Sherlock?" Tiffany uncharacteristically screams at me.

"Yeah, it'll make my day."

***

At 9:00 AM, we get out of the limo Tiffany sent for us on the Midway Airport tarmac. The Richmond company jet, fueled and ready to fly, awaits.

"It's about time we began travelling in the comfort we deserve, Dad."

"Actually, Kelly, I was planning on taking us on a trip to Montana, but I thought it would be more fun to go nose-to-butt."

Tiffany arrives in her own limo only a half-hour late. Even though we're going up and back on the same day, Tiffany has packed two suitcases.

As she approaches, I have to ask, "I guess he wrote you back."

"Of course he wrote me back. Once I get a guy on the line, they don't hang up, they get hung up."

By a noose.

"Let's get on the plane," Tiffany says. "I need a nap after getting up so early this morning."

***

Bozeman, Montana is a charming place. Set in the Gallatin Valley between two mountain ranges, the town is postcard picturesque. Its main street, aptly named Main Street, harkens back to times of simplicity in Western America. There's an Elks Club, Public Library, hardware store, bars, cozy restaurants, and, of course, Heeb's grocery store. One of the three cabs that operate in town takes us past a corner where a horse stands on top of a building.

"How'd that horse get up there?" Care asks.

"Jumped," the driver replies.

"They do things differently in Montana, Care," I tell her.

"Well, here's the place," the driver says, stopping at a restaurant in the front of a hotel. The sign reads: Ted's Montana Grill.

Tiffany pays the tab and tips the guy what she'd tip if she were in Chicago. It makes the driver's day.

In the jet before landing, Tiffany changed from her traveling pantsuit to a sexy little Western number, which included a short leather skirt, a tee shirt inscribed with *Come Home to My Range*, and a pair of calf-high cowboy boots. If Buck does show up, he won't be able to miss her.

"What's that mean, Dad?" Care asks as we stand under

Ted's sign that reads *Home of the Bison Burger.*

"It's the way they buffalo you to eat here, Care."

Ted's Grill is actually perfect for what we need to accomplish. The tables are spread out in a large room in front of a second-story terrace and the hotel check-in desk. Tiffany can sit right in the middle. The girls and I can be at a table off to the side and be able to see and hear everything without being conspicuous.

I work out a plan with Tiffany I'm positive won't work, but what the heck.

"Just chat him up, Tiffany. Don't let on who you are until we get an idea who he is. Ease into the conversation, ask if he has any tattoos, if he's ever been to Chicago, has a family, been married before."

"Ten-four, Mr. Sherlock."

"Whatever we do, you can't scare him away."

"The only way he'll get scared away is if he thinks he can't handle me."

As we all sit, Tiffany takes a compact out, opens the mirror, takes a look, decides she's already perfect, and returns the case to her Hermès purse. She nervously waits a minute, then turns to me to signal that she's totally bored and hates to wait.

I should text her *Patience is a virtue*, but I hate texting.

The lunch crowd begins to fill Ted's. The waitress hands out our menus, which are all bison all the time. When in Rome, do as the Romans do, I guess.

Five minutes go by. Tiffany's thin patience has become anorexic.

A guy walks into the place wearing a western shirt and Salomon Quest GTX boots. He's about the size of Cato without the paunch, beard and thinning hair. He's older than the guy with the fish, no surprise there, and looks a bit different. His hair is styled, shirt and jeans pressed, nice socks. He breaks into a big smile when he spots Tiffany, and rushes to her table. I can hear him say, "Mother Nature sure has done well by you."

I have to "Shussh" Kelly and Care to stop their excited giggling.

Tiffany doesn't stand to greet him, but does put out her hand to shake, which he takes and plants a kiss upon. What a charmer.

"Hi, I'm Bob, Bob Smith."

"Mary Jones."

Clever alias couple.

He sits. "As soon as I saw your picture I couldn't wait to meet you."

"Yeah, I have that effect on men," Tiffany tells him.

"You certainly did on me."

"Come here often?" Tiffany asks.

"Often enough."

"What's your sign?"

"Open for business," he says with a laugh.

"Aren't you the clever one?"

Detective's intuition: I've never met this guy. I've only seen two old pictures. The descriptions from his brother and wives have been sketchy at best, and there are no sock samples hanging out of his pocket, but there is absolutely no doubt that this is Buck Crouch. I can feel it.

Oh jeesh, I'm sounding like Jupiter.

"I'm surprised you didn't bring your fish along," Tiffany tells him.

"I thought you might like that picture," he says.

"Nothing better than reeling a big one in, is there?"

"Little Miss, you sound like my kinda nature girl."

I can't take any more of this dating pitter-patter. I tell the girls, "Wait here," get up, walk slowly over to their table, and stand between the pair, looking towards Buck.

"You're a tough one to come by," I say.

"Pardon me?" he says.

I put out my hand to shake and look him right in the eye. "Buck Crouch, I'm Richard Sherlock, Detective Richard Sherlock."

He's been had and he knows he's been had.

"How'd you find me?"

"Everybody's got a weakness," I tell him.

"And yours is women," Tiffany answers. "Any guy with two wives and a girlfriend was bound to have his horns out wider than a cell phone tower. I guess you could say we had your number."

"Well, I certainly hope finding this out will not mean we're going to end our promising relationship," Buck says to Tiffany.

"I lied," Tiffany admits. "I hate nature, and fishing is only for people who can't afford restaurants."

"Lied on the internet—who would ever guess?" he says. Buck stares at Tiffany, stares at me, and does something I would never expect: he breaks into raucous laughter. "This is hilarious."

"Why?" Tiffany says.

"I get outed by a detective named Sherlock. How weird is that?"

"I didn't get to pick my name," I tell him like I've told countless others.

"Is your real name Watson?" he says to Tiffany.

"No, it's Tiffany, Tiffany Richmond. Sound familiar?"

"No."

"You almost got away with it, Buck, almost," I tell him.

"Hey," he says, "up here the law's *catch and release*. You might have caught me, but now you got to let me go."

Buck's still laughing as Care and Kelly come over, wanting to get in on the fun. "Who are you, the Nancy Drew twins?"

"I'm Kelly, and this is my sister Care. Nice to meet you."

"Join us," Buck says. "The more the merrier. Have you ordered?"

"We were considering the bison," Kelly says.

Tiffany asks, "May I see your Cubs tattoo?"

"I'd be more than happy to show you a lot more," Buck says, rolling up his sleeve, "but this could be a good place to start."

We all take a look.

"Go Cubs, Go."

"You know anyone else who has one of those?" I ask.

"Oh, sure."

"Are they still alive?"

"As far as I know," Buck says.

The waitress takes our order. All of us do bison, except Tiffany who orders a Tuna Salad Niçoise. Why they would have a tuna salad in a bison restaurant is beyond me.

"Most people get caught right away when they try to disappear," I tell Buck.

"Ya got to do your homework," Buck says.

"Did you have help?"

"Nope."

"How long did it take you to plan?" I ask.

"Six months. I had to get all my ducks in a row before I left the pond."

"Why'd you pay off your credit card?" I have to ask.

"Didn't know I had it at first. Then I decided it was the last piece of Buck Crouch that needed to be buried."

"A lot of people have been looking for you besides us," I tell him.

"You have no idea, Detective."

"Why'd you just up and split?" I ask.

"I had my reasons."

"Two wives?" Tiffany wonders out loud.

"That was a couple of them," Buck says.

"Have you been up here in Montana the whole time?"

"Mostly. Takes time to set up a new life for yourself."

Oddly enough, Buck seems to be enjoying himself, as if getting caught gives him the opportunity to get things off his chest.

"The fates and fortunes of the world came down upon me and I decided I didn't want to deal with certain stuff anymore."

"Such as?" I ask.

"I didn't want my idiot brother or anybody else begging me for money, my women were getting on my nerves, I got a new jerk for a boss, and had enough money to never have to worry. So I disappeared."

"And you figured you could scam the Richmond Insurance Company," Tiffany adds to his list.

"What?"

"You know what I'm talking about," Tiffany says.

"What scam? I'm not scamming anybody."

"Oh, yeah," Tiffany argues. "Sure, you want nothing to do with claiming the big money from the policy?"

"What the heck you talking about, gorgeous?"

"My million bucks you're trying to grab."

"You got a million bucks?"

"Actually, more than that."

"With your looks and a million bucks, Sweetpea, what are you doing on an internet dating site?"

"Trying to find you."

"Well, you found me. Now would you like to go back to my place and see my etchings?" Buck asks Tiffany.

"We have one stop to make before we do any finger painting," Tiffany tells him.

"Where?"

"Chicago."

"I don't think so."

"You might as well come clean, Buck," I tell him. "We can file enough charges to send you up a river where the fish never bite."

"What charges?"

"Let's see," Tiffany says. "Faking your own death, trying to collect on a life insurance policy when you're not dead, and lying on your internet dating profile."

"What life insurance policy?"

"The one for a million bucks."

"The only life insurance I had was through the underwear company and that ended when I walked out."

"Then why did you try to fake your own death?" Tiffany comes right back at him.

"I didn't fake my own death and I didn't lie on my profile."

"Oh, come on, you're not thirty-something."

"Well, maybe I stretched the truth a little bit."

Tiffany goes the angry route. "We know what you did and you're going to tell it all in front of the judge."

Buck stares Tiffany right in the eye. "God, you're hot when you get mad."

I get in the middle of this. "Let's back up here—"

Tiffany doesn't let the conversation go into reverse. "Admit it, Buck!"

"I didn't fake my own death. What are you people, crazy?"

"Then explain how your body showed up in a Wisconsin ravine a year ago," Tiffany shouts.

"Body in a ravine?"

"Yeah, laying there all ABC'd," Tiffany says.

"ABC'd?"

"Already Been Chewed."

Buck can't keep his eyes off Tiffany. "Anybody with an imagination like yours must be great in the sack."

"Wouldn't you like to know?"

"Absolutely."

"Don't say that stuff around my kids," I admonish the pair.

"Oh, sorry."

"That's okay, Dad, I'm mature," Kelly tells me. "And Care doesn't know enough to even ask about sex."

"I do too," Care argues.

The bison burgers and salad arrive. I have to admit, they're pretty good. We all take a break as we munch 'em down.

"You people are all nuts," Buck says. "I don't know anything about a body and I certainly don't know anything about any insurance policy."

For some reason, I'm starting to believe him.

"The policy you've had since you were one."

"One what?"

"One year old."

Buck looks at me like I'm hallucinating.

"What did I do, go buy one with my leftover diaper money?"

"Your father bought it for you."

"My father never had more than two gin bottles to rub together."

"Have you talked to him since?"

"I did at his funeral, but he didn't have much to say."

"He was probably still mad at you," Tiffany says.

"He purchased a whole life policy on you and paid the premiums for years," I explain.

"That's news to me."

"If you didn't have life insurance, why would you write a will?"

"The only will I ever wrote was a few months ago, which nobody's read except me."

"How about your body?" Tiffany asks. "The one they found ravaged by a bunch of wild animals."

"My body's right here," Buck says to Tiffany. "I'm in it and if you'd like to examine it more closely, I'd be more than happy to oblige."

"Explain to us why you disappeared," I say.

"Look," Buck says, "I didn't do anything wrong, didn't fake my own death, and don't know about any insurance policy. The time was right. I didn't like my life, so I left to start a new one. There's no crime in that."

"Why would you leave a house that was paid off?" I ask.

"Let Blanche and Travianna fight over that dump. I could care less about the place."

"Did they know about each other?" I ask.

Buck shrugs his shoulders.

"Well, they do now. Travianna moved into the house with Blanche," I tell him. "It wasn't a real smooth transition, but they're getting along a lot better."

"Well, they do have one thing in common."

"Why didn't you marry them?" Kelly asks.

"I'm hardly a one-woman kind of a guy," he says and looks over at Tiffany. "But for you, gorgeous, I might make an exception."

"Blanche also sold all that fine artwork of yours on the walls."

"That crap wasn't mine," Buck says. "Give me a little credit, would you?"

"If it wasn't yours, whose was it?"

"That's what I got out of my old man's estate."

"Listen, Buck—" Tiffany says.

"My name's not Buck, it's Bob, Bob Smith."

"How long did it take you to come up with that one?"

"There's a method to my madness, honeychild."

"You're going to have to come with us back to Chicago," I tell him.

"Why?"

"To prove you're not dead."

"I already know I'm not dead."

"The court doesn't."

"And that's my problem?"

"You have to go. There's a million dollars about to be paid out," Tiffany says and adds, "And I need a new car next year."

"Look," I try to reason with the man, "there is a major insurance fraud being carried out and your name's on top of it."

"Bob Smith?"

"Buck Crouch."

"Didn't you just tell me Buck Crouch was found dead in a ravine in Wisconsin?"

"Yes."

"Sounds good to me. Buck's dead, Bob's here. Time to move on."

I try to convince him. "Listen—"

"I don't care," he says. "I didn't do anything wrong. It's not my money. If you people have a problem, you work it out. I'm going fishing."

Buck/Bob stands up, looks over at Tiffany. "I'm really going to miss you. We could have been so happy together. Sure you wouldn't consider a long weekend in the woods?" he asks in great expectation.

"Sure, after you join us in court."

"If you want a little courting, I can do that, but actual court, no way."

Tiffany quickly pulls out her phone, lifts it to her eye, but before she can snap the shutter, Buck reaches over and covers the lens.

"Sorry, no pictures."

"Why not?"

"I'm not very photogenic."

Buck pulls his hat down low to cover his face, turns, and heads for the door.

"Buck," I call out to him, "there's one more reason you might want to come with us."

"What?" he says without turning around.

"You might want to meet your son."

"What son?"

"The one you had with Jupiter."

"Oh my God."

## CHAPTER 22

The plan was for Buck to go home, pack up a few things, and meet us at the Bozeman airport in an hour.

After waiting two hours, Care says, "I don't think he's coming, Dad."

"You're probably correct, Care."

"We should have had someone go with him," Tiffany says.

"I suggested you do that, Tiffany, but you refused."

"Me with Mr. Touchy-Feely Nature, in his place, alone. Oh yeah, I'm going to sign up for that duty."

"That new Lexus doesn't come cheap, Tiffany."

"Try texting him," Kelly says.

Oh yeah, that'll work.

We give up on another passenger and jet off into the Big Sky sky. It's going to be tough to fly commercial again, especially when I fly the crummiest airline, in the smallest middle seat, on the cheapest fare, on a flight with more stops than a UPS driver during the Christmas rush.

A limo waits for us on the Midway tarmac as we taxi to a stop. I sit in the jet's comfy seat until the stairs open and come down, and see a woman come out of the limo and rush to meet us. If this were Hawaii, she'd probably have leis.

It's Bree Bisonette, pronounced "Biz-o-nay," standing waiting to greet us.

"What the hell did you think you were doing?" Bree screams at Tiffany louder than the roar of the jet engines. "You're going to cost us another hundred grand!"

"Well, that's a fine 'how do you do?'" Tiffany says.

Bree yells at me, "You know what she tried to pull?"

"No."

"She sends the million-dollar check, unsigned."

"Gee," Tiffany says, "I wonder how that could have happened?"

"Seedy Sheehy has already petitioned the court for damages! We don't stand a chance."

"Well, let me tell you something," Tiffany returns in kind. "Buck Crouch is alive. He said he didn't fake his death, doesn't know a thing about any policy, and he lied on his dating profile."

"Where is he?"

"In Montana."

"Is he going to testify?"

"Maybe."

"What do you mean, maybe?'"

"He's thinking it over," Tiffany tells her quite unconvincingly.

"A lot of good he's going to do us in Montana if he's not here to testify, Little Tiffy."

"We need a little more time."

"We don't have it." Bree keeps the volume on high. "The signed check is going out this afternoon."

"You can't do that."

"We don't have a choice. Sheedy's accusing us of fraud. The insurance commission's involved, and they're threatening to revoke our license."

"Well, if you think I'm letting those little things get in the way of my communion money, you're way off first base, Ms. Bree Biz-o-net-zero."

"Enough, you two." I separate the combatants before someone breaks a nail scratching an eye out.

We get into the limo. There is plenty of room in the back for all of us, but Bree chooses to sit in the front. The second Tiffany starts to yell at her, she pulls up the glass privacy panel between the seats.

End of conversation.

"Tiffany, we have to think this thing through. There's a lot more to this story, and we have to figure it out before we make another move."

"But it's a million dollars, Mr. Sherlock, for a guy who's not dead."

"Once we figure the whole case out, we'll figure out a way to get the money back. I promise."

"Can we do that?"

"Of course." I have now traversed past the *White* and descended into the *Blatant Lie* category. I feel like I'm in a cheap suit channeling Dewey Diddier.

The check was delivered and signed for at 4:55PM.

*** 

The case is over, except for the shouting.

Yeah, right. Who am I kidding? If it had more holes than Swiss cheese before, it's now holier than a kitchen strainer.

I take the kids to dinner at a local Italian spot, where there's no bison in the Bolognese sauce. I'm quiet, lost in thought, on the pensive side. My kids obviously realize my discomfort.

"Dad," Kelly says softly, "what's the matter?"

"I'm confused."

"You know what's good when you're confused?" she continues.

"No, what?"

"Shopping," she answers and goes on to explain, "Breathing the fresh air inside an air-conditioned mall, walking freely into stores to see the new styles, trying on different combinations, then using your credit card to bring huge smiles to the face of your daughter." Kelly finishes with "I promise, you'll feel so much better."

"Kelly, eat your spaghetti."

"Dad," Care says between bites, "do you think Mr. Buck was lying?"

"I'm not sure. Do you?"

"No."

"Why not?"

"He might lie about the size of his fish, but I don't think he was lying about the insurance policy," Care says.

"Why not?"

"I don't know, just a feeling."

Like father, like daughter.

"You want to know what I think, Dad?" Kelly asks.

"The only thing you think about is shopping," Care tells her sister.

"Buck's telling the truth, but he's not telling us the whole story," Kelly says.

"You got that right," I conclude.

Kelly smiles big at her sister. "Maybe we should get him in a room, tie him down, turn on the hot lights, and squeeze him until the truth comes out."

"Yeah, Kelly, that'll work. We don't even know where he is."

I sit confused. "You want to know what I think?"

Neither answers, so I take it as a "yes."

"I think we're making an assumption, which maybe

shouldn't be made."

"What?"

"We're assuming the Buck we met is Buck. Maybe he's not. We have no current picture, fingerprints, driver's license, or Costco card. Maybe this guy's a phony? First rule of life: Assume Nothing."

"Then who could it be?"

"Maybe somebody who knew what Buck had and wanted it for himself."

"You think that guy could have murdered Buck and took his place?" Kelly asks.

"I hope not. If your mother found out I took you to lunch with a murderer, I wouldn't be able to see you two until after college."

"What are we going to do, Dad?" Care asks.

"I haven't the faintest idea."

***

Italian food is great because you always take home enough for another meal. As soon as the doggie bags are put away, the kids head for the TV.

"Turn it off."

"No TV? We can't go without TV. We'll die."

I enter the front room carrying my recipe box, pens, and push pins. "It's time for *The Original Carlo*."

We start with questions. Whatever comes to mind, blurt it out and write it down.

If it's not Buck, whose body is it? How did Jupiter get the Heeb's pictures? Why did Buck leave the way he did? If he planned it so well, how'd he forget about the credit card bill? What does he have against photography? What are the chances of us flying on the company jet again? How many socks did Buck have to sell to be the #1 salesman? Did Travianna punch Blanche or did she have help? Why is Cato such a jerk? Would Estalita give us the recipe for the Philippine treats? How could two people live in a singlewide trailer? Why didn't Buck pick a better name than Bob Smith? Why would anyone walk away from a house worth at least four hundred grand? Is Draconian really Buck's son? Was that really Buck eating buffalo burgers? Does Tiffany really need a new car?

Within an hour, the *Carlo* is filling up.

Next, we move onto what could be possible.

Buck and Cato in cahoots. Buck knew about the policy all along. The geocacher who posted the coordinates also hid the body. It's a conspiracy and everyone's involved. There's more than one policy to collect on. There was a pay-off not to autopsy the body. It wasn't really bison meat in those burgers. Buck wrote the silly will to throw us all off. The rest of the money is out there and it's a lot more than we thought. There are more people involved in this mess than we ever imagined.

One piece of the puzzle at a time goes onto an index card and up onto *The Original Carlo*. Problem is the more pieces we put up, the harder the puzzle is to solve. And the only aspect I'm sure of is that we haven't yet found all the pieces of the puzzle.

This is pretty exhausting. If you think a puzzle in front of you is thrilling and exciting, you're wrong. It's a pain. The girls crap out in two hours and head for bed. I stay up, do fifteen minutes on the Oriental Oscillator, write down a few to-do's for tomorrow, and stare at the *Carlo* in hopes an incredible revelation will come into my head and put us on the road to realization.

Yeah, that's going to happen.

# CHAPTER 23

The kids don't like getting shaken out of bed.
"Come on, get up."
"We want to sleep."
"Get up. The early bird gets the worm."
"Who wants worms?"
"Fishermen."
Bree Bisonette agrees to meet us in the coffee shop on the lower level of the Aon Building, where Richmond Insurance is located, but only on one condition. "Don't bring the airhead with you."

Being before noon, this will not be a problem.

The kids munch on donuts as Bree and I sip coffee.

"If Buck got a life insurance policy when he was a baby, wouldn't Cato get one too?" I ask.

"Seems logical."

"Can you find out?" I ask and add, "And see if he cashed it in."

"I can do that."

"Have you had any luck finding out how the premiums were paid?"

"All I can tell you is the policy was purchased through an agency in Kenosha, which closed ten years ago. All the money came through them."

"Could you get me whatever you have on the agency?"

Bree asks, "What are you trying to accomplish here, Sherlock?"

"I'm following the money."

"Hopefully, the million that went out our door."

"I like to start slow and work my way up, Bree."

Bree sits back, gets contemplative, and asks, "You really believe that was Buck you met in Montana?"

"I'm not sure what to believe."

"There is something else you should know," she says.

Uh oh.

"Seedy Sheedy must have known someone at the bank because our check was processed at 5:11PM and came out of our account at 9:01 AM this morning."

"Why is this pertinent?"

"If it's fraud, Seedy Sheedy is now in the middle of it."

"And that would surprise you?"

"There's a big difference between lying in court and taking a piece of the pot in a phony insurance scam," Bree says.

"I have to say it's more like *Time's money*, Bree."

"Unless you're the idiot Tiffany, who can't tell time."

\*\*\*

Next stop on the Detective Express is Jupiter's humble quarters. The temp has already reached 85 and the kids decide to stay in the car. When it comes to scary Goths, sweaty discretion is the better part of valor.

Jupiter, surprised to see me, steps outside to talk. With no Draconian present, Kelly and Care join us on the driveway.

"I got good news for you, Jupiter, and I have bad news."

"Take the good news first," Care suggests.

"Buck, or at least a reasonable facsimile, is alive."

"You're kidding."

"He's in Montana, just like you said."

"That's impossible."

"What do you mean, 'impossible'? You said your chakra was tracking him like Lojack."

"Buck's dead." Jupiter is adamant in her opinion.

"No, we ate bison burgers with him," Care says.

"I got the DNA back," Jupiter tells us. "There was a bone fragment that wasn't toasted, and it matched Cato's DNA perfectly."

"How did you get Cato's DNA?"

"Give me some credit. The guy's a total slob."

"You went Cato dumpster diving?"

"Some things in life you just got to do."

Better thee than thou.

"They're identical twins, the DNA is the same, and after I get Draconian's used Kleenex into the lab, I'll be able to prove he's Buck's son." There is a surety in Jupiter's voice, which I'm not sure is warranted.

This case is twisting more times than a Chubby Checker 45.

"Don't forget the bad news," Care reminds her.

"Okay, give me the bad news."

"The check went out, the money is in the estate, and I wouldn't be surprised if it's already been disbursed. In other words, Cato is already spending it."

"Then we have to stop him."

There's that "we" again.

"I don't know if that's possible, Jupiter."

"I'll contest the will."

"What good would that do? The will is a joke."

"I'll prove paternity."

"You're too late."

"Sherlock. My son's a mess, he needs help."

"The check's already been cashed, Jupiter."

\*\*\*

Our visit with Jupiter was a real load of laughs, about as much fun as having Draconian over to the house for a play date.

It's getting not only hotter and muggier but close to noon, a safe time for the girls to call Tiffany.

"Tiffany, it's us, and we got good news and bad news for you," Kelly and Care speak into one phone. "You want the good news or the bad news first?"

"Bad news," Tiffany replies.

"Buck's dead."

"He can't be dead, we saw him yesterday."

"The hippie lady had his DNA done on his ashes and it matched his brother's."

"That's impossible."

"DNA doesn't lie, Tiffany," I join the conversation.

"Then who was the guy at the bison burger place?"

"We don't know," Care and Kelly both say.

"Bob Smith," I tell the group.

"He was a fake Buck?" Tiffany asks. "Like counterfeit?"

"He lied to us, Tiffany," Care tells her.

"Just like he did on his dating profile," Kelly adds.

"This doesn't make any sense," Tiffany says.

"Sure it does," I say. "Everybody lies on the internet. You said so yourself, Tiffany."

There is a pause for Tiffany's brain cells to get in sync and attempt to process the new information.

"So, what's the good news?" she asks.

"We're back on the case. Dad's not giving up and we're going to get to the bottom of this fishy fish tale." Kelly's quite proud of her verbal alliteration.

"Great," Tiffany says. "What are we going to do next?"

"Have lunch. We're really hungry." Care's always hungry.

"Where are you taking us?" I ask.

***

We meet at a trendy spot named Native Foods Café, located in the once working-class neighborhood of Wicker Park, which was made famous by the writing of Nelson Algren. If Nelly were alive today, I'd doubt if he'd order the Portobello Jibarito special.

"We have to get that million dollars back, Mr. Sherlock. Now it's a matter of principle."

"When did you get principled, Tiffany?" I ask.

"First time was in high school, when I wore skinny jeans."

"Hate to tell you this, Tiffany, but once the horse is out of the barn, it's tough to get him back."

"Oh, no," Care says. "We're not going to see Buttonwillow again?"

Our food arrives and my phone rings at the exact same time.

"Another girlfriend, Mr. Sherlock?" Tiffany snarkily asks.

I see the name on the screen. "Bree Bisonette, Tiffany." I return her tone.

"Even you can do better than her, Mr. Sherlock."

"Hi, Bree."

"Write this down," Bree tells me without pre-conversation niceties. "The agency owner's still alive and living in Racine. When I called, his wife said he was out fishing." She gives me the name and address, and quickly hangs up, as if she knows Tiffany is close by and doesn't want to get infected via cell phone transmission data.

Never in all my days of detecting have I ever had a case where so many of the people liked to fish. I wonder if I'll end up catching anything.

## CHAPTER 24

Welcome Snivley's home is a few miles south of the Racine marina, a block or two off Lake Michigan. The moment I see the guy get out of the Ford F-150, I know it's him. Who else but a guy named Welcome would wear a hat festooned with fishing lures?

"Excuse me, Mr. Snivley."

He stops, seeing me, Tiffany, and two kids approaching.

"Well, howdy. How are you?" Welcome is very welcoming.

"We're from the Richmond Insurance Company," I explain.

Hearing the name, his immediate reaction is "I'd like to help. But I'm out of the business and I can't help you to get Richmond to pay off on your policy."

"Your reputation precedes you, Tiffany."

I keep walking towards the elder gentleman. "No, sir, that's not what we want to discuss," I call out.

"Well, then, young feller, tell me what can I do for you?"

I give him a hand with the cooler he's pulling out of the truck's club cab. I hope my helpfulness is to be rewarded.

"My name is Richard Sherlock." I put out my hand to shake. "You owned the Welcome Agency?"

"For thirty years."

"How did you ever get your name?" Care asks.

"My parents were very friendly," he answers.

"Is Snivley some foreign word for being nice?" is Tiffany's follow-up question in her quest for name knowledge.

I quickly get off that topic. "I'm investigating a fraud, possibly perpetrated by one of your past clients."

"Who?"

"Leonard Crouch."

"I don't hear any bells ringing inside my noggin."

"It was a life insurance policy bought for him when he was a baby," I explain.

"For about two years those policies went like hotcakes," Welcome says proudly.

"There were actually two policies bought, one for him and one for his twin brother, Cato."

Welcome Snivley reaches down to unlatch his cooler. "Well, let me think about it a spell."

"What's in the cooler?" Care asks.

"Today's catch."

"Can we see?"

Welcome pops the top and four fish are resting on a bed of ice.

"They look gross," Kelly says. "Are they dead?"

"Hopefully."

Care takes a closer look. "The reason their eyes stay open is because once they're dead, the muscle doesn't work to close them."

"I don't think fish have eyelids," Welcome says.

"Well, then, that too," Care says.

The girls carry the cooler, and we follow Welcome to a shed in his back yard.

"Is Crouch the name on the policy or the name of the insured?" he asks as he takes the fish out of the cooler and lays them on a block of wood.

"Would they be different?" I ask.

"Could be." Welcome takes a knife the size of a machete off the wall, and WHOMP, whacks the heads and tails off the fish.

The kids jump back. Tiffany jumps back behind the kids.

Welcome continues, "I could buy a policy on you, but since I'm paying, my name would be first." Welcome slices each fish up its belly and empties out the innards into a bucket along with the severed heads and tails. This is attractive as well as appetizing.

"What are you going to do with the guts?" Care asks, pointing at the bloody remains in the bucket.

"Bury it in my garden. Wanna help?"

"Not really."

Welcome stops. "Ya know, years ago, there was this woman who bought policies on her kids, who I think were twins. She'd show up every year with cash to pay the premiums. Talk about a real looney-tooney."

"What was so nutty about her?"

"She'd show up one year looking like Jackie Kennedy and the next like Homeless Hattie."

"Maybe she just had an odd fashion sense," Kelly says.

"Or wasn't very stylish and copied the wrong people," Tiffany says.

Welcome continues, "Then one year, she shows up with the money and asks me to write a letter telling the beneficiaries they could cash out, or let the cash value pay the additional premiums."

"So, the kids never knew about the policies?"

"Maybe not."

"Did you write the letter?"

"Yeah, but she never gave me an address where to send it."

"What did you do?"

"Sent the letters to her."

"Do you remember what her name was?"

"Smith. Imelda Smith. I hear she's still around."

"Where?"

"She's out ripening."

Welcome fills in the details on a scrap of paper, and thankfully wipes the fish blood off before handing it over.

"Thanks, Welcome."

"You're welcome."

"No, you're Welcome," Tiffany says.

***

I should have realized when I saw the smaller sign under the big sign for Ripening Acres that read *A Special Place for the Memory Impaired,* our visit might be challenging.

As we drive through the front gates Tiffany asks, "Do you think you'll end up in a place like this, Mr. Sherlock?"

"No."

"Why not?"

"One, I can't afford it. Two, I have daughters, who will be more than happy to change my Depend when I can't hold it any longer."

"That responsibility always falls to the youngest child," Kelly informs Care.

Ripening Acres is a very nice place. Spread out over a couple of acres of Wisconsin farmland, it's divided into Living, Assisted Living, and Special Care sections. All are neat, ordered, and spotlessly clean. We find the main building, enter, and pass by a fully stocked library, card room, large eating area, exercise room, and infirmary.

"Excuse us," I say at the receptionist's desk. "We'd like to see Imelda Smith."

"Are you family?"

"No, but we're here because of her family," I explain.

The woman gives us an odd look. "Because of her family... what does that mean?"

I'm not prepared to answer, but Tiffany has no problem.

"She might be my long-lost great-aunt on my mother's side." Lying must be contagious during this case.

"Really?"

"I kid you not," Tiffany says with a straight face.

I wonder where she ever heard that expression.

The woman hands over a clipboard with a pen on a metal string and says, "I'll need you to fill this out."

I waste no time completing the form.

"Wait over there, please."

There are chairs for waiting guests. We sit and watch as members of the upper demographic pass by walking, walking with walkers, or being pushed in wheelchairs by able walkers. At first, it seems a bit on the depressing side, but after the initial shock of what age does to a body, I see the folks talking, smiling, and seemingly satisfied in their surroundings.

"Imelda Smith." A male voice rings out from down a hallway to our left.

"Yes." I return the call.

"She's eating. Do you want to see her now or wait until she's finished?" the orderly says, approaching.

"Which would be best?"

"Neither."

The man turns to return from where he came, and we all follow him to a smaller room with long tables inside.

"Enjoy your visit," he says, pointing to the far corner of the room where a young woman in caregiver clothes is spooning food into a petite woman of maybe eighty pounds, equal number of years, with more lines on her face than a Chicago city map.

We approach.

"Imelda, my name is Richard Sherlock—"

Imelda continues eating.

"Appetite seems pretty good," Kelly says.

"She doesn't look it, but she can put it away," the caregiver remarks.

"Is that a smoothie you're eating?" Tiffany asks.

No answer.

"It's yogurt," the caregiver explains.

"You should give her a protein bar," Tiffany suggests. "I bet that would get her in gear."

"Imelda," I speak to her again, "tell me about your sons."

She peers up at me, her eyes somewhat focused, and she spits up juice as she says, "I got to get to the meeting."

"What meeting?"

"Tonight's."

I ask the aide, "Is there a meeting tonight she's going to?"

"No, she always talks about going to a meeting."

"But you don't know what meeting?"

"Can't be late," Imelda says weakly.

"Imelda, do you have a son named Buck?"

"Buck?"

"Yeah, and one named Cato."

"Gotta get to the meeting," Imelda says. She stops eating, collapses back into her chair, and falls asleep.

The aide cleans her up.

"Does she always talk about meetings?" I ask.

"She'll talk about that for a week, next week she'll talk about something else. This is not all that odd. A lot of the old folks mutter stuff like this."

"She ever mention her family?"

"Sometimes."

"What does she say?"

"That they should go to the meeting with her."

Imelda starts to snore.

"How long has she been here?" I ask.

"She was here before me, so at least six years."

"Do you know anything about her?" I ask.

"She's sick."

"I mean about her family."

"No."

"Who could tell us?"

"Miss Greystroke."

Imelda doesn't return our "Nice to meet you," "Enjoy your lunch," or "Next time we come, we'll bring party games." Although she does awaken for a few seconds to say, "See you at the meeting." Then she loudly fills her diaper.

It's been nice, but it's time to go.

Five minutes later we sit in Miss Greystroke's office.

"Are you any relation to Sherlock Holmes?" she asks after my introduction.

"No." I want to ask if she's any relation to Tarzan, but I don't.

I hint around the purpose of our visit and she responds, "I can't release personal information on one of our patients."

"She must have a relative in charge of her care. Could you give us that name?"

"As far as we know, she has no living relatives," she says and adds, "Why do you want to know?"

"Imelda has come up in our investigation of a possible insurance fraud."

"At eighty-one?"

"You can't trust anybody these days," Tiffany answers.

"Could you tell us who pays for her care?" I ask.

"She does."

"What does she do, go to the ATM once a week?" Tiffany asks.

"The money comes through her estate."

"Would you give us the name of the executor of the estate?"

"If I do, will you leave?"

***

We get lucky. F. Carlton Huff is in his office when we arrive unannounced.

As soon as I utter the words "Insurance Fraud," his ears perk up.

Huff hurriedly taps computer keys, waits for the page to load, looks at it carefully, and says, "No money's been drawn out of her account except the usual."

I try to look around him at the computer screen, but he quickly exits the page.

"She's loaded, isn't she?"

"Miss Smith has no immediate money concerns."

"Married?"

"No."

"Do you know if she had any children?"

"Not that I'm aware."

"Living relatives?"

He shrugs his shoulders.

Tiffany asks, "Gay?"

"Never asked."

"Could you tell us anything about the woman?" I plead.

"All I can tell you is Imelda learned early on that a little money compounded over a long time becomes big money."

"One more question?"

"You can ask."

"When she dies, where does the rest of her money go?"

Huff stares at me.

I put my hands out, as if to say, "Okay, I'm ready for your answer."

Silence.

I wait another thirty seconds until F. Carlton Huff says, "I said you can ask, I didn't say I would answer."

## CHAPTER 25

"I'm going to sue."

"Sue who?"

"The estate."

"On what grounds?"

"That Draconian's Buck's son."

"I don't know if that will do you any good," I tell her.

"Why not?"

"If the money's already disbursed, the estate will be dissolved, and there'll be no estate to sue."

"That would be a bummer."

Jupiter's not a happy camper. She sits in our front room, sweating along with the three of us. The a/c is acting temperamental this morning.

"How's Draconian?" Care asks.

"Better. He's been on the computer studying famous musicians."

"Who?"

"Brad Delp, Chris Cornell, Per Ohlin, and Phil Ochs."

"Never heard of 'em," Care says. "What does he think about Taylor Swift?"

"Probably that she's not too swift," Jupiter says.

There's a pause before I ask, "Jupiter, did Buck ever talk about his mother?"

"Never."

"Why not?"

"He never knew her. She split when he was a baby."

"Why?"

"I'm not sure he knew. He was raised by his grandparents."

"Which ones?"

"On his dad's side."

"Ever meet them?"

"Nope. Met his dad once. Total dweeb."

Enough nothing on the topic. I decide to move on.

"Jupiter, how did you get the pictures from Heeb's?"

"I didn't. They're phonies," she admits and adds proudly, "I'm pretty good with photoshopping."

"You thought that would convince me to find Buck?"

"Worked for a while, didn't it?"

"Amazing how your doctored shots matched the picture

taken at the bank."

"Sherlock, there's a ton of guys in Montana wearing boots, baseball caps, and plaid shirts."

I'm toying with the idea of telling Jupiter more about the Buck we met in Bozeman, but hesitate. Would it get her hopes up? Would she believe it after receiving the DNA results? What good would it do? I don't have to toy long, since Kelly speaks up.

"The Buck we met in Bozeman wasn't wearing a baseball cap."

"What Buck?"

"The Buck Tiffany found in Bozeman," Care tells her. So much for toying with ideas.

"Did he have on hiking boots, real expensive hiking boots?" Jupiter asks.

"Jimmy Choo doesn't make hiking boots," Kelly answers.

"We're pretty sure he was a phony Buck," Care says.

"Why?"

"He didn't know about the insurance policy, could care less about his old house, and admitted he lied on his dating profile."

"So he was just some guy trying to get in on Buck's money?" Jupiter asks.

"No, he wasn't doing that either," I tell her.

"So why do you think he was there?"

"To meet Tiffany."

Jupiter's confused, and she gets more confused as she looks over and sees *The Original Carlo* in all its glory.

"What're all the index cards doing stuck to that awful painting?" she asks.

"We laid out the case to help us see it better," I say, slowly getting off the couch and going to the painting.

"It looks like a bad acid flashback," Jupiter says.

I wonder, are there any *good* acid flashbacks?

Jupiter's exasperated. "Do you have any idea what's going on, Sherlock? You're the detective."

"Kinda."

"Give me the *kind* in kinda."

"It's a conspiracy of some kind. It could be as bad as a murder or a scam to grab a million in insurance money. I'm pretty sure it's a group effort. Problem is, I'm not sure who's in the group. It could be Cato and the wives, Cato and the lawyer, police chief, coroner, imposter Buck, and geocacher. Or any combination of all or some of the above."

"I feel left out," Jupiter says.

"You were up there, but we took your cards off when you were coming up the stairs," Kelly says.

"We'll put you back after you leave," Care tells her.

"Groovy."

"I'll have Draconian's DNA back from the lab soon," Jupiter says. "I'm not giving up."

"That's the spirit," Care cheers her on.

"Which lab?"

"DNA's"R"Us."

***

The following morning I drop off the kids at Tiffany's condo building. Tiffany gave instructions to the doorman to let them in, and not disrupt her beauty sleep until at least eleven.

"Remember what I told you, girls."

"Yeah, Dad, we got it."

I go on my merry way, although the merry doesn't last long once I reach my first stop.

"Some guy comes to the door this morning with this letter we have to sign for." Blanche is still in her nightshirt, which is hardly attractive.

"Blanche thought it was from the lottery telling her she won," Travianna explains.

"It says we have to clear out of here," Blanche says, passing the letter to me.

The letter is from seedy Arnold Sheedy. "It's a bunch of legalese gobbledy-gook meant to get you two to leave."

"They're not going to turn off the electricity and our toilets, are they?" Blanche asks.

"No. They're trying to scare you out."

"Well, I don't scare easy," Travianna says.

"I do," Blanche says.

I explain, "Before they could do anything, they'd have to transfer the title into Cato's name, get a warrant from the Sheriff, and then get the court to order an eviction."

"And those are good things?" Blanche asks.

"In your case, yes. All that takes time."

"I told you so," Travianna tells her roomie.

"But I wouldn't be spending a lot of money on a new kitchen in the meantime, if I were you," I add as a warning.

The house is empty without all the awful artwork and stuffed animals. Buck's motif is lost forever.

"Did Buck ever mention a woman named Imelda Smith?" I ask the two.

"Oh, please, not another girlfriend," Travianna says.

"No."

"She isn't that lady who bought all the shoes in that foreign country years ago?" Blanche asks.

"No, but you did get the Imelda part right." I pause, then say, "She might be Buck's mother. Did he ever mention her?"

"Nope."

"His father?"

"He didn't care much for his old man."

"We didn't either."

"If he wasn't drunk, he was on the way to getting drunk," Blanche, who would know a drunk when she sees one, says.

"What was his name?" I ask.

"He liked to be called either 'Buck One' or 'Big Buck.'"

Charming fellow, no doubt.

"Did you know Buck's grandparents, the ones who raised him?"

"Nope."

"He ever talk about them?"

"One time Buck told me," Travianna says, "'When it comes to parents, I got the short end of the stick.'"

"That's why he didn't like or want kids. I think he was afraid of the responsibility," Blanche adds.

Travianna adds to Blanche's addition with "And commitment."

"By the way," I say to Travianna, "when you and Buck shared your apartment, did you find any of his stuff when you moved out?"

"Not much."

"Whatever it was, do you still have it?"

"If she didn't sell it," Travianna says, pointing to Blanche.

"Mind if I go through it?"

We go outside into the dusty and dirty garage. Buck's car sits lonely as a wallflower at a high school dance.

"There it is." Travianna points to a box on a shelf.

I lift it down, take the top off and find it empty as a bulimic's tummy.

"I remember now," Blanche says. "It had a bunch of books in it."

"Books about what?"

"Numbers."

"Buck always did the Sudoku," Travianna says and adds, "At least at my place he did."

"What happened to them?"

"I think they went on the *Any Item for a Dime* table."

Travianna looks like she'd like to smack Blanche in her other eye.

I peer inside the car. Empty.

"You got the keys?"

"In the ignition."

I reach in, take the keys, move around to the rear, open the trunk, and find one box.

It's filled with a smattering of oddball items. A compass, fishing license, shotgun shells, ruler, shoelaces, Swiss Army knife, nudie playing cards, a set of dice, Farmer's Almanac, a number of unfinished crossword puzzles, waterproofing spray, pencils, pens, paperclips, and way in the back, a very old check register. The latter I take out and peruse where Buck once spent his money. Unfortunately, nothing is out of the ordinary. Inside the register is a folded lined page, the kind used by accountants for listing debits and credits. On this particular sheet are dates, numbers, and one or two checkmarks running down in three columns. There are no totals, subtotals, or explanations in the margins. It makes absolutely no sense.

"You sure Buck didn't leave any files or records or old receipts around?"

"When he left, there was nothing left," Blanche says.

I push the trunk closed. "You talk to Cato lately?"

"Nope."

"You might want to keep it that way."

***

I am sans children and so-called assistant on this day, due to my placing Tiffany and my girls on a *Special Assignment*, so

I decide to make a stop they wouldn't enjoy making.

"That chick is hotter than an aged jalapeno, Sherlock."

I sit in Larry Flemm with two m's' office. It hasn't changed much, just like Larry.

"I need to see the copies of Buck Crouch's credit card statements. The ones that were past due."

To my surprise, Larry goes into his desk drawer, pulls out a file, and hands it to me.

The forms are right on top. I page through the four or five pages quickly, and hand the folder back to Larry.

"That was quick."

"I'm not sure what I'm looking for and now I'm not sure I've found it." I'm lying. Maybe I've joined the liars' club or been immediately affected by a liar's disease, merely sitting in Larry's office.

I reach onto his desk, find a blank piece of paper, take a pen out of his cup holder, and write five or six lines on the page. Next, I pull out my wallet, remove my last fifty bucks, and pass it all to Larry.

"I need to know what this lady has been doing for the last fifty years." I pause and add, "And I need it soon."

Larry reads the name on the page. "Not much to go on, Sherlock."

"You're a true professional, Larry. I have all the faith in the world in you."

"I'll do it on one condition."

"What, Larry?"

"You bring the little lady over when you pick it up."

"Larry, you drive a hard bargain."

Larry gives me a huge toothy smile to seal the deal.

"Larry," I tell him, "I think you got some bologna stuck in your teeth."

*** 

Yet another stop on the Detective Express. I'm on a roll.

"What are you doing here?"

"I wonder if Estalita will give me the recipe for those Philippine candies? My kids loved 'em."

"She ain't around."

"Mind if I wait?"

"She won't be back soon."

"Where is she?"

"Around somewhere else."

Cato Crouch isn't much of a welcoming host. I should introduce him to Welcome Snivley, and he could get a few pointers.

"By the way, Cato, did you ever get any responses from the internet dating site you were on?" Before he can answer, I explain, "I'm looking to start dating again and I want to know if I should use a picture of me with a fish."

"No."

"No, you didn't get any responses? Or no, I shouldn't use a fish?"

Cato steps out of the trailer, closes the door behind him, and comes down the two steps. "Go home, Sherlock. The case is closed. We got the money. Buck's dead. Cryin's over. It's history."

"Are you sure?"

"Positive."

"Then who was the Buck I met in Montana the other day?"

"I couldn't tell you. You didn't invite me to the party."

"If I arrange another one, you want to go?"

"Buck's dead."

"Not the one I met."

"Imposter, then."

"I don't think so."

"Nobody cares what you think."

He might be right. Nobody listens to me either.

"I've got more loose ends in this case than a frayed rope, Cato."

"That's your problem, not mine, Sherlock."

"I just can't let it alone."

"Again, your problem."

"Not if I can make it your problem, Cato."

"Are you threatening me?"

"This is all a scam. I know it, you know it, and Buck probably knows it too."

"Go home, Sherlock. The fat lady's already hit her last note."

***

Ten or fifteen years ago, the latest breakthrough in modern medicine was something called Total Tomography. A person, who probably was perfectly healthy but wanted to live forever, would go to an MRI center and have about a thousand images taken of his innards. All the major organs would be represented and a few extra added-attraction organs were included if you signed up for the Platinum Plan instead of the cheaper Gold or Silver Plan. Next, a 'specialist' imagographer—a name I just made up—would put the scans into a computer and evaluate them against the established disease data which was available at the time. A couple weeks later, the imagee would go in and meet with the imager doc to go over scans. The imagee, who had no idea what he was looking at, and the doc would then come up with predictions of what diseases were hiding right outside his front door. At this point, the imagee was getting scared to death, being told all that could go wrong in the future, but not to worry because the doctor would prescribe exercises, nutrition plans, prescriptions, and other expensive methods to catch the bad body vibes in the bud before they had a chance of sprouting in the liver, kidneys, or spleen, one of the lesser organs included in the Platinum Plan scans.

I had a friend who opted for the deal. He was thin, fit, and perfectly healthy at the time. During the post-scan interview, the first suggestion the doc made was "You have to start exercising more."

"But I already run seventy-five miles a week," the patient responded.

"Then maybe you should pick up the pace."

The next suggestion was more of a warning: "You have some possible weakening of your arterial walls in your heart. Probably heredity."

"My mother's eighty-three, my dad's eighty-five, and both grandparents lived into their nineties."

"Past performance is no prediction of future performance." A phrase evidently borrowed from a financial professional who was not too good at making predictions either.

Total Tomography never became the medical panacea the tomography industry thought it would become. It faded away faster than a bad MRI scan.

TT has been replaced by the next big thing, which is called DNA sequencing, where the 23 chromosomes of your genome are coded, classified, and crosschecked with a whole lot of other data to predict what will go wrong with your body in the future. Millions of dollars are being invested by drug companies the world over in your personal genome. Personally, I'd prefer to keep my genome to myself.

Yes, there is a point to all this.

Jupiter dropped off the stolen urn with Buck's ashes at DNAs"R"Us to be analyzed.

I make a visit. And at first, they can't find Jupiter's account.

I finally talk to Barry, who overhears my conversation with the receptionist, pulls me aside, and says in hushed tones, "What are you doing here?"

"I want to know how you got DNA out of a can of ashes."

"Shhhhh."

"Why so quiet?"

"I told her not to say anything to anybody." He speaks in a quietly frantic tone.

"Why not?"

"Why do you think?"

I don't have to contemplate long. "You traded your services for her services."

"Shhhh."

"Fine. Just tell me how you did it and I'll be gone."

"There was an unburned piece of tooth inside."

"How could there be? The body was cremated."

"It happens," Barry says.

"Did you DNA the rest?"

"No. It was a bunch of ashes."

Barry is sweating profusely.

"One last question."

"Hurry."

"Was Jupiter's weed worth it?"

"Totally, dude, totally."

# CHAPTER 26

"**O**kay, what did you find out?"
"Nothing."

"What do you mean 'nothing'? You had all day."

"Dad, by the time we went to the spa, got our mani-pedi, did some hydration therapy, had our tea tree/avocado/sea salt facial, the day was pretty much shot," Kelly tells me.

"I wasn't big on that avocado thing, Dad," Care admits. "It made me look like a frog."

The *Special Assignment* I assigned Tiffany and the girls to perform was to open, sort, and inspect the box of Buck's unopened mail.

"Nobody sends mail anymore, Mr. Sherlock, that's so 1990's."

"Well, if nobody sends it, Tiffany, why is there so much of it?" I ask, pulling the box toward me.

"Some businesses can't afford to make robocalls, Mr. Sherlock."

We stand in the front room of Tiffany's condo. The lakefront spreads out eighty floors beneath us and the central air keeps us as cool as cucumbers in the fresh vegetable aisle.

"Sit," I order.

I dump the box in the middle of a Persian rug and start the process.

"This pile is for anything not personally addressed to Buck. This pile is for any mail addressed but obviously an offer to buy something you wouldn't need. The last pile is for anything possibly personal. Go."

All hands go into the pile like kids to a grab bag. Envelopes get thrown around like Frisbees.

The first pile is the biggest and the first to go right back in the box: Pennysavers, ads, weekly shoppers, real estate brochures, coupon books, Bed Bath & Beyond percentage-off offers, and a bunch of really worthless junk mail.

The second addressed pile has to be divided twice. One set from unknown and one set from well-known, established companies. All were offers for Buck to buy insurance, medical plans, land, real estate, or some financial service. I have the girls open each piece, and if it's a form letter, it goes right back into the box.

The third pile has nineteen pieces of mail. Two are from Bank of America, wanting to renew his credit card, debit card, and checking account. One was a statement from the credit card account he had just paid off. The amounts matched with what I remember seeing in Flemm's office. The Neptune Society sent an offer for ash disposal. Three were bills from utility companies, soon to be sent in pink if Blanche and Travianna didn't pay up. Three were dinner invitations from firms selling estate plans, and three were dinner invites if you signed up for free drug trials and were already suffering from the particular disease. All dinners were to be held at expensive restaurants. I thought about taking these home and getting a few free meals for myself. The remaining six envelopes were from charities, some recognizable, asking for a personal donation. I read each of these, and some were quite touching in their emotional appeal.

"I get those all the time," Tiffany tells me as I read.

"Aren't you special."

"Yes, Mr. Sherlock, I am," Tiffany answers. "Quite special."

I stack the third pile, put a rubber band around it, and set it aside.

We're done.

"What other fun activities do you have planned for us?" Kelly asks with a sassy tea-tree, sea-salt glow on her face. "Because the last one was pretty lame."

"Go home, mop the kitchen floor, scrub the toilet, and clean the mold inside the shower. That sound like fun, Kelly?"

"Maybe for you, Dad, but include me out." My older daughter has such a way with words.

***

Back at the apartment, I put three new cards up on *The Original Carlo*: Charities, Free Dinners, and B of A. I have no clue what significance they may or may not have.

I made the girls come home with me. I don't want them getting too used to central air, and I want to see the colors fade on their faces faster than a rainbow at twilight time, as they walk into our apartment.

As the kids watch TV, I stare at the index cards and try to make sense of nonsense. I get an odd thought, can't see an answer before me, and pick up the phone.

Blanche answers. "Yo."

"When did Buck's father die?"

"A year ago," she says.

"Did you go to the funeral?"

"There wasn't one."

"Any service?"

"We didn't go."

"Did Buck?"

"No, but he paid for it."

"How did you know that?"

"He complained about the cost of cremation."

***

I don't sleep well. Oddly enough, it's not my sore back that's keeping me awake, but the utter confusion going through my brain. One unresolved thought bounces against another like atoms inside a supercollider.

At nine the next morning I rouse the girls out of bed. "Get up."

"No, we're on vacation. We get to sleep in."

It takes me about a half-hour to get them up and out of the door.

"Where are we going?" Care asks as we hit the humidity and head for the car.

"The bank."

"Are we going to get money so we can go to the mall?" Kelly asks, suddenly awake.

"No."

We arrive at the Bank of America closest to Buck's house and walk inside. I proceed to the line for the teller's window, pulling out the letter found in Buck's mail.

"Dad, what are we doing here?" Care asks.

"Looking for a safe deposit box."

"Didn't we already do that?" Kelly asks.

"Kelly, knock it off."

"Dad, not only are you making us do boring stuff, you're making us do it twice."

I don't answer, because it's my turn at the window.

I push the letter in the slot and ask, "My name's Leonard

Crouch and I know you cancelled my account, but did you also close the safe deposit box?"

The woman goes on her computer, searches, and says, "Yes."

"When?"

"Over a year ago."

"I've been having problems," I whisper to her. "I can't remember if I cleaned the box out or not. Early-onset Alzheimer's."

"Wait," she says.

Kelly and Care stare at me like I'm loony.

"Must have," she says. "The box was cleared for a new customer."

"Whew," I sigh. "Now all I got to do is remember where I put whatever I had in it."

"Good luck." She pushes the letter back through the slot, looks up at me, and asks, "Would you like to reopen your account, Mr. Crouch?"

"Not now, but I'll try to remember to do it later."

***

We get back in the car and head for our next stop.

"Dad, we're bored," Kelly informs me.

"In life, you make your own good time."

"No, Dad, that's your job."

When we reach our destination, Kelly exclaims, "Oh no, not another rerun."

I remind the girls, "Don't touch anything."

The door is open. I don't knock. We barge in to find our so-called expert napping at his desk. I clear my throat. "Ah, excuse us—"

Larry Flemm with two m's pops out of his somnambulistic trance.

"Don't scare me like that, Sherlock."

"What'd you find out on Imelda?"

"Who?"

"Imelda Smith."

Larry comes somewhat to, and says, "Oh yeah," and adds, "Not much."

"Fine, give me the 'not much.'"

Larry picks out one file in a stack of two, opens it, and reads, "She was born in Chicago during the Depression. Father worked at a bank, mother was a mother. Went to Lane Tech, worked at Northern Trust, then fell off the map for a couple of years. She shows up again when both parents die in an automobile accident."

"Siblings?" I interrupt to ask.

"None that I could find."

I have to remind myself that Larry, when he was at the CPD, wasn't known as *a great looker-up of stuff.*

"Go on."

"She drops off the map again until two years later when she's living in Milwaukee working at a medical clinic."

"Imelda became a nurse?"

"If she did, she was self-taught." Larry reads down the one-page listing. "Then she disappears again."

"Could she have gotten married?"

"There's no record."

"Could she have had some medical problems?" I ask.

"If she did, it would explain the next set of holes in her history, which last until she's forty-six."

"I'm listening."

"She ends up working at a halfway house in Kenosha."

"Doing what?"

"I don't know."

Bad answer.

"That job lasted until she was seventy-two when she had her first stroke," Larry says, reading the last line on the page.

"That when she went into the care facility?"

"Ripening Acres."

As far as I can tell, this has been a total waste of time.

"Where'd you get all this, Larry?"

"Usual spots, plus I got a buddy at the IRS. Oh, you owe me another hundred bucks."

"For what?"

"My buddy at the IRS."

"Put it on my account."

"You don't have an account."

I stand to leave. The girls stand with me.

"Sherlock, weren't you supposed to bring the little lady with you on this visit?"

"I brought them both with me, Larry."

"No, Tiffany."

"Next time, you might want to specify which little lady."

I turn to leave.

"Goodbye, Mr. Flemm with two m's," the girls say and leave the office without touching anything.

*\*\*

I take the kids to Uno's on Wabash. It's the best pizza in the entire world. I call Tiffany, tell her to join us, and hopefully pay the check.

"I can't believe this is happening, Mr. Sherlock."

"Tiffany, I know this is hard for you to comprehend, but sometimes in the insurance business, you have to pay off on a claim."

"No, not that," Tiffany says. "It's that he isn't writing me back."

"Who?"

"Buck."

"I thought he wasn't your type."

"I'm trying to get him to come to Chicago and tell the Judge he's not dead."

"That's not going to happen."

"He's not answering any of my emails, even the ones I've sent a picture with."

"Maybe he's off the dating site, Tiffany."

She stops. "You know, I never considered that."

We finish our pizza with plenty to take home. The check sits until Tiffany thankfully picks it up.

"There's still one stop we can make today," I tell the group. "And if we hurry, we still have a couple of hours of daylight to do it in."

"Where, Dad?"

"It's a surprise."

*\*\*

By the time we get out of the restaurant, it's twilight time. Tiffany refuses to ride in my car, so she cabs home.

"Are you going to tell us where we're going, Dad?"

166

I don't have to answer because I turn on a street they've already been on. I can feel the fear quotient in the car rise like the thermometer did this morning.

"I'm not going in there," Kelly says.

"You can stay in the car, then."

"I could melt in the car."

"Or," Care says to her sister, "you could go inside and get a stake through your heart."

"Pick your poison, girls," I tell them, parking and getting slowly out of the Toyota.

"I'm going with Dad," Care says.

Care jumps out of the car, leaving her sister, and follows me to Jupiter's front door.

"What are you doing here?" Jupiter asks, seeing the two of us.

"Is Draconian home?" Care asks as if she's going to follow it up with "Can he come out and play?"

"No, he's not here."

Care turns and yells to Kelly, "Come on, the coast is clear."

As Kelly joins us, I tell Jupiter, "I need the ashes back."

"Why?"

"Because they don't belong to you."

We go inside and I immediately regret it. The kids are going to see the pot plants in the kitchen and start asking questions I don't want to answer.

"Draconian out having breakfast?" Kelly asks.

"I don't know where he is," Jupiter says. "He's been acting kind of weird lately."

"How could you tell?" Care asks.

"I don't know where he's been going. He just up and leaves," Jupiter says with fear and concern.

"Band practice?" I ask.

"I think they folded."

I wonder how the music industry will survive without the Scumbag Death Cult's melodious renditions of death and destruction.

"Don't worry, Jupiter, he's probably just going through a phase of a phase."

The urn is on the table where she cuts the crystals. I pick it up. She doesn't fight me for it.

"All the DNA is complete. Draconian's Buck's son, no doubt

about it."

"I'm not sure that fact will do you much good now."

"I'm going to call a couple of those lawyers I see on TV and sue."

"Good luck, Jupiter."

I look around to see Kelly and Care staring into the kitchen. Uh oh.

Before we leave on our trip home, I ask, "Who wants to hold Buck's ashes so they don't spill?"

There are no takers.

Back at our apartment we sit on the back porch until the once-again-working air conditioner does its thing inside.

The inevitable question comes up.

"Dad, is Jupiter growing those Japanese trees into the shape of rhinoceros and stuff?" Care asks.

"God, how lame are you?" Kelly snaps at her sister. "She's growing weed, you idiot."

"Weeds? The kind you have to pull?"

"Marijuana, dummy," Kelly pours it on.

"How do you know that was marijuana, Kelly?"

"I watch cable TV."

The teen years are going to be tough.

Once we're back inside, I ask, "Could one of you go get the top of the box that was holding Buck's mail?"

Neither volunteers their service.

I retrieve it myself, move their ice cream dishes to the side on the coffee table, place the box top upside-down, and empty the urn into the cardboard. A puff of dust rises from the ashes.

"Gross!"

"What are you doing? That's disgusting."

I take a pen and begin to sift through the remains. "I'm looking for dental records."

Cremains aren't merely ashes, but bits of charred bone, which are grey or dark grey in color, with a texture resembling coarse sand. It takes about 2-3 hours to cremate a body at around 1800-2000 degrees. Once cooked, a magnet is used to remove any metal from hip replacements and such. To complete the process, the bone fragments are pulverized into the same powdery sand as the rest of the remains.

Why anyone would want these remains on the mantle in their living room, I really don't understand.

I find bits that didn't get fully crushed and separate them. These pieces are whiter than the rest. Maybe after the case is finally over, I'll make a little mosaic with the pieces spelling out *BUCK*.

With the initial shock over, the kids put their noses into the ashes.

"Nobody sneeze," I tell them.

I sit back as they sift through Buck and come up with a few more bits and a couple of questions I quickly realize I can't answer.

A few cases back, I met both Titus Pyre and Thelma Lament, husband and wife, and proprietors of the Pyre/Lament Funeral Home, Mausoleum, Crematorium and Cemetery. I call their number.

"I'm not sure you'll remember me, but this is Richard Sherlock."

"Of course I remember you, Richard. The live ones I always remember," Titus tells me. "How are you?"

"I have a few questions. Would you mind helping me out?"

"Shoot."

"Can you get DNA from cremains?"

"Sure. How do you think they identify burn victims?"

Never thought of that.

"Teeth are best." Titus answers my next question before I ask it.

"Why?"

"Harder." Titus adds, "Some more unscrupulous cremators will remove the teeth before pulverization."

"To remove the gold and silver?" I answer before he has a chance.

"Although we would never do that."

"Do they ever cremate more than one body at a time?" I ask.

"It's against the law," Titus tells me.

"That's not what I asked."

"But that's the only answer I'm going to give." He chuckles.

"Titus, you are a gentleman and a scholar. Thank you very much and please say hello to Thelma for me."

"Will do."

The kids finish separating the chunks from the sand. I go into the kitchen's junk drawer, find a small, unused paintbrush, an old envelope, and return to our worktable. I sweep the fragments into the envelope and the remaining remains back into the urn.

"This was actually kinda fun, Dad," Care says.

"And you people say I don't know how to have a good time."

## CHAPTER 27

My allotted kid time for summer vacation is coming to a close. I'll have to return Kelly and Care to their mother on Saturday morning. In some ways, I will miss them and in others, I'll be glad to no longer hear Kelly begging me to go to the mall.

I know one day in Montana wasn't much of a summer vacation, but days and nights in the posh surroundings of Tiffany's condo, trips to her spa, rides on corporate jets, and fancy dinners out on the town are a heck of a lot better than a long weekend at the tacky Wisconsin Dells, shopping for cheap trinkets, and eating at fish boils.

In a week or two, they'll both be back in school, and we'll go back to our Tuesday nights and every-other-weekend schedule. Ah, the life of the divorced dad.

My desire to figure this whole mess out is starting to wane. My interest is fading like Buttonwillow at the end of a nose-to-butt trek. It bothers the heck out of me that I know now almost as much as I knew when I entered this mess. The fact is that even if I do figure out the chicanery involved, it won't make a bit of difference. The money's already gone. Buck, whether he is Buck or not, isn't coming back, dead or alive. Cato will still be a jerk. The wives will get evicted sooner or later. The dead Buck in the ravine is going to stay ashed up. And, no matter what happens, Tiffany's going to get a new Lexus, no doubt about it.

***

The call comes in at 10 AM.

"Get over here, Sherlock! We're being invaded."

What is this, *Revenge of the Jedi*?

"Hurry."

"Calm down, Blanche."

"I can't. There's too many of them to fight off."

"Put Travianna on the phone."

The calmer of the two wives gets on the phone and tells me what's going on.

"Hold your ground until I get there."

The next words out of my mouth are "Code Red, Code Red!"

By the time we get over to the house, the aliens, who are actually agents, are swarming like ants at a picnic. There are signs up, from the street to the front door, and one very obnoxious woman seems to be in charge.

"Don't worry about them," the woman tells the throng, pointing at Blanche and Travianna. "They're squatters."

I—and the kids—approach the woman, who immediately asks us, "Are you an agent or a broker?"

"Neither."

"The house won't be open for offers until tomorrow," she tells us. "And if I were you, I'd bid well over the asking price."

She hands me her business card, and puts out her hand to shake. "I'm Titi Poon, Sackrider Realty." She pauses, then adds, "Broker of this wonderful, unique property."

"Which isn't yours to sell yet."

"Oh, don't be silly," Titi Poon says, walking quickly away to escort new brokers into the house.

Blanche and Travianna are doing their best to tell the real estate swarm everything that's wrong with the house.

"The basement floods." "There's asbestos everywhere." "Rats." "You have to flush the toilet twice."

"Blanche—" I call out to get her attention.

"I thought you told us he couldn't sell the place yet, Sherlock."

"I did."

"Then why is this happening?" Travianna says.

"Good question."

I re-approach Titi Poon but before I get a word out, she says, "There's not too many good fixer-uppers left in this neighborhood. If I were you, I'd act quickly."

"How'd you get the listing of a house that remains in an unsettled estate?" I ask.

"In real estate, you have to be aggressive."

"But the title remains in Buck Crouch's name, not his brother Cato's."

"Who?"

"Cato Crouch."

"Arnold Sheedy gave me the listing. Now there's a guy who knows a good broker when he sees one," Titi says. "We've worked together a hundred times."

"You can't do what you're doing," I tell her.

"It's only a matter of time," she says. "We'll get the offers in, and by the time we have a deal, the estate will be transferred."

"You can't show a house your client doesn't own."

"And you can't let a small technicality stand in the way of doing business."

Titi goes off to glad-hand.

By this time, the broker's open house is winding down. Agents are leaving.

Ms. Poon comes up to me one more time with a big smile and a hearty handshake. "And if you have a house you want sold, remember, 'Titi Poon will put the *sting* in your listing.'"

Finally, it's over.

Blanche and Travianna sit on the front porch steps. Both are worried wrecks.

"This can't happen."

"Buck would have wanted us to keep the house."

I put my hand out to calm the pair. "Here's what to do."

They listen, which is odd since no one ever listens to me.

"Get down to the Cook County Health Department, tell them your kid has a case of German Measles, and they'll give you signs for your house that say: *QUARANTINED*. Then you write in underneath: *Due to Highly Contagious Deadly Flesh Eating Bacteria*. Put the signs up on every door and one on Titi Poon's For Sale sign in the front yard. If anybody comes to the door, just cough and moan a lot."

I get the kids back in the car.

"Wow, Dad, that was trippy."

Driving away, I'm totally lost in thought. Why would Cato put the house up for sale now? Even if he sells it, it won't go through because it can take weeks to change the title. Cato must be one in-a-hurry, greedy dude. He just carried away a million in cash.

"Dad, what are we going to do today? It's our last day on vacation with you and we should get to do something really fun."

"I have a better idea," I tell them. "You're both moving on in your educational process, one to middle school and one to high school, and maybe this is a good time to sit down and discuss what are going to be your new goals, expectations. As well as talk about how you can make the best of the next level of education."

"Oh, Dad," Care says, "that sounds like advice."

"Dad, we hate your advice," Kelly says. "We never listen, and if we do hear something, we forget it right away."

"What do you mean? I give great advice. What about 'Learn something new every day'?"

"Oh, that was like so lame."

"How about 'Finish what you start'?"

"Dad, I promise you, I'll finish middle school," Care tells me.

"And I'll finish high school too," Kelly says, "unless something better comes along."

"Like what?"

"A really rich guy, who has air conditioning and a car that's not thirty years old," Kelly says.

"He won't want you, Kelly, because you don't have a dowry."

"What's a dowry?"

"Look it up when you get into high school."

Disgusted with me, the girls call Tiffany.

"Hello, little dudettes."

"Tiffany, Dad's being mean to us. He won't take us anyplace on our last day of vacation."

"Where do you want to go?"

"Someplace fun," Care says.

"Like shopping."

Tiffany says, "Let me talk to your father."

I hear this and suddenly can't wait to be scolded by my so-called assistant.

I take the phone but don't speak until I pull the car to the side of the road. "Safety first, ladies." They hate it when I refuse to talk and drive at the same time.

Kelly and Care both roll their eyes with a "Can life get any lamer?" attitude.

"What, Tiffany?"

"I talked to Daddy and he's really mad we had to pay off on the claim when the guy is still alive."

"Tiffany, did you tell him the guy in Bozeman may have been an imposter?"

"No. Why would I do that?"

"Because he may have been an imposter."

"Daddy told me not to quit. 'It's always darkest where the sun don't shine,' Mr. Sherlock."

And my girls think I give bad advice.

"Tell you what, Tiffany, there's a couple loose ends I need to clear up. I'll do that if you take the girls today."

"Deal."

"Meet me at my apartment as soon as you can, and bring lunch."

\*\*\*

I make a major decision after we arrive home.

No matter how much I have to go into credit card debt, I'm buying a new air conditioner. It takes me fifteen sweaty minutes to force some cold air out the window unit this time.

Tiffany shows up in about an hour, bringing some frou-frou food the girls pretend to like. I eat it without asking what it may be. Sometimes it's safer that way.

As the girls chatter like monkeys at the zoo, I sit and stare at *The Original Carlo*. For some reason, I'm getting a second wind, or maybe a third, on this case. The fact that so much doesn't make sense is driving me senseless.

"We're going out on the lake, Mr. Sherlock."

"Well, if they're going in the water, make sure they swim in front of the lifeguard."

"They don't have lifeguards on yachts, Mr. Sherlock."

"You're taking them on a yacht?"

"Yes. Where else do you go to get on the lake?"

Silly me, how did I not know that?

"Where are you going, Dad?"

"I certainly hope somewhere to get my money back," Tiffany adds to Care's question.

"A halfway house in Kenosha."

"If I were you, Mr. Sherlock, I'd go to both halves."

\*\*\*

The Bright New Life Recovery and Rehab Center isn't very bright, lively, or new. Shakespeare was right: "What's in a name?"

It's comprised of three buildings: two are dorms and the

third is for administration, a clinic, meeting rooms, and a day room/dining room, which has a big-screen TV the size of Vermont. An old guy, who looks like he's had a few personal battles of his own in the war on drugs, is named Jack Babalew. He's the boss.

"Is this for you?" he asks as we take the tour.

"No."

"We can't take kids under eighteen," Jack tells me before asking his next question.

"Actually," I interrupt, "I'm here about a person who used work here, Imelda Smith."

"Imelda Smith?"

"Yes, you do know her?"

"The love of my life," Jack says with a pleasant nostalgia in his tone.

"Were you two an item?"

"No. Imelda wasn't the romantic type."

"What type was she?"

"The acutely addicted type." He stops, looks me right in the eye. "What's this all about anyway?"

"I'm an insurance investigator in the middle of a possible fraud case, where Imelda Smith's name and money have popped up like weeds in a fallow field."

"Well, I certainly wouldn't want anything bad to happen to Imelda," Jack says with a very odd tone in his voice.

We pass one of the dorm buildings where a number of men are inside cleaning, or outside gardening and doing chores.

"When Imelda first came, she was a chronic. That means she couldn't leave the facility. After about a year, she entered our progress program, where you're allowed out to work, take care of your kids, or whatever. Then for the last years, she didn't live here, but used the place as a spot to come to when she felt she was slipping off the wagon."

"She pop in often?"

"Often enough. Imelda never quit battling her demons. I can't remember her missing a meeting."

"Where'd she live?"

"Apartment in Kenosha."

"She work?"

"She never told me how she made her money, but I'm sure she made a lot of it."

"How'd you know that?"

"She kept us out of bankruptcy twice."

"Her family visit while she was here?" I keep the questions coming.

"I don't think she had one. This place was pretty much her family."

"Was she ever married?"

Jack shrugs his shoulders. "Imelda was different. Real quiet. Some addicts will talk your ears right off, but not Imelda. She kept everything locked inside her. I always figured that's why she was addicted and stayed addicted."

"She's still alive, you know."

"If you want to call that living," he says.

We're winding our way back to the administration office.

"You start this place, Jack?"

"Thirty-seven years ago."

"Why?"

"A lot of addicts stay in the drug business. They become counselors or workers. That's what I did, and it blossomed from there."

"If you're a fox, wouldn't it be best to stay out of the hen house?" I ask.

"Well, sometimes it's best to stay close to who you are," he says. "You can make a pickle out of a cucumber, either a gherkin, bread and butter, or make it kosher, but down deep it's still a cucumber."

***

On the way home, I swear the temperature hits one-ninety. I get off the 94 and head for the lake. I wind down through Waukegan and Lake Bluff until I hit Lake Forest and decide to take a walk along the shore in front of massive estates, one of which Tiffany will probably own someday.

The lakefront is public property for all citizens to use, but in Lake Forest there is a nonresident usage fee of $10. I guess that's not too bad to use a beautiful beach, but in addition, all the parking lots near the lake are city-owned and require a permit to use, and guess what? You have to be a Lake Forest resident to get a permit. Leave it to the rich to find ways to keep the tramps out, which are, in their eyes, anyone who can't afford to live in Lake Forest, like me.

I keep going south until I hit Winnetka, park for free, and head towards the water.

The ride in the car has done a number on my back. Luckily, I keep an old back brace in the trunk, which I strap around my middle before I take off on my stroll. The brace is quite big and it makes me look like I'm either wearing a flak jacket or carrying a load of explosives. I get some weird looks.

The breeze coming off the lake cools the temps down about fifteen degrees. Whew. Walking along, I see sailboats and powerboats out on the lake and wonder which one my daughters are on. Lucky them, unlucky me.

Using my photographic memory, I picture *The Original Carlo* and notice the error in my ways. I haven't connected the dots.

How could I have missed the similarity of Smith? Did Buck or imposter Bob make a conscious choice of his last name?

What is the connection between Cato and Estalita, except for being married? Is there something more between the two? Is it a marriage of convenience, and if so, what would make it so convenient?

Cato could have set it all up. He cashed his life insurance policy in, so he must have known Buck had one too. I wouldn't put it past him to write a phony will or bribe the doc to cremate the body. Problem with Cato, he just doesn't impress me as a guy with enough brain cells to come up with such an elaborate plan and then pull it off.

Why did Buck disappear in the first place? He had two wives, one girlfriend, time to find additional women, and plenty of money to do it all with. The part about his getting fired is silly; no company fires their top, sock-it-to-'em salesman. Why would the Buck/Bob we met in Bozeman have no interest in anything left behind, including a $400K house, stuffed trophies, and a lot of really bad art? He wouldn't even have to go through a divorce or divorces if he wanted to wipe his slate clean and start over. Talk about a lucky guy.

Why did Jupiter start off lying to me, change her story when she saw cash on the horizon, then push the Draconian angle when it was obviously too late?

Imelda seems to be the most dot-connectable of the bunch. If she's Buck and Cato's mother, where was she during their formative years? Drunk and in the gutter? I've known my share of alcoholics, but I never met one who was an astute investor who invested his or her money instead of drinking it all away.

I can't quit the case. I need answers. If I don't figure this all out, I won't sleep for a month, which would make it two months in a row.

I get back in the car and make one more stop before the day is over.

## CHAPTER 28

Herman McFadden is an investment whiz, computer hacker, and a porn-addicted fat guy.

A few years back, I got him out of a particularly nasty murder charge, and he's been beholden to me since. I don't hesitate to pull in favors. Herman lives in a spacious two-bedroom apartment on the North Side. The place needs to be spacious, since Herman weighs upwards of four hundred pounds, and that's when he's on one of his diets.

I knock. There's no answer.

"Herman, it's me, Sherlock."

I hear noises, probably the building sagging as the weight shifts inside the second floor.

The door opens. The cool air rushes out. It feels marvelous.

"Nice belt," Herman says. His massive size fills up the doorframe like a fog covering the Golden Gate Bridge.

"It's not a belt, it's a brace; my back's going out again."

I wait for Herman to shift away from the door and walk inside.

"Guess what, Sherlock?"

"You're doing Zumba?"

"No, I lost thirty pounds."

It's hard to notice, since Herman losing thirty pounds is akin to one container falling off a cargo ship.

"How?"

"The brown rice and Oolong tea diet," he explains as he sits in a new lounge chair I haven't seen before. "All them Chinamen are thin 'cause all they eat is brown rice."

"How about Buddha?"

"He had a thyroid condition."

I move some porn magazines to the side, and check for any wetness before I sit on the couch. "Why don't you watch porn on the internet like all the other guys, Herman?"

"I'm a purist."

Herman takes a bowl of rice off a side table and puts a set of chopsticks through his fat fingers. "What do you want, Sherlock?"

"A favor."

"What else is new?"

"Are you using chopsticks because they're harder to eat

with?" I have to ask.

"No. I dropped my silverware tray on the floor and I'm scared if I get down to pick it up, I won't be able to get back up."

"I'm in the middle of a wild one, Herman. I need your help."

"Let me repeat," he says. "What else is new?"

It takes me about twenty minutes to go through the whole Crouch case. I'm pretty sure Herman is paying attention, although oftentimes he seems more concerned with balancing a hunk of rice from the bowl and into his mouth.

When I finish, he's finished.

"There's more rice in the cooker," he says, handing me the empty bowl. "Get me a refill, would ya?"

I obey his wish and when I return, he asks, "So what do you want me to do?"

"Estalita Crouch. I haven't been able to turn one leaf over on her."

"You Google her?"

"I don't have a Filipino Google app."

"What else?"

"I can't find the Montana Buck, Bob Smith, or much on Imelda Smith."

Herman washes his second bowl of rice down with a pitcher of Oolong tea.

"What do you think, Herman?"

Herman lets loose a burp that could shatter safety glass.

"Well, let me see what I can do."

Herman hits a button on his chair's armrest, which makes the chair seat motor upward and then tip forward, putting Herman easily on his feet.

"This is the greatest invention since the garage door opener, Sherlock. It used to take me ten minutes to get up, and that was with a rope on a weighted pulley."

Herman shuffles over to his dining room table where two wooden chairs await his butt. He moves his financial charts and graphs to the side, sits, and logs in.

"You know where Estalita's from in the Philippines?"

"Probably Manila."

While Herman taps keys on his computer keyboard, I go into the kitchen, find the silverware, pick it up, wash it along with the other dirty dishes, bowls and whatever; I should have been a housewife.

As I return to the dining room, I see Herman is not a happy guy.

"When do you need this Sherlock?"

"Yesterday."

Herman lets loose a second burp, which sets off car alarms in the street.

Enough said.

\*\*\*

By the time I fight the reverse commute back into the city, it is well past 7PM.

There are enough half-filled cardboard containers on Tiffany's kitchen island to feed the population of Beijing. I don't hesitate and dig in. The food may be cold, but it's delicious.

"Dad, we have to get a boat," Kelly tells me. "Being out on the water is so invigorating."

"You're fifteen, Kelly, you don't need any more invigoration."

"Please, Dad."

"I can't afford a car. How do you think I could afford a boat?"

"Maybe you should get a second job?"

"Easy for you to say, Kelly."

Care fills me in. "Kelly was more invigorated by the crew than by the water, Dad."

"Oh, please, don't tell me."

"Dad, I think I'm going to love high school," Kelly says with a dreamy look in her eye. "I think I'll major in gender studies."

And I thought the *terrible twos* were bad.

"Buck still hasn't written me back, Mr. Sherlock," Tiffany tells me. "I can't believe it. I always get a call back."

"There's plenty of fish in the lake, and plenty of guys holding them up on dating sites, Tiffany."

"Maybe he broke his finger and can't type."

"Yeah, that's it."

Tiffany perks up a little bit; a thought must have entered her mind. "Oh yeah," she says, "Bree Bare-her-butt-o-nette's looking for you."

"My cell plan doesn't include Wisconsin. What did she

want?"

"She said that lawyer guy's suing for more money."

"Seedy Arnold Sheedy?"

"If that guy gets any more of our money, my dad's going to have a canary."

"You mean a 'coronary'?"

"Whatever."

"I'll call her."

I've finished off six of the cardboard boxes. The Kung Pao Chicken was the tastiest, followed closely by the Sesame Shrimp. A cup of Oolong tea sure would taste good right now.

"Come on, girls, we're leaving."

"Do we have to, Dad? We like it here."

"So do I, but it's time to return to reality. Thank Tiffany for all she's done for you and how she's made your vacation so special."

The two gush their appreciation as they group-hug. I stay on the sidelines where I obviously belong.

\*\*\*

Saturday morning, I let the girls sleep in, and I rearrange the index cards on *The Original Carlo* about thirty-seven hundred more times. There has to be a rhyme and reason to this puzzle, but I just can't seem to put the square pegs in the right holes.

My back is killing me. The Aleve doesn't help, nor the twenty minutes on the Oriental Oscillator. I put the back brace back on and suffer in silence. When the kids do arise, I make them French toast, a favorite for their last vacation breakfast with Dad. I have them go in and pack up what stuff they're taking back to their mother's house.

At eleven, we're in the car heading towards Sauganash.

"Well, girls, I hope you enjoyed our vacation time together."

"We liked the Tiffany parts, Dad," Care says.

"I bet you can't wait for next year to do it again."

"Yeah, especially the Tiffany parts," Kelly says.

"I feel it is so important that we took this time and really bonded together as a family." My sarcasm is so thick it drips off my tongue like sixty weight motor oil.

"Dad, when are you going to pick up Buttonwillow and bring her back to our barn?"

"I'm not. As of drop-off time, that duty transfers to the person in charge, which will be your mother, who just happens to be the person who purchased the very hungry animal in the first place."

"I'm not sure she'll like that, Dad."

"Hey, I told you people, 'Don't buy anything that eats.'"

I pull in the driveway of what used to be my house.

"All right, both of you give me a kiss."

I get a lousy peck on the cheek from each before they scatter out of the car with their stuff and head for the front door.

It's locked.

I yell out, "The key's under the mat."

Care lifts up the mat and searches underneath. She doesn't find a key, but something else. Both girls run it back to the car.

Care hands me an envelope, addressed to *Richard Sherlock*.

"Your mother has to use my last name? How many Richards does she know?"

Ever since my divorce, my ex-wife has decided that the best form of communication is to write me notes. Seeing we didn't speak much in the last couple years of marriage, this isn't all that surprising.

"What does it say, Dad?" Care asks.

"Get back in the car. Your mother says she needs another week to recolor her aura."

## CHAPTER 29

I might be dating myself, but when I was a kid my mother took me to the store right before Labor Day and bought me a box of #2 pencils, three pens, and a spiral notebook. I doubt if she spent more than five bucks total.

Times have certainly changed.

"Why can't you use the calculator I gave you, Kelly?"

"The ugly one from the Save-a-lot Credit Union you got free? No way."

"Why do you need a scientific one?"

"I don't know. I'm not in school yet," Kelly says, "but that's what's on the list."

Each of my daughters has a school supply list longer than my left leg. Scientific computers, regular computers, special notebooks, book covers, pencils, pens, markers, highlighters, erasers, water bottles, gym clothes (two pairs), gym shoes, composition books, double-sided tape, combination locks, and two kinds of glue, hopefully one not for sniffing. The Back To School section of the Target store is bigger than their cleaning supply aisles, and probably twice as profitable.

I walk out of the store five hundred dollars poorer.

"Okay, Dad. Now we need clothes."

The rest of the weekend the kids must try on hundreds of pairs of pants, shoes, tops, outfits and other *accessories* that they "just have to have."

Add another four bills to improve their looks to the five I spent to improve their minds.

At least all the shopping took my mind off the case. Pretty lousy consolation, exchanging absolute frustration for abject poverty.

\*\*\*

On Monday morning, I awaken with new thoughts and theories to test against what currently sits upon *The Original Carlo*. Before doing any exercises or rolling around on the Oriental Oscillator, I go right to work.

After two hours, I have canned every new idea I had, and my back is twice as bad as it was yesterday. I lie on the floor with a heating pad on my lower back, my feet up, arms out, toes curling in, all in the attempt to bring a little relief to my spine, which is tighter than a lug nut on a tire. At ten the kids get up, walk in the room, sprawl on the couch, turn on the TV, and finally notice me lying on the floor like a deformed pretzel.

Kelly asks, "What fun things do you have planned for us to do today, Dad?"

"Same as I had last week: none."

"Bad answer, Dad."

"Bring me my phone, would you?"

Kelly doesn't move. She has her brain's audio app set on *Ignore any requests for help or orders to work*. Care rises, gets my phone, and hands it to me.

In a few seconds, I say, "How was your weekend, Bree?"

"Boring. How was yours?"

"Expensive."

"You have to get down here, Sherlock. You know what's hitting the fan," Bree tells me.

I ask, "Is the 'fan' the one person in the world that likes me?"

"No."

We meet Bree Bisonette in the coffee shop downstairs in the Aon Building, around eleven-thirty.

"How can he sue us? He already got his million dollars."

"Sheedy's making a case that we systematically held the money for an inappropriate amount of time. He's suing us for breach of contract, interest on the million, his legal fees, and emotional pain and suffering."

Kelly interrupts her munching on a bear claw to ask, "Could we sue you for the emotional suffering we've endured for not being taken on a proper vacation, Dad?"

"Be my guest."

"Mr. Richmond has had it with this case," Bree says. "He wants it put to bed immediately."

I know Bree would like to be the one to do the last part personally with Mr. Richmond. Some loves never die.

"I don't know what we're going to do, but you better do it quickly."

"Me? What do you want me to do, Bree?"

"Figure it out. Get us out of this mess. Get our money back."

"Bree, you hear yourself? You're sounding just like Tiffany."

"Oh, God. I never believed I could sink so low."

***

There is an old adage in the detective business: *When in doubt, go back and start over.* It's not a very clever adage, which says a lot about the detective business.

I make a phone call.

"Sure, we'd love to help" is the answer to my first question.

After I hang up, I tell the girls, "Get ready, we're leaving."

Care asks, "Where are we going?"

"On a hike."

"Is Tiffany going with us?"

"No, Tiffany hates nature."

We stop by the apartment to pick up an extra set of clothes.

"What do we need another outfit for, Dad?"

"You never know when you need to be cool."

I've been on I-94 so often I'm getting to know it better than my own street. It takes us about two hours to get to Slinger, Wisconsin, where the Forty Double D's wait for us on the side of the road.

I make the introductions. "Deloris and Debbie Diggler, this is Kelly and Care."

Kelly has a look of amazement on her face as hands are shook.

"You didn't wear hiking boots?" Deloris asks.

"Do we have time to go out and buy some?" Kelly asks.

"We're going to rough it," I explain.

The sisters lead the way. This is no easy hike. There is no trail and much of the ground is soggy. We stay mostly where the water ran during the spring, but have to climb over fallen tree trunks and jump over puddles. The humidity and heat are stifling. Debbie and Deloris treat it like a walk in the park.

"You can get there faster in the early evening because the mosquitos will pick you up and carry you most of the way," Deloris says.

"But when you get there, you'll need a blood transfusion, since most of yours will be sucked out," Debbie finishes the thought.

Charming.

It takes about forty minutes before we stop.

"That's where we found him." Deloris points.

The spot, Buck's temporary gravesite, is between two mature pine trees. I walk over and stand on the mound of earth where the body was buried and look upward. I can see where the ski slope becomes a drop so sheer even an extreme skier would need a parachute to come down safely. There are few trees between where I stand and the top of the cliff. If a body was thrown off, it would roll pretty much unencumbered all the way down and hit so hard that it would dig itself into the wet ground.

"Where'd you find the geocache?" I ask.

Debbie stands on the spot. "Right here." She reaches down and picks up the metal box, opens it, and says, "Need any coupons for the Outdoor Store?"

"I could use some new boots," Kelly says.

"No, we're good," I call out.

The sisters and I wander around. I really have no clue what I'm looking for. Kelly and Care sit on a log, exhausted from the excursion. Enough said about youthful energy.

I come to a conclusion: There's no way anyone could carry a body from the road into this ravine and plant it like a crocus. I totally agree with Sheriff Cliff's theory. If it was Buck Crouch on top of that hill, he either got down here by tripping over his own feet, was pushed, or given the old "One, two, three, heave-ho."

Rain falls on our way back to our car. At first it is a relief, then the wet turns into a glue that plasters our clothes onto our skins like an ad onto a billboard.

"Can I ask one more favor of you?" I say to the sisters.

"Sure."

"Can we borrow your shower?"

By the time we've all changed into our additional sets of clothes and wished the Diggler sisters, "Thanks and all the best," it's well past four o'clock.

We're in the car and Care notices immediately we're not on the way home. "Where to next?"

"Since we're already up here, I'd like to stop by and say hello to an old friend. That okay with you?"

"Sure, why not?" Care says.

"Kelly?"

I see in the rearview mirror she's lost in thought.

"Kelly, earth to Kelly."

"Dad," she says, "do you think I have a chance of having boobs as big as the Diggler sisters?"

Oh jeesh.

It takes us twenty minutes to get to our next stop.

"We'd like to see Imelda Smith."

"Oh, sure," the receptionist tells us in a much more welcoming tone than on my previous visit. I must have made a good first impression.

"She's in the room down the hall from the day room. You better hurry, she's scheduled to be moved out this afternoon."

"Thank you."

The kids follow me down the hall, past the dining area, and into the day room where most of the occupants are napping, watching TV, or existing in some somnambulistic state of being.

I don't see a hallway. I ask an orderly, "Imelda Smith?"

He points around a corner and says, "First door on your right."

We follow his directions.

We find Imelda all alone in the middle of the room. She lies quietly, her hands resting on her chest. She looks a little better than the last time I saw her, with a lot more color in her face.

"Should we wake her up, Dad?" Care asks.

"No, I don't think so."

"Why not?"

"I don't think she'd be much for conversation today."

"Why not?"

"She's dead."

"AHHHH!" Kelly screams and runs out of the room.

Care moves a little closer. "I've never seen a dead person before, except on TV."

"It's a whole new experience in person," I tell her.

"You know, she doesn't look all that bad," Care says.

"No matter how good you look, if you're dead, you can't look good."

We're back in the car on our way to our last stop of the day.

Kelly's angry. "Why didn't you tell me she was dead, Dad?"

"I didn't know."

"I bet I'm now emotionally scarred for life," Kelly informs me. "And it's all your fault, Dad."

"You want to know how she died, Kelly?"

"Well..." she hesitates, "sure."

"Imelda shopped till she dropped."

\*\*\*

We find F. in his office. He's a bit surprised to see me.

"If I guess, will you tell me if I'm right?" I ask.

"Guess all you want," he says.

"She left all her money to the Bright New Day Recovery Center."

"Good guess." F. Carlton Huff smiles.

## CHAPTER 30

It's close to seven when we get back into the city. I'd take the kids somewhere nice for dinner, but with the back-to-school expenses and two new wardrobes, my one credit card has hit its limit. I don't like to do it, but with only twenty bucks in my wallet, I stop at Superdawg and let the kids chow down on red hots and fries. I abstain.

While they munch down over-condimented wieners, I call Herman.

As soon as he hears my voice, he tells me, "There's no such person as Estalita Crouch, Sherlock."

"Sure?"

"Of course I'm sure. Cato Crouch has never been married."

"But she's wearing a rock on her left hand the size of a shot glass," I explain.

"So is Ludmilla, the woman I was supposed to marry."

Herman got left at the altar the day of his wedding dance. I was his best man, and Kelly and Care were flower girls. Herman was so devastated, being jilted, he ate the entire wedding reception's six-foot Domino's pizza in one sitting.

"She have a maiden name?" he asks.

"Duarte."

During the pause, I hear his fingers tapping the keys.

"How about the other people, Herman?"

"I'm working on it, Sherlock. I'm working on it."

"You can put Imelda Smith last on the list."

"Why?"

"She died."

"Was it something you said?"

"Very funny, Herman."

There is one more stop I'd like to make, but it's too far to drive this late at night. I get the girls back to the apartment. I crank up the a/c unit and we settle in for the night.

"Are we going to work on the case tonight?" Care asks.

"No."

"Why not?"

"I'm sick of this case. I got no idea what's going on, the people involved are either dying or can't be reached, and the money has already been paid out. Even if I do figure it out, what would be the point?"

"Gee, Dad, you don't have to snap at me."

"I didn't snap at you, Care."

"Yes, you did."

Kelly adds, "Yes, it was definitely a snap, Dad."

"Sorry."

My frustration has hit its peak. I take the sheet I use when I sleep on the couch, unfold it, and drape it over *The Original Carlo*.

"But if you don't solve the case, Tiffany won't get a new Lexus."

"Heaven forbid."

"Dad," Kelly interjects into our conversation, "if we're not going to work on the case, can we do something fun tomorrow?"

Before I have a chance to say "No," Kelly adds, "and it can't be any hike in the wilderness or visiting dead people."

"What do you have in mind, Kelly? Another trip to the mall?"

"I was thinking more along the lines of a massage, mani-pedi, and a facial."

"No problem, Kelly."

"Really?"

"And I'll personally do all three myself. What time should I put you down for your treatments?"

"Oh, Dad, that's creepy."

"Fine, you do them on me."

"That's even creepier."

The downstairs door buzzer in the kitchen goes off.

Who the heck can it be? It's after nine. I won't even answer the phone after nine.

Buzz, buzz.

It's probably the drunk on the second floor who can't find his keys. He's good for a *let-me-in* at least twice a week.

The buzzer rings again and again. The girls make no effort whatsoever to get off the couch and answer it.

"Who is it?" I push the button and yell into the little speaker.

"It's Jupiter. I have to see you."

I hear panic in the other room. "Draconian's coming up to drink our blood."

"Don't let 'em in, Dad."

"This is an emergency, Sherlock. I have to see you. Please, I'm desperate."

I hit the release button.

"Oh no, we're all going to die!" Both girls scamper for the bedroom, slam the door, and lock it from the inside. I can hear them pulling furniture to barricade the door.

I open the front door to see a quite distraught Jupiter.

I call out in the direction of the bedroom, "You can come out. She's alone."

Jupiter walks in.

"You have to help me."

"What happened?"

"Moonjava's gone."

"Who?"

"Draconian. He's gone."

The girls come out of hiding and join us in the living room.

"Where did he go?" I ask.

Before she plunks herself down, Jupiter looks up and asks, "Why do you have a sheet over the ugly painting?"

"*The Original Carlo* isn't ugly, it's unique," I explain.

Jupiter plops down on the couch, and her head goes in her hands. Obviously she's shed a lot of tears lately. "I don't know where he went," she says, on the frantic side. "Maybe he's been kidnapped?"

"Who'd want him?" Kelly unfortunately thinks out loud.

"How do you know he's gone?" I ask.

"He hasn't come home in days."

"Maybe the Scumbag Death Cult got a gig out of town?" Care suggests.

"Yeah," Jupiter says, "in Hell."

"Oh no," Kelly says. "There's Goth clubs up here on earth."

"Those guys he was reading about on the internet," Jupiter says. "They were all were musicians who committed suicide."

This isn't the least bit funny anymore.

"Don't think that, Jupiter."

"What am I supposed to think?"

"Anything but that."

"We have to put a missing person's report out. Get those freeway signs to light up."

"Draconian's eighteen, Jupiter. He can't be treated as a missing child, he's too old."

"This can't happen, Sherlock. I know I've been a lousy mother, but this can't happen."

I tell Kelly to get Jupiter a glass of water, which she does, amazing as that may seem.

The three of us watch the tears fall from Jupiter's eyes.

We sit with little left to add to the conversation for a few very long moments.

"Jupiter, I'll take you home. Let me look and see what he took. I'll be able to tell if there was anything suspicious."

I get Jupiter off the couch, grab my wallet and keys, and tell the girls, "If the buzzer rings, don't let anyone in."

"No problem, Dad. No problem."

***

If a person is about to do something personally drastic, he or she will usually leave a few clues. From what Jupiter expects, that something would be a suicide note.

Thank God, I can't find one.

Jupiter stands to the side and watches me poke through Draconian's room. I look behind the Kurt Cobain and Joey Ramone posters. Nothing. Under his bed, there are old Abba Zabba candy wrappers. In the corner where the carpet has come up, I find an old guitar pick. His white make-up, black nail polish and eyeliner remain on a counter. Thirty-seven cents is left in his drawer. These are not good signs. It's hard to tell what clothing he took and what he left behind since there is a pile of dirty clothes in one corner, and his drawers are stuffed with piles of clothes in no order. Draconian doesn't believe in folding.

"Do you know what clothing isn't here?" I ask Jupiter.

"His boots, cape, jacket, and jeans."

"All black, right?"

"Moonjava wasn't much on color coordinating."

"His guitar gone?"

"Yeah."

"Any other personal items?"

Jupiter shrugs a "No."

"Any pictures, mementos, favorite roach clip, dark glasses, piercing, chain, or autographed picture of Johnny Rotten?"

She shrugs again.

"Did you notice any weed missing?"

"No, and that I would have noticed right away."

It takes me a whole hour to go through the room. I wash my hands really well when I'm finished.

This doesn't look good, but I don't share my thought with Jupiter.

"I'm going to make some calls tomorrow, Jupiter. I got a few favors I can call in. I'll get his description out on the street. Do you have a recent picture of him?"

"Yeah."

"I want you to get some sleep. Don't convince yourself of the worst. I'm sure he's out there. Maybe he found a Goth girl. Who knows? If you can, write down names of his friends, people he hung out with, get the names and addresses of his bandmates, give me a list of where he used to hang out. Stop worrying."

Jupiter nods her head unconvincingly. I'm not sure she can tell I'm mostly lying, but sincerely hope she can't. She goes off to find the picture. I wait for her at the front door.

"Here."

Wouldn't you know it? Draconian is no exception to the rule. A Goth ain't a Goth without a picture of himself up against a tombstone.

## CHAPTER 31

I can't sleep. I toss and turn, which is extremely painful on my back. The individual aspects of this case bounce around in my brain like a runaway tractor across a plowed field. I give up on sleep before the sun comes up. I load up on Aleve, do some exercises, eat toast, put on my brace, leave the girls a note, get in the car, and drive to Batavia.

I knock on the trailer door until Cato comes out.

"What are you doing here?" he says, half-asleep. "And where did you get that ugly belt?"

"It's a brace, not a belt, and I just happened to be in the neighborhood and thought I'd stop by to get that recipe from Estalita."

"She ain't home."

"Do you know where she keeps her recipes?"

"No. Go away."

I don't move. Cato is starting to wake up. He's not a guy who looks good first thing in the morning, and he seems a few steps down from that today.

"You just pocketed big bucks, Cato. Why the heck are you still living in this dump?"

"Maybe I like it here," he says.

"Ambiance?"

"What the hell do you want, Sherlock?"

"Answers."

"About what?"

"Did you know your brother was going to disappear? How do you think he died? Was Imelda Smith your mother? Where's the rest of Buck's money? Who was the guy I met in Montana? And do ya think the Cubs have a chance to repeat?"

Cato gives it some thought and counts down on his fingers as he says, "No. I don't know. Who? What extra money? How the hell would I know? And only if their pitching holds up."

"How about elaborating just a bit?"

"If you don't have pitching, you'll never make it in the play-offs."

This isn't working out as I had planned.

"Do you know what I am, Cato?" I ask in all sincerity.

"Obnoxious."

"Besides that?"

"Worthless, stupid, and wasting your time?" he answers.

"I'm the stain on your shirt you can't get out. The bad smell in the basement that won't go away. The unlucky penny always in your pocket." I pause. "I'm not quitting until I get to the bottom of all this."

"Why bother? The court ruled. The money's gone. The ship's sailed. The clock's run out. Go home, Sherlock. The race has been won."

Cato turns, re-enters his trailer, slams the door, and probably is on his way back to bed.

Maybe that's where I'll go too.

*** 

The kids must have been watching from the front windows because as soon as I'm out of the car, they both come running up.

"Dad, Dad!"

"What?"

"Blanche and Travianna called," Care says.

"We have to go right now," Kelly adds.

"Why?"

"They're being invaded again!"

The kids get in the car, I lock up the apartment, and within fifteen minutes we arrive at Buck's house.

I can't believe what I'm seeing.

Four people have surrounded the property, banging on doors and windows, screaming comments: "Let us in." "We're calling the Sheriff." "Come out before we storm the place."

The person at the front door, who is leading the charge, wears a hazmat suit and sounds familiar.

"What are you doing?" I ask the germ-a-phoebe.

"We have to get in."

"Why?"

"I have a showing."

Behind the sterilizing mask is Titi Poon. I know this from her knee-jerk reaction of plunging her gloved hand into a pocket and bringing it out to hand me her business card.

"There's nobody sick in there. Them squatters have got to go."

"If you're so sure nobody's sick, why'd you wear the hazmat

197

suit?"

"I had it in my closet and haven't had a chance to wear it lately."

I look to my left and see Travianna staring out from behind the drape. "Why don't you let me go in and talk to them?"

"With or without a suit on?"

"Don't worry, I got shots before I came over."

Titi stands back. I signal Kelly and Care to join me, and rap on the door.

"Blanche, Travianna, let me in."

The door opens a crack, eyes peer out.

"It's just us," I tell the eyes. "Let us in."

We enter.

"That woman's scarier than the alien in *Alien*," Travianna tells us as Blanche relocks the door.

"That flesh-eating bacteria worked for a while," Blanche says. "Maybe we should have upped the disease to the Ebola virus?"

Care peers around the room and asks, "Do you miss having all those dead animals around?"

"In a way," Travianna answers. "They were the only pets I've ever had I didn't have to pick up after."

"We have to do something, Sherlock," Blanche says. "We don't have any place to go if we get booted out of here."

"One of you has to go downtown to the Board of Realtors' office and sign a formal complaint."

"What? That we got squatter's rights?"

"No, that they're selling a house before they have the title."

"We can't go down there together," Travianna says. "One of us is going to have to stay here and defend the fort."

"Good idea," Blanche agrees.

"I'll hold off Titi Poon," I tell the pair. "But you got to get down there and do it today."

They each push out a fist, showing their resolve.

"Right on."

The girls and I go back outside to the porch.

"Titi, I'm telling you, you're playing with fire here." I speak at the breathing hole in her suit. "You try to sell a house that your client doesn't own and you'll lose your license."

"He told me he owns it."

"Do you have it in writing?"

"No."

"Have you seen the title?"

"No."

"Do you have a signed listing agreement?"

"I can't stand around and wait for piddly paperwork."

"Look, Titi, in this market the longer you wait, the more the house is going to be worth, and the more commission you're going to get."

"Hmmmm."

Obviously, Titi Poon has an extra 24th chromosome, the greed gene, and I've hit it.

"Well, I always thought he priced the place too cheap," she admits.

"You'll only have to wait a couple days, Titi. Plenty of time to up the price ten grand."

"Hmmmm. Hummmm."

Disaster averted.

We wait for Titi and her crew to pack up and leave before we exit.

Kelly asks, "Do they make those hazmat suits in any other color than white?"

"I'll have to get back to you on that one, Kelly."

"I'll be waiting."

Care asks, "Is it against the law to stuff people the same way they stuff dead animals?"

"You can do it in Egypt, but only if your pyramid is ready to be occupied."

&ast;&ast;&ast;

Tiffany is waiting for us when we get back to our apartment.

"Little dudettes, what are you doing here?"

"Mom needed more time to work on her aura, so we got stuck with Dad again," Kelly tells her.

"Where have you been?" Tiffany gets out of her cooled car holding a package.

"There was an alien invasion over at the Crouch house. Dad had to stop it."

"How?"

"Light saber," I tell her.

"Well, Mr. Sherlock, while you have been running around playing Hands-on Solo, I've been working on the case."

"And what have you uncovered in your search, Chewbacca?"

"I don't know who that is, but I can tell you that Buck Crouch is definitely alive."

"Really? How'd you find that out?"

"He was seen back at Ted's Montana Grill eating a Buffalo Burger."

"So?"

"Now I have proof."

Tiffany opens the package, pulls out a glass and hands it to me. I roll it around in my hands, hold it up to the light, and peer through it. The glass is unwashed.

"Okay."

"I made a deal with a waiter at the restaurant," Tiffany says. "If Buck came back in, he'd take the glass Buck used and send it to me. Now we have his fingerprints, Mr. Sherlock." Tiffany beams at her cleverness and revelation.

I stand holding the glass. "But you touched it, the waiter had to touch it, and now I've touched it."

"But I got his prints. All we have to do it match it to something in his sock drawer and we have proof."

"As they say on CSI, the evidence has been compromised, Tiffany."

"Dad's right," Care says. "I watch that show all the time."

"Darn."

"What was he doing back at Ted's?" I ask.

"Eating, Mr. Sherlock. The place is a restaurant."

My turn. "You don't have to snap at me, Tiffany."

"I didn't snap at you."

"Yes, you did," Kelly tells her. "We know a snap when we hear one."

"But I thought I had the case all wrapped up," Tiffany says.

"Welcome to my world."

"Well, what are we going to do now?" she asks.

"We have a couple more stops to make in the next couple of days."

"Where?"

"Larry Flemm's."

"Larry Flemm with two m's?" Kelly asks.

"No way I'm going there," Tiffany says. "That guy's a creep with two p's."

"Okay, then you go see Herman McFadden."

"Herman!" Tiffany explodes. "That guy makes Larry Flemm with two m's look like a Chippendale dancer."

"What do you want to do, Tiffany?"

"Find Buck Crouch, get our money, and go look at new cars."

"You won't do anything I ask you to do."

"Yeah."

"Why not?"

"Three words, Mr. Sherlock: Herman the Vermin."

"If you won't do what I need you to do, what are you going to do?"

"Maybe I'll do something you haven't thought of."

"Like what?"

Tiffany puts her nose up and says, "I don't know because I don't know all the stuff you've already thought of."

Enough is enough.

"Fine, Tiffany, do what you want. I've had it with you."

I turn my back on her. Kelly and Care stare at me. They want to be on Tiffany's side, but they know I'm right.

I start to walk up the path to the front door and my phone rings.

It's Jupiter.

We converse for a few seconds. I hang up, turn, and head back towards the three females. I totally ignore Tiffany and say to Kelly and Care, "Get in the car. We have to go."

I get no argument.

***

"Calm down, Jupiter."

"I can't."

Jupiter is a mass of negative emotion. She's had so many tears running down her cheeks, rivulets have formed. Her ears are bright red, her hair is matted like an unwashed Rastafarian's, hands are shaking like a Parkinson's patient, and voice is cracking like cement during an earthquake.

I get her seated on her couch. The girls sit on crystal crates.

"I guess you didn't listen when I told you to quit worrying."

"I tried to get ahold of his bandmates, went to the alley where he used to hang out, called every number on his cell phone. Nothing."

"You have to keep trying."

"I'm psychic. I know when something's wrong."

"You're convincing yourself before you have any proof, Jupiter."

"The negative vibes are hitting me like arrows from an automatic bow."

"Stop it. You can't do this to yourself. Draconian could be in the middle of some mosh pit somewhere."

Jupiter puts out more words, but for the life of me, I can't make heads or tails out of them. She's a total, unmitigated, emotional wreck.

"Jupiter, I'm going to the police. I'll get the word out on him. But I want you to get some sleep, and tonight, go to all the Goth clubs you can find, take his picture, and ask every kid there if they've seen him. Can you do that?"

"Yes."

"We're going to find him, Jupiter. We're going to find him."

# CHAPTER 32

B efore I can get a word out, I'm interrupted.
"Wait."

"What is it? Eczema, whooping cough, psoriasis, tired blood, or mealworm disease?"

"That's not funny, Sherlock. I could be knocking on death's door."

"And nobody would be home, Jack."

"For your information, I got Celiac's Disease." Jack holds his lower stomach like a pregnant woman trying to pass gas.

"What is Celiac's Disease?"

"Intestinal disorder from too much gluten."

"Jack," I ask, "have you ever seen gluten, or a picture of gluten, or a hunk of it on a loaf of bread?"

"No."

"Two years ago, did you ever hear anyone mention the word?"

"No."

"Do you know why?"

"No."

"Because gluten doesn't exist. It's just some nonexistent snake oil, conjured up by a bunch of food manufacturers to get you to pay an extra fifty cents for a box of Post Toasties."

"Sherlock, I'm telling you, I got it. You might as well start writing my eulogy."

Wait, Jack Wayt is one of my best friends from the Chicago PD. We pretty much came up together through the ranks and stayed that way until I got fired.

"What disease did you have last month, Jack?"

"Irritable Bowel Syndrome."

"And what happened, Jack?"

"False alarm, but I decided that will be the last time I self-medicate."

"Jack, please, no descriptions in front of my kids."

Kelly and Care give him a *disgusting to the max* look.

"Sorry, kids. A little too much information, huh?"

"Ah, yeah."

Jack has a bit of hypochondria in him. Nobody on the force gets more out of the health insurance plan than Wait, Jack Wayt.

"Jack, I need a favor."

"You always need a favor, Sherlock."

"I like to be consistent."

I pull out Draconian's graveyard photo and hand it over.

"Looks like a happy-go-lucky fellow" is Jack's initial reaction.

"He disappeared. Mother's going out of her mind."

"He has a mother?" Jack asks.

"We all have a mother, Jack."

"I wish mine was the mother of all healing," Jack says.

"I need you to spread the photo around, especially to cops who got a Goth or punk rock club on their beat."

Jack rubs his stomach and burps.

***

We're becoming regulars at the café in the basement of the Aon building.

"This guy's worse than a deer tick, Sherlock."

"What do you want me to do, Bree?"

"Get him off me."

"What has he done now?"

"He's in court lying through his teeth," Bree says. "Claiming we systematically colluded to withhold all payments by false accusations saying the evidence was compromised and misleading."

"We did do that, didn't we?"

"But now Seedy Sheedy says he has proof we tainted the evidence."

"What evidence?"

"He didn't say."

"Why aren't you talking to Dewey Diddier instead of me, Bree?"

"Dewey told me he used the same lie a couple times himself and it worked great."

"Sheedy's bluffing, Bree. All he wants to do is settle."

Bree's at her wits' end. "Maybe we should?"

"Mr. Richmond settle?" I ask facetiously. "That's not going to happen."

Kelly and Care are on their second scone, oblivious to my problem.

"Dad, can I have a Coke?" Kelly asks.

"No. You know a Coke has eight tablespoons of sugar in each serving?"

"Can I have a Diet Coke?"

"No. That's even worse."

"There's no sugar in a Diet Coke."

"But there's stuff in it that tricks your body into thinking you just drank something sweet and then you go and eat double the sugar from something else to make up the difference."

"Well, then, what we can have?" Care asks. "We're thirsty."

"See if they have any Oolong tea."

Bree gets my attention back. "Sherlock, you got to do something. This case is getting worse and worse by the minute."

Me? Why is it always me?

"You're missing something, Sherlock. I know you are."

"Easy for you to say, Bree."

"Just find it and get this over with."

Oh jeesh.

# CHAPTER 33

As I stated before: When in doubt, go back and start over.

"Remember, don't touch anything."

"Yeah, yeah, Dad, you don't have to tell us again."

I do my best to be a protective parent, and this is the thanks I get.

We find Larry napping at his desk again.

"Hello, Mr. Flemm with two m's," my girls call out.

Larry almost falls out of his chair.

"Don't do that!"

"Sorry, Larry."

"What do you want, Sherlock?"

"You didn't happen to find out what happened to the rest of Buck's money, did you?"

"What money?"

"Buck must have had other accounts—an IRA, savings, piggy bank—but there's no record of any of them."

"Why would I care?"

"Because that money could have been used to pay off his one credit card."

"Sherlock, a lot of people don't have any money except what they got in their pocket."

And I'm one of them.

"Buck was the same way."

"I have a hard time buying that one, Larry."

"Suit yourself, Sherlock."

"Did you go through his old checkbook?" I ask.

"Yeah."

"Did he write any checks to anyone named Smith?"

"Pretty common name."

"Imelda Smith."

"No."

"Sure?"

"I think I would remember someone named Imelda."

Darn.

"When you talked to your buddy at the IRS, did he say Buck filed a tax return this year?"

"Ya know, Sherlock, you owe me money for my chat with my IRS plant."

"I've been so busy on the case, it slipped my mind."

Larry rubs his thumb against his two forefingers and waves them my way.

"Okay, okay, I'll put you on my expense account this month, Larry."

My expense account will get for him about as much as it gets for me: nothing.

"Come on, Larry, did he file?"

"No."

"Now was that so hard to say, Larry?"

"Yeah, because nothing's free, Sherlock, nothing."

"You're on my list, Larry, you're on my list." I make sure not to mention what list.

Outside Larry's building, the only thing hotter than the sidewalk is the inside of my car. We might as well live inside a crock-pot on high.

"Dad, you got to get a car that has an air conditioner that works," Kelly complains.

"What do you want me to buy first, the boat or a new car?"

"Both."

There is a weird beep in the back seat.

"Dad," Care says, "Tiffany just texted me."

"Whoopee."

Care reads off the phone's screen, "She says she's not speaking to you."

"Lucky me."

There is a pause, and another beep.

Care continues, "She says she will be speaking with Buck no later than tomorrow."

"At a séance, through someone who speaks to the dead?"

"I'll ask." Care taps back to Tiffany.

A beep.

"She says it's none of your business, but she'd like to tell me and Kelly at lunch."

"Find out where."

"Coco Pazzo on Hubbard Street."

"Tell her we'll be there in twenty minutes."

Tiffany might not have much when it comes to grey matter, but she's got great taste in restaurants.

\*\*\*

Tiffany has reserved two tables: a table for four and, right next to it, a table for two.

"You may inform your father," Tiffany says to Care, "he can sit there."

I take the table for two as the three of them sit at the table for four. I sing a few bars of *Lonely Table Just for One* to set the mood.

"You might want to remind your father that I'm not speaking with him."

"Dad," Care says, "Tiffany's not speaking to you."

"Thanks, I would have never known that if it wasn't for you, Care."

The waitress passes out menus and says in a very bad Italian accent, "Benvenuto."

I'll bet any money the woman speaks exactly like me when she's at home.

Tiffany asks if they have an "odd year Chianti from the southern part of Italy?"

"Sì."

Kelly asks, "Do you have any Oolong tea?"

"Scusi?"

"The three of us will have iced tea," I say, ending the drink orders.

Coco Pazzo is one of the new gourmet Italian restaurants which are currently the rage in Chicago food circles. Little on their menu is recognizable as any item you'd see at Olive Garden, and most are absolutely unpronounceable even if you live in the Vatican. Tiffany orders a salad and the girls want pizza. So much for adventurous gourmet choices. I point to an item and ask the waitress, "This good?"

"Eccellente."

The drinks are served. Tiffany sips her wine and gives me a snarky, nose-turned-up sneer.

Nice to see you too, Tiffany.

"I'll bet Buck is trying to get ahold of me right now," Tiffany tells the girls.

"Really? How'd you do it?" Kelly asks.

"Well, when you have an unresponsive and not very clever person you're forced to work with, you have to take the bull by the tail and swing him around to another way of thinking."

"Exactly," Kelly says.

So much for loyalty from daughter number one.

Tiffany removes a folded sheet of paper from her Louis Vuitton purse. She unfolds it and holds it up for the girls to see, but not I.

Care reads, "Nature Boy, where are you?" Care pauses before continuing. "I remain smitten. But you haven't written. Come on and give me a shout. 'Cuz I can't wait to measure your next big trout."

After Care's sparkling reading, Tiffany plops the page down on the table.

"You put an ad in the newspaper?"

"Did you hear something, little dudettes?"

"Yeah, it was Dad asking you if that's an ad in the newspaper."

"La, la, la, la, la," Tiffany chants. "I can't hear him."

The headline and the poem are accompanied by a photo of Tiffany in hiking boots, Daisy Duke shorts, and a low-cut, sleeveless leather vest, smiling sexily while holding a fishing pole. At the bottom of the ad is the line *Can't wait to hear from you*, and Tiffany's email address.

I don't know how many people live in Bozeman, Montana, but every male from puberty to elderly is going to be hitting *Send* in a matter of hours.

"How big is the ad?" Kelly asks.

"Full page," Tiffany says. "I wanted to make sure all those oh-nature-al people can't miss it."

"I don't see a problem there," I blurt out.

Tiffany says to Care, "Would you please tell the person at the next table that he's alone and has no one to talk to."

The food comes.

Kelly and Care's reaction to their pizza is "Why isn't it round?"

"It's a flatbread pizza," I tell them.

"Isn't all bread flat?" Care asks.

"Try it, you'll like it."

I have no clue what I'm eating, but boy, is it tasty.

When we're finished eating, I stand and say, "Well, this has really been a slice, no pun intended, but we still have stops to make today, girls. And you have to come with me."

"Why, Dad? We'd rather go help Tiffany."

"Yes, I know that, but if I need to speak to Tiffany, she

won't speak to me, so I'll need you to call and talk to her for me."

"Gee, I didn't think of that," Kelly says.

"Me neither," Tiffany says.

"Let's go."

Outside the restaurant, while Tiffany waits for the valet and before we walk up Hubbard to the spot I found on the street, I say to my girls, "Tell Tiffany 'thanks' for lunch, and please thank her for me, not only for the food but for the stimulating conversation."

Care repeats my comment verbatim.

I smile and give Tiffany a wave. We get about twenty feet up the street when I have a thought.

"Kelly," I say, "go back and ask Tiffany if she knows who Buck was having lunch with the day the waiter lifted his fingerprints." I pause, and add, "If she doesn't know, ask her to find out."

By the time Care and I reach our car, Kelly returns to say, "Tiffany said, 'She'll see if she can fit it into her schedule.'"

So glad I asked.

***

"I can't find him anywhere. I went to all the punk bars, coffee shops, record stores, and alleys behind all of the above, and nobody's seen him."

"Did you use the graveyard picture?"

"Yes. And they all said they had one just like it."

"No one recognized him?"

"One couple did, but most others were too stoned to remember."

"Did the couple give you any clues?"

"No, but they gave me a half-off coupon to hear the Sloppy Seconds at Reggie's Rock Club."

"You should go."

Jupiter remains a nervous wreck.

"It's bad, Sherlock, I can feel it."

"Jupiter, you can't give up."

"I don't know what else to do."

"Go to the Greyhound bus station. If he went anywhere, he probably could only afford the bus."

"Moonjava got carsick as a kid."

"Show his picture to anybody who works there."

"But he didn't have any money," Jupiter says.

"Go to pawn shops. If he needed money, that's where he'd go first," I suggest.

"Did you notify the police?" Jupiter asks.

"Yes."

"Did they find him?"

"Not yet."

Jupiter's waterworks go on. "This is all my fault. I should have been a better mother, got him into Little League instead of music, and never helped him with his make-up."

"It does you no good to blame yourself, Jupiter."

The tears stream down her cheeks.

"Don't worry, Draconian's going to show up." Care tries to make Jupiter feel better. "It's not like he doesn't stand out in a crowd."

"With those blackened eyes, maybe he's moved in with a bunch of raccoons?" Kelly takes a different tack.

Jupiter shrieks in emotional pain.

"Kelly," Care tells her sister, "you're not helping."

"Keep looking, Jupiter," I tell her. "Keep looking."

We're back in the car when my phone rings. I pull over to the side of the road and take the call.

It's Travianna.

"We're as good as homeless."

We arrive at Buck's house in fifteen minutes. There's no place to park. Red, white, and blue streamers adorn the house. Titi Poon is outside the front door giving out numbers to prospective buyers as if she's working behind a deli counter. I hear her announce, "There has been a change in the listing price to four-twenty-five."

The girls follow me around to the back of the house, where I pound on the door. "Blanche, Travianna, it's me, Sherlock. Let me in."

Travianna opens the door, checks to be sure I'm not an imposter, and lets us in.

"We're land-barren," Travianna announces.

Blanche is at the kitchen table finishing up a half-pint of Old Crow.

"Didn't you go downtown and file the complaint?" I ask.

"Yes, but they wouldn't listen to me."

Welcome to my world.

"Why not?"

"They said the title was transferred and they had every right to sell the place."

"Cato?"

"No."

"Who, then?"

"Some company named AS Enterprises."

"Who the heck is that?"

"I asked, and they said, 'AS Enterprises.'"

Something's screwy here.

"Do we have to let those people in?" Blanche asks.

"You better. The last thing you want is for the Sheriff to come over right now and evict you for being squatters."

"Sherlock, you got to help. We don't even own a tent."

"I'll go out and talk to Titi Poon. You two stay here and don't do anything stupid."

By the time I get out to the front porch, Titi Poon is announcing, "This is the only house in the neighborhood under five-fifty. Keep that in mind when you're making your offer."

"Titi, may I speak to you a minute?"

"You want a number?"

"No."

"You want to make an offer?"

I pull her aside. "Look, the people living here have been totally kept in the dark and have made no plans on their next home. If you promise to leave them alone until the new buyer closes escrow, I'll make sure they hire you as their agent when they buy their next place."

"Hmmmmmmmm."

"More commission, Titi."

"Hmmmm. As long as they get out or stay in the garage while I'm showing it, you got a deal."

I go back in the house. Blanche is pretty much in the bag by this time, and Travianna's gonna have a heck of a time moving her.

"You don't have a choice," I tell the two. "You got to get out while she shows the house, but you can come back after that."

Neither is too happy with the deal I made, but it's better than sharing a sleeping bag in the park tonight.

"And if Titi asks you how much you want to spend on your new place, tell her around a million. That'll keep her at bay for a while."

All I can think about as we drive away is: Who the heck is AS Enterprises?

*\*\**

"Dad, why do you keep taking us to places where we can't touch anything?"

I don't have a good answer, so I don't answer. I knock.

It takes about three minutes of wait time for the door to open.

"Hey, little flower girls, how nice of you to stop by."

"Hello, Mr. McFadden."

I try to look around Herman to see if any porn magazines are lying around, but looking around Herman is impossible.

"What are you doing here, Sherlock?" Herman asks. "I told you I'd call when I was ready."

"I got more to add to the mix, Herman."

"Do your favors ever stop?"

"No."

"And why are you wearing that ugly belt?"

"It's not a belt. It's a brace for my back."

"Come on in."

Herman shifts to the side and we're able to squeeze in.

Trying to be the hostess with the mostest, Herman waddles into the kitchen and announces, "Well, I got either some old cheese or really old lunch meat. Would you like some?"

"We're good out here, Herman. Thanks anyway," I yell as I pick up and hide his X-rated reading material.

"You don't mind if I have a light snack, do you?"

"It's your place, Herman, do what you want."

A few minutes later Herman waddles back into the front room carrying a bowl of rice and a cup of tea. He plops down in his new chair and starts shoveling rice into his mouth.

"What happened to the chopsticks?" I ask.

"Got so frustrated and hungry, I bit into one and almost broke a tooth."

Kelly's nose sniffs the pungent aroma wafting in the air. "What are you drinking?"

"Oolong tea."

"Can I try some?"

"Sure, there's a pot of it on the stove."

The girls get up and head for the free tea.

"Herman, you find out all that stuff I asked for?"

"No."

"You find out anything?"

"Yeah, three things."

"Do tell."

"First, Cato and Estalita aren't married."

"You already told me that."

"Well, it still counts as one of the three, Sherlock."

"Okay, fine. But if they're not married, how is she able to be in the States?"

"Either a tourist visa, Green Card, or she's an illegal."

"Do you know which one?"

"I'm working on it."

The kids re-enter the room, sit on the couch, take one sip of the tea, and almost turn green.

Yuck.

"What's number two, Herman?"

"Buck and Cato are the sons of Imelda Smith. After birthing dem babies, she evidently fell off the wagon. Since the baby daddy was more of a drinking partner than a parenting partner, it was his parents who raised the kids. Buck Senior was around, but wasn't much of a daddy." Herman stops to scoop up more rice and shove it down his throat.

"Didn't Imelda come from money?" I ask.

"Yeah, that was how she paid for the booze and the drunk tanks she'd go in and out of. Oddly enough, she was no dummy when it came to money. She caught the tide of the internet and day-traded her way into some pretty serious coin."

"Her ex get any of it?"

"Probably, but she must have cut him off because he cut her off from seeing the kids. At one point when she was sober, she put most of her money in the hands of a finance guy who put it in a trust and divvied the money out only when she was sober."

"F. Carlton Huff."

"If you already knew that, Sherlock, why the heck did you ask me to find out?"

"I thought you'd enjoy the challenge."

"Gee, thanks."

"Imelda bought the life insurance policies on the boys?" I ask.

"She did. Guilt's a powerful motivator."

"Is there any way of knowing if she had any relationship with the boys once they became adults?"

"Ask your buddy F. Carlton."

"I did. He wouldn't tell me."

"Some detective you are."

"All right, what's the third thing you found out?"

"I'm not telling."

"What do you mean you're not telling?"

"I'm not telling because you should have figured this out by yourself."

"Come on, Herman."

"No. You can do it, Sherlock."

Jeesh.

Care pipes up, "This is just like us doing our homework."

"Yeah," Kelly says. "How does it feel, Dad?"

"Think it through, use your brain, break it down, figure it out," Care mimics.

My words once again.

"Okay, fine, Herman, give me a hint."

"Why would a man leave his entire life behind him and just up and split?" Herman asks.

"Another woman?"

"He already had three, and probably one in every town he sold socks in."

"Buck wanted to get away from his wives?"

"He wasn't married."

"Fatal disease?" Kelly asks.

"No."

"Gambling debts?" I try.

"No."

"The Mafia was out to get him?" Kelly tries.

"No."

"Give me another hint," I plead.

"Money."

I look at Kelly, Kelly looks at me, and Care says, "He won the lottery."

"Bingo."

"What?"

Care shrieks and jumps up and goes into her touchdown victory dance.

"I'm glad to see one member of the family can figure things out," Herman says.

It makes all the sense in the world, but I ask anyway, "Are you sure?"

"Of course I'm sure. It's public record if you win the lottery."

"Did he win like a billion dollars?" Kelly asks.

"He didn't win the big one, but he picked five out of six or six out of seven and took home six mil."

"Why can't you win the lottery, Dad?"

"Because I can't afford to buy a ticket, Kelly."

"Hard to believe you didn't see this one, Sherlock."

I'm floored. "He splits, removes all traces of himself, changes his name, and disappears. No brother, no girlfriends, no long-lost relatives chasing him for what they think is their fair share."

"You can't blame the guy," Herman says.

I pause. "Then he falls off a mountain and dies before he has a chance to spend a dime?"

"I'm going to put an 'I doubt it' on that note, Sherlock."

"So the guy in Montana was Buck?" I ask.

"I wouldn't be too sure of that either," Herman says.

"Then who was the dead guy?"

"I don't know," Herman says. "He didn't stop by to introduce himself."

My mind is racing a mile a minute. "Maybe Buck didn't win the lottery, but somebody else did and Buck used the ticket?"

"Now you're thinking, Sherlock."

"This could be murder?"

Herman shrugs the fat on his shoulders.

"Or maybe Buck and Cato are working together?" I suggest.

"Could be."

"Dad," Kelly says, "maybe Buck knew it was this Russian lottery scam, reported it to the feds, and he's now in the witness protection program?"

"Yeah, right."

Care says, "I think that it was Buck, and he used a

counterfeit ticket to get the money."

The possibilities are endless.

"I got one more angle to work on, Sherlock, and I'm calling it quits on this one," Herman says.

"No, you got two."

"More?"

"I need to know who AS Enterprises is."

"Who?"

"They're the ones who got the title on Buck's house."

"Buck doesn't care about his house," Herman says. "He's got millions. Why would he care about that dump?"

"Just find out who they are, please?"

Herman harrumphs and says, "Sure you people don't want any cheese?"

## CHAPTER 34

M y brain is in overdrive. So many scenarios and what-ifs are going through my head I can't concentrate on anything else. I order a pizza for dinner.

"Dad, we had pizza for lunch."

"Yeah, but this time you're getting a round one."

When the pizza arrives, I open the box and put it on the front-room coffee table. The kids dig in. I lean over to get myself a slice and it happens. It all comes full circle in one split second.

My back goes out.

The pain shoots through my lumbar vertebrae like a 30-ought-6 through a pumpkin. I freeze up, double over, and crash to the floor like a Saddam Hussein statue after the takeover.

"Dad, what's the matter?" Care jumps up and rushes to my aid.

"Something the matter with the pizza?" Kelly asks.

"No."

"Thought you mighta got a bad piece of pepperoni," Kelly says, munching away.

"Go get the Aleve, the heating pad, and the Oriental Oscillator. Hurry."

I'm on the floor, face down, can't move, breathing like an out-of-shape marathon runner with the pain shooting through me faster than electrical current in an execution.

"Want me to walk on your back?" Care asks.

"No."

After four Aleve and twenty minutes of the heating pad, the jolting pains are subsiding, but I'm still as stiff as a board.

"Put the oscillator here, then roll me on top of it."

Care and Kelly logroll me onto the contraption.

"Care, take my feet. Kelly, take my arms. Lift and push me back and forth like you're rolling out pie crust."

"You've never taught us how to bake, Dad."

The kids jostle me around like a sack of dead fish.

After one minute of rolling, I yell, "Stop."

The girls drop my feet and arms. I can barely speak.

"Get the thing out from underneath me."

Kelly yanks it out as if she's Dr. Ratman Rattigan pulling a tooth.

"Ouch."

I'm flat on my back. Motionless, I feel no pain at first, but when I try to lift my head, the pain comes back with a vengeance. My feet point at the couch, my head at *The Original Carlo*. I'm a beached whale at low tide.

"Just let me lie here. Don't touch me."

The girls go back to their pizza.

"Want another slice, Dad?"

"No, but thanks for asking, Care."

By the time my two have devoured the pizza, I say, "Take the cushion off the couch. Care, you lift my feet and, Kelly, you move the couch closer, and gently, very gently put my feet up."

This is much easier said than done. Care drops one of my legs and Kelly bumps me as she shoves the couch in closer. "Ouch." But it does get done and I'm still alive. With the weight coming straight down on my lower back, much of the pressure is released.

"Now get my pillow, lift my head up, and put it underneath."

The two are getting better, but Clara Barton they'll never be.

I lie like this for a few moments with no pain.

"You know what you remind me of, Dad?" Kelly asks.

"No, do tell."

"You look like one of those Arabian shoes that curls up at the toes."

"I think he looks like a human Skee-Ball game."

"A Slinky stuck between steps."

"One of those bendable straws you get at 7-11."

I'm thrilled to be such a good source of comedic material.

The position actually works. I can't move an inch, but I'm pain-free. I hear another weird beep, but not from my back.

"Hey," Kelly says, "I got a text from Tiffany."

"Let me see." Care crowds over to read.

"She says she needs help."

"Tell her I'm floored, hearing her request," I say from the floor.

Kelly texts back. Another beep. "She needs our help, not yours, Dad, because she's still not speaking to you."

"Silence is golden."

Kelly reads, "She's got seven hundred responses with

pictures from her ad and needs help sorting them out."

"The power of the press."

"She says she can't believe the size of some of the trout," Care says.

"In some instances, size does matter."

"What should we tell her?"

"Tell her we're all backed up over here and you'll call her tomorrow."

Kelly relays the message and the beeps stop.

"Would one of you go get me the hand mirror in the bathroom?"

"It's okay, Dad, you don't have anything stuck in your teeth."

"Would one of you just go get the mirror?"

For the next hour, I lie on the floor adjusting the mirror so I can see *The Original Carlo*. This works great except for the fact that I have to read all the index cards backwards, a small price to pay for literacy.

Care stands on one side of the painting, and Kelly on the other.

"Put Imelda on the top, Buck to the left, and Cato to the right." From this point on, I direct, and cards are placed and replaced by the girls.

Patterns I never imagined begin to appear. I now have answers for the sons' life insurance payouts, Buck's one credit card, why Buck abandoned his house, the will in the safe deposit box, and a couple of relationship issues.

The girls pin and re-pin the cards and offer suggestions: "Travianna and Blanche are lesbians." "Benny Ficus, Buck's boss, did him in because he cheated on his expense account and was going to hang it on Buck." "The geocacher planted the body to be the ultimate find in geocaching history."

"Anything's possible, girls, anything."

The best part of this exercise, if you can call my static movements an exercise, is I am able to specify the necessary questions that need answering. In detecting it is oftentimes more important to know which question needs asking more than the answers we might get.

The door buzzer rings two hours later.

"This time one of you has to answer it," I inform the girls. "I'm kind of tied down right now."

Care runs to the kitchen, presses the button. "Who is it?"

"Jupiter."

"Is Draconian with you?"

"I wish."

Care buzzes her inside the building. She carries a guitar as she enters our apartment.

"Are we going to do a sing-a-long?" Care asks.

"No."

At the moment Jupiter sees me, she asks, "Why are you laying on the floor on your back, checking your make-up in a hand mirror?"

"I'm not primping. It's the only way I can see the note cards. My back went out. I can barely move. Excuse me if I don't get up."

Jupiter sits on the couch, strums the guitar.

"It's Draconian's. I found it in a pawn shop."

"How do you know it's his?" Care asks.

"It's got the Scumbag Death Cult's logo on the back." Jupiter flips the guitar over to show a sticker depicting a vampire's stake thrust through a used condom.

Exactly what I wanted my kids to see right before bedtime.

"That's attractive," Kelly critiques the logo.

"When I saw it hanging in the pawn shop," Jupiter says, "I thought I was going to die."

"No, this is a good sign," I speak up. "If he was going to do himself in, he wouldn't take out a loan. This says he needs money for something."

"You really believe that?" Jupiter asks.

"Yes. This should give you hope, not despair."

Jupiter strums the strings again. "God, I hope you're right."

"Did you go to the bus station yet?"

"No."

"Go tomorrow and bring his picture with you," I tell her. "Ask if you can see the security camera footage."

"You think they have cameras there?" Jupiter asks.

"They have cameras everywhere."

Jupiter's breathing a little easier.

"And go to the concert tomorrow night. If he shows up anywhere, it will be with his own people," I add.

"Can we go too, Dad?" Kelly asks in knee-jerk reaction fashion.

221

"Are you big Sloppy Seconds' fans?" Jupiter asks before I can speak.

"Oh," Kelly says, "I was hoping for Katy Perry."

"Jupiter, go home, get some sleep. I'll call my police buddy in the morning and give you an update."

Jupiter stands.

"This is good news, Jupiter. Trust me; it's good news."

The kids pretty much wipe out after ten o'clock. I have Care bring me a sheet, and cover me like a corpse. I lie for another two hours, staring into the hand mirror, reading the cards, but mostly running scenarios through my head. The only reason I stop is to carefully flip over onto my stomach, and slither on my belly like a dying reptile, all the way into the bathroom. It takes me another twenty minutes to straighten up enough to pee.

Boy, is this a relief.

I slither back to the front room, assume my previous position, think for another hour, and make a decision.

Oddly enough, I sleep like a baby.

# CHAPTER 35

The kids wake me up at 10 AM. I haven't slept this late since my honeymoon.

I can move, not well, but I can move.

"You're on your own for breakfast this morning," I tell the kids as they help me get upright.

If I were two foot taller and had a couple bolts in my forehead, I'd be a *dead* ringer for a modern-day Frankenstein.

I let the girls get me to the bathroom, where I slowly get undressed and into the shower. I let the scalding water hit my lower back until the hot water in the hot water heater gives out.

"Ahhhhhh."

A pounding comes on the bathroom door.

"I'll be out in a minute."

"Dad," Care yells through the wood, "Mr. McFadden's on the phone and says he's done."

I open the door a crack and Care hands me my phone.

"Herman."

"Sherlock, how tall was the body they found in the woods?"

"Five-nine."

"How tall was Buck?"

"Five-nine."

"Was Buck alive when they measured?"

"As far as I know."

"Did you know that when you die, your body reverts to its longest height?" Herman asks.

"No, I didn't know that."

"That doesn't surprise me."

"Herman, what's this all about?"

"This is all I'm going to tell you, Sherlock. From this point on, you're on your own."

"Shoot."

I sit on the toilet, wrapped in a towel for the next ten minutes, totally and absolutely mesmerized with what Herman's relating. The report is so complete I don't have to ask questions.

When he finishes, my reaction is "Unbelievable."

"You're welcome," Herman says before I can thank him.

"One more thing, Herman," I get in before he hangs up. "Did you find out who AS Enterprises is?"

"It's some silly company name some jerk used because he's buying property and doesn't want other people to know who he is. Now, that's it, no more. I got a lot of porn to catch up on, Sherlock."

"Thanks, Herman."

Kelly hands me a set of clothes through the door. I get dressed very slowly, emerge from the bathroom, and go straight but slowly to *The Original Carlo*. I take a long look. I don't have all the answers, but I now have the right questions.

And there is only one place I can get the answers.

I am so focused I don't see Kelly and Care standing staring at me.

"Dad, you okay?" Care asks.

"No, but I'm better."

"What are we going to do today?" Care asks.

"Plenty."

"Any shopping on the list?" Kelly asks.

"No." I see the clock. It's a little past eleven. "One of you get Tiffany on the phone."

"She's not speaking with you, Dad."

"Fine, you two can be the go-betweens."

"Cool."

By the time I get the sentence out, Care has already dialed.

"Her phone's not on. Tiffany's probably still beauty-sleeping."

No big surprise there.

"Leave a message."

I get to the dining room table, sit down, and dial my phone.

"Bree, it's Sherlock." I don't wait for a return pleasantry. "Call Sheedy, tell him we'll settle."

"Settle? Richmond Insurance never settles," Bree bursts out.

"Tell him we want to meet in his conference room this afternoon at four."

"You sure you know what you're doing, Sherlock?"

"Not really, but I'm close."

"Do you want Dewey Diddier there?"

"No. Don't take 'no' for an answer from Sheedy. This has got to go down today."

Next call I make is greeted by "Wait."

"Jack—"

"The symptoms are getting worse, Sherlock. My life has already passed by my eyes twice."

"Was one time better than the other?"

"Yeah. How'd you know?"

I tell Jack what I need him to do.

"You sure about all this?" Jack asks.

"No, but I'm pretty sure. That enough?"

"For you, yeah."

"And did you get any sightings of the Goth kid I told you about?"

"No, but it's hard to tell. All those kids dress exactly alike, like they just checked out of Motel Hell."

"Keep looking."

"We will."

"See you at four."

Care and Kelly run up holding a phone.

"Tiffany's on the phone," Kelly tells me. "She doesn't have a lot of time because she's in the middle of her toy-lay."

Care asks, "What's a 'toy-lay'?"

I take the phone. "Tiffany—"

"La, la, la, la."

I hand the phone back to Kelly. "She's still not speaking with me."

"Go ahead, Dad, shoot."

"Tell Tiffany I need her to come over here, pick me up, take me to three places, and bring me back downtown."

Kelly relays the message, not very well, but Care fills in what she misses.

Before I get an answer, I add, "In exchange, she can have you two in the afternoon to help go through all her email responses."

"Tiffany says 'Deal.'"

"Get her here by noon."

"She said, 'No prob.'"

Untruer words have never been spoken.

I start down at noon, and by twelve-thirty I'm downstairs when Tiffany arrives.

As I get to the car, Tiffany sees me and asks the girls, "What happened to him?"

"His back went out."

"Serves him right for being so mean to me."

"I wasn't mean to you, Tiffany."

"Did somebody say something? Because I didn't hear anything."

"Care, tell Tiffany to drive us over to Buck's house."

Care repeats.

"Why?" Tiffany says.

Care repeats.

"I'm thinking about making an offer on the place."

"Really, Dad?"

"Sure, if Tiffany will loan me the down payment."

"La, la, la, la."

When we pull up to the house, Titi Poon is ushering in another set of prospective buyers. I'm too sore to get out of the car.

"Kelly, Care, go in and get Blanche and Travianna, and bring them out here."

The two run in. I wait. Tiffany pretends I'm not in the car.

The girls run back out. "They're not here, Dad."

"Check the garage."

Two minutes later, the four of them return.

"Titi Poon says she's already had four offers," Travianna tells me.

"Don't worry about that now. Here's what I need you to do."

I explain in detail, write down the address, and just to be sure, I end with "See you there at four. Don't be late."

I wave as we leave.

"Tell Tiffany we have to go to Batavia, where Cato lives."

Before Care has a chance to repeat, Tiffany says, "I hate those tacky suburbs."

"Tell Tiffany a deal's a deal."

***

Tiffany stays in the car, afraid she'll get infected with some horrific trailer park bacteria. "Tell your father he should have told me and I would have worn my hazmat suit," she spouts.

Kelly and Care climb the two steps and knock on the trailer park door while I wait on terra firma.

When no one answers, I call out, "We know you're in there, Cato. Come on out."

One minute later he emerges. The only thing that looks worse than the look on his face are the pajamas he's wearing. I would never have thought Spiderman pj's would come in his size.

"What do you want, Sherlock?"

"Busy this afternoon?"

"Yeah, my schedule's pretty well booked."

"Well, you might want to consider moving things around because there's a meeting in Sheedy's office today at four."

"He's no longer my lawyer."

"Yeah, I figured as much," I tell him. "But you still might want to be there, Cato."

"Why?"

"Because I know where your money went."

I turn, the girls follow, and help me to and into the car.

"What was that all about?" Tiffany asks.

"Fishing expedition."

"Mr. Sherlock, what's fishy? I didn't see a pole. Tell me." Tiffany's more forceful this time around.

"La, la, la, la," I sing-song my reply.

When we get close to the city, I say, "Would one of you please inform Tiffany to take the Kennedy and get off at Addison?"

"Where are we going?" Tiffany snaps back.

"Herman's."

"That's the third stop?" Tiffany shrieks. "If I would have known that, I wouldn't have made the deal."

"A deal's a deal."

We pull up in front of Herman's. I tell the girls, "Go up, knock, and he'll give you an envelope. Don't go inside and—"

Kelly interrupts, "Don't touch anything. Yeah, Dad, we got it."

The girls run out of the car. I sit with Tiffany. I know she is dying to chat, but her misplaced promise and pride won't allow it.

"Sure am tired of this heat," I say.

I look over to see her biting her tongue.

The girls return to the car with the envelope and a small foil-wrapped package.

"What's that?" I ask, pointing at the package.

"Either old cheese or really old meat," Care says.

\*\*\*

I'm twenty-five minutes early. Actually twenty minutes early, since it takes me five minutes to get out of the car.

"You guys have a good time going through the Buck pictures. I'm sure you'll be seeing a lot of nice fish."

"What are you going to be doing, Dad?" Care asks.

"Putting a puzzle together."

"Tell whoever just spoke this is no time to be playing games," Tiffany tells Care.

I ignore the comment.

"I'll pick you up later when the game's over." I say and close the door quickly before they can argue, and Frankenstein-walk into the Oriental Building.

I decide to wait in the lobby for Bree and Wait, Jack Wayt before going up to Sheedy's conference room.

Jack shows up first. He's brought a friend.

"Wait—Sherlock, you look worse than I do, and I'm at death's door," Jack says, greeting me.

"My back went out."

"Oh, yeah, that happened to me once," Jack says. "I thought I was done for."

Jack's never met a disease that didn't almost kill him.

"I'm Sherlock." I put out my hand to shake.

"Ernie Schmidts."

"I appreciate you stopping by. You'll either thank me for what you're going to hear, or end up hating my guts for all the work I'm going to give you."

"Aren't you the guy who punched out his boss on TV?" Ernie asks.

Am I ever going to get out from under my past black cloud?

Bree shows up next. Dewey Diddier is with her.

"What are you doing here, Dewey?"

"I thought I might come and pick up a few good lies I could use some day," Dewey answers. "Seedy Sheedy is one of the best."

"If you're wrong on this, Sherlock, and we settle for more money than we've already shoveled out, Mr. Richmond will have my head," Bree tells me.

"But maybe he'll want the rest of your body with it," I

suggest to her. "There's a silver lining to every cloud, Bree."
    Bree hesitates, to ponder the possibility.
    "Ready, people?" I ask.
    Up the elevator we go.

## CHAPTER 36

As I enter the conference room, Cato, Blanche, and Travianna are already seated. I sense there hasn't been a lot of friendly chitchat going on. Jack, Ernie, and Bree sit while Dewey roams around the room, searching for dropped quarters.

I open the satchel I brought along, find the Aleve, and pop two in my mouth. Next, I tighten the brace around my waist and decide to stand because if I sit down, I may never get up.

We all wait a few minutes in a cloud of silent mistrust, foreboding expectations, and overwrought tension, until the side door opens and in rushes Seedy Arnold Sheedy.

"You better be ready to make a deal, because I got people to see and places to go," Arnold announces.

Dewey Diddier takes out a note pad and pen, determined not to miss a good lie.

"Thank you all for being here," I begin. "Yes, we'll be ready to take the case to conclusion, but there's a few aspects I need to go over before we wheel and deal."

"Hurry up," Sheedy says.

Before I get my first words out, the door of the conference room opens, and in walk Tiffany, Kelly, and Care.

"What are you doing here?"

"I knew you were trying to pull a fast one on us, Mr. Sherlock," Tiffany says. "Whenever I know you don't want me there, I'm here."

"Us too, Dad," Kelly says.

"Does this mean you're talking to me again, Tiffany?"

"For now."

It was nice while it lasted.

"Dad," Care says as her eyes search the room, "why aren't there any snacks?"

"I have some old cheese or really old meat if you're hungry," I tell her, showing her the foil-wrapped pack.

"I'll pass."

"Can we get on with this?" Seedy Sheedy asks.

I straighten my torso one last time before beginning.

"There's an old saying in the detective business: When in doubt, go back and start at the beginning."

Jack and Ernie nod their heads.

"Cato and Buck Crouch, identical twins, had two parents, Buck Crouch Senior and Imelda Smith. Actually, we all have two parents. Well, at least until test tube babies were invented.

"I'm not going to say Buck and Imelda were bad parents. Let's just say they had other priorities. One of which was drinking themselves into oblivion most of the time. Buck Senior's parents, the twins' grandparents, stepped in to raise the two boys. And for the next couple of years, Imelda and Buck drifted in and out of the picture. Imelda was worse than Buck in the inebriation category, and when the boys were two, she began falling on and off the wagon. A year later, Imelda's parents died and left her with a pretty good stack of cash. Luckily, she was in a state of sobriety at the time, and made the wise move to take out life insurance policies on her two kids. When baby daddy Buck Senior got wind of the windfall, he wanted his share. Imelda refused. Buck went to court and claimed 'Unfit Mother,' and kept Imelda away from her kids." I pause. "How am I doing so far, Cato?"

Cato doesn't speak, but his ex-lawyer does.

"If I want to listen to a life story, I'll watch the Biography Channel," Arnold says.

"Excuse me," Care says, "but the Biography Channel died when they ran out of people to biography."

"Thank you, Care, for the interesting tidbit of information."

"You're welcome, Dad."

"Fast forward to the boys reaching adulthood," I continue. "Imelda, still in and out of sobriety, writes a letter telling the boys about their insurance policies and that they can cash in if they want. Problem is, she sends both letters to Cato's address, evidently because she doesn't have Buck's."

I peer over at the brother. "What did you do with the money, Cato?" I don't wait for his answer. "I'll bet some you drank, some you gambled, and the rest you wasted."

"You don't know what you're talking about, Sherlock," he tells me.

I glance over at Arnold, who's tapping his fingers on the table as if he's marking time to a Scumbag Death Cult cover.

"So Buck goes off and becomes a super sock salesman, and Cato continues to be pretty much the also-ran in a family of two. The twin brothers couldn't be more different. Cato has lots of problems, none of which I'll go into here, unless you want to supply a list, Cato?"

"Maybe later," Cato says.

"Buck has one big problem: women. He just can't get enough. He has one to take care of his house." I point to Blanche. "He has one to relieve pressure while he's at home." I point to Travianna. "One to supply him with weed. Really good weed, I might add. Plus he has women scattered around the cities and towns where he sells socks."

"I'll settle for two hundred grand right now," Arnold pipes up, "if I don't have to listen to any more of this crap."

"I think it's fascinating," Bree tells Arnold. "Please continue."

"Well," I say, "years go by and something unexpected happens in Buck's life. He decides to make a change."

"Was it one of those male menopause things and he buys a red sports car?" Tiffany asks.

"Not exactly."

I have to raise a finger towards Care, warning her not to spill her beans just yet.

"This is where I need a little help. Cato, I know Buck didn't tell you why, but did he tell you he was splitting town?"

"No."

"Whether you're lying or not doesn't really make a difference. I'm just curious." I pause. "Did he tell either of you?" I ask Blanche and Travianna.

"No," Blanche answers.

"Me neither," Travianna says.

"But he did tell you about his house, and if anything happened, you should go move in with Blanche?" I say to Travianna.

"How'd you know that?"

"I didn't, but thanks for telling me."

Travianna's shocked. "You're welcome, I guess."

"In the next few months, Buck carefully lays out plans and one day disappears without a trace. And nobody did it better than Buck. Poof! He was gone with everything he wanted to take in his wallet."

The seated begin to look at one another like poker players trying to find a tell.

I continue, "The first to react is you, Blanche."

"Me?"

"Yes. You either had the credit card, the numbers on the credit card, or you applied for a new card in Buck's name, and went on a spending spree."

"No, I didn't."

"Yes, you did. A skip tracer found all the bills, and I seriously doubt Buck bought a lot of clothes on the Home Shopping Channel or cases of half-pints of Old Crow."

Blanche swallows hard. She could use some Old Crow right now.

"So. Buck's gone, Travianna's moved in. Cato knows there's a million dollars of insurance just waiting for him if he can prove Buck's dead." I look over at Cato. "You never got around to giving Buck Imelda's letter, did you?"

"This is all new to me, Sherlock."

"Yeah, but even if I'm wrong, it's a great story, don't you think?"

"No."

"Cato's first claim to the money was amateurish and was turned down flat. So, he does what most red-blooded Americans do when they want to skirt the rules: he hires a slimy lawyer."

"Hey, watch it," Arnold screams out.

"Sorry, Mr. Sheedy, I meant to say 'seedy,' not 'slimy' lawyer."

"That's better," Bree calls out.

"So Cato tells Arnold a story full of trumped-up lies in an attempt to hide his own wrongdoing. Arnold not only sees right through Cato's malfeasance, but realizes there's a million bucks just waiting to be claimed.

"Arnold tells Cato the law requires a wait of seven years, but Cato doesn't have seven years to wait, he's already broke. A death certificate is what's needed to speed up the process. And the best way to get a death certificate is to have Buck's dead body or at least a reasonable facsimile at their disposal. "

"This is absurd," Arnold says. "I'll lower my price to one-fifty and we can all go home."

"Before I continue, I'd like to introduce a special guest we have with us today, Mr. Ernie Schmidts."

Ernie stands, as Jack and I applaud, and waves to the crowd.

"Ernie is a member of a federal task force, which deals with international crime."

Ernie sits and Seedy Sheedy starts to sweat.

"I'm going to pause here to add an educational section to my presentation. Why? Because it's never too late to learn something new. Right, girls?"

Kelly and Care are immediately embarrassed.

"If you didn't know, if it's anything to do with faking your own death, disappearing without a trace, or phony documents, Manila in the Philippines is the place to be. Birth certificates, passports, death certificates, cremains, and just-off-the-table corpses are available for a price. I know the next time I'm out body shopping, I'm going to Manila."

Except for the principals, the others can't believe what they're hearing.

"Yep, that's right. Cato and Arnold invest in a 5' 9", 170 lb. body, which they have tattooed with a Cubs logo on one arm, similar to guess who? Buck.

"Their problem now is how do they get it here? UPS doesn't do bodies and it won't fit into a FedEx envelope. They have to hire someone who will swear the body is a relative and is heading back home for burial."

Arnold screams out, "This is crazy. Elmore Leonard couldn't write a plot this stupid."

I point at Arnold and Cato. "You two made a mistake here. You both should have gotten better references, because the woman you hired, Estalita Duarte, wanted more than just an hourly wage for transporting a coffin. She wanted to be part of the team, a partner, not merely a lowly employee. You really can't blame her."

"You can't prove any of this," Arnold argues.

I stare right at Cato, whose eyes shoot to his shoes, and I explain, "The body arrives, you pack him in the car, drive up a ski trail in the late fall and heave-ho him off a cliff. Snow covers him the entire winter, and when spring comes, you go in, find what's left, flip him over, being careful to preserve the Cubs tattoo, bust out his teeth, bust more bones, bleed him dry, cut up his fingers, and make sure he'll be the perfect appetizer for the forest animals to nibble on."

"There's a job I wouldn't want," Travianna says.

"You get lucky when the body is found by some geocacher, and even luckier when the coroner cremates the poor soul before identifying him."

"Ridiculous," Cato says. "I never went to no Philippines, bought no body, and threw no corpse off a cliff. That was Buck in that grave. Everything matched: height, weight, tattoo, everything. You're trying to hang your fairy tale crime on me."

"How tall are you, Cato?"

"Five-nine, just like the corpse."

"How tall was Buck?"

"The same," Buck says, then adds, "Identical twins, duh."

"Blanche, stand up." I motion to Kelly to come over as I pull out a tape measure.

"How tall did you say Buck was?" I ask Blanche, who's sitting next to me.

She stands up and puts her hand to her chin. "This tall."

I hold the tape and Kelly unrolls it to the floor.

"How tall, Kelly?"

"Five foot ten inches."

"See?" I say. "Bodies don't match."

"But we all shrink as we age," Arnold says with a smirk on his face.

"Yes, but when we die, we stretch to our longest length."

"How'd you know that?" Cato asks.

"Jack told me." I point to my cop buddy.

Jack says, "Sherlock's right. I had to take that into consideration when I bought my coffin."

"Good luck proving all this, Sherlock," Arnold says.

"You're right, Arnold. I can't. But explain to me why your Buck wasn't in his Salomon GTX boots when he died. Why there was no ID, wallet, or money found, or why he wasn't wearing socks. He was a sock salesman, for Christ sake."

"You can't prove a thing," Arnold says.

"I doubt if I'll have to. That's why I invited Ernie along." I pause, try to straighten up by arching my back, but it only makes the pain worse.

"Fast forward again to just a few weeks ago. Cato and Arnold are ready to reap from their own Grim Reaper when Richmond Insurance refuses to cough up the dough, a function they're especially adept at doing. I get involved, and stuff starts to go wrong. First, I find Buck's safe deposit box, and inside it, a last will and testament dated when Buck was a mere youth."

Arnold speaks up. "Which specifically specified who got the

estate."

"Me," Cato adds.

"Correct," I agree with Sheedy and Cato. "Major problem diverted, but you then go and break my first rule in life."

"And what would that be?" Arnold asks.

"Assume nothing," Kelly blurts out.

I can't believe it. One of my daughters has listened to some of my advice.

"Exactly! You assumed it was Buck's will, but it wasn't. Buck's will is somewhere in Montana. The will you saw was Buck's daddy's will, which was truly a joke, since Daddy didn't have a dime."

"That's it." Arnold jumps out of his seat. "I've had enough of this absolute absurdity." Arnold begins to march around as if in front of a jury. "First, we have a death certificate in Buck's name, a recognized legal document. Second, we have Buck's body, and whether it's one inch off, who cares? And third, we have DNA from Buck's urn that matches Buck's DNA. Dispute all that, Sherlock."

"You didn't happen to get that DNA from an aged, 1960's hippie drug dealer named Jupiter, did you?" I ask.

"Yeah, when she came in to shake me down with some crazy story of her punk kid being Buck's son."

"Damn. I told her not to say anything to you until we were ready." I'm back to nobody listening to me.

"Come on, Sherlock, if you don't got a good answer, we're quitting this silliness and talking money," Arnold snaps at me.

"Jupiter didn't have Buck's DNA, she had Cato's. She fished it out of his trash, if you want to know. And the DNA that came out of the urn—"

"Yeah, that was Buck's," Arnold screams out.

"No." I turn to the brother. "Cato, give us a smile, would you?"

Cato sneers, "No."

"Although he's not in a cheery mood right now," I smile at Cato, "you all know Cato is quite challenged in the tooth." I speak directly to Cato. "I have one word of advice for you, Cato."

"What?"

"Floss."

I get a few laughs from the peanut gallery after that one.

"What Cato did was grind up a few of his old molars and put them into the urn's ashes, planning to hold them as a last resort to prove it was Buck's DNA in the urn, since he thought identical twins would match perfectly. But Jupiter beat him to the punch when she absconded with the urn, had it analyzed, and tried to use it as proof of paternity.

"If you think I'm nuts here, Cato, all you have to do is offer up your DNA to the court, and I'll bet it will match exactly with the teeth fragments in the urn."

"We're identical twins. You can't tell one DNA from the other," Cato says with a gap-tooth smile upon his face.

"Well, not quite. DNA changes over time if you didn't know. Your DNA and your brother's would not be identical, just like the two of you."

"There's more holes in this story than Swiss cheese," Arnold says.

I should unwrap Herman's cheese and offer him some, but I don't, for fear that it actually is old meat.

"I don't know what the split was between the two of you, but I do know that you, Arnold, became skeptical of your partner in crime and decided to restructure the deal. You'd settle for Buck's house and walk away. Cato could have the million in insurance money and all would be fine. Well, that's at least what you told Cato."

"I never made any such deal."

"And no title for any property went into my name," Arnold adds.

"Maybe not you, Arnold, but AS Enterprises got the title, a company where you're the only principal."

If he could, Arnold would be chewing on Herman's cheese right now.

"As I promised you, Cato, I know where your money is. Well, maybe not exactly where it is, but what happened to it."

Cato is silent for the first time since the beginning of my show-and-tell.

"A money transfer was set up by none other than your attorney, to move the funds to an offshore account, which we can trace. But unfortunately for you, the money was again transferred to another account, which might be more difficult to find."

Cato's face has turned the color of his remaining teeth, a

somber yellowish grey.

"But don't despair, Cato. If you find Estalita, you'll find your money. You might want to ask Arnold. I have a feeling he might know where she is. But you better get to it quickly, because Mr. Schmidts will be on the trail too."

Tiffany jumps out of her seat. "Hurry up, Ernie. You got to find our money. I've already picked out my new car."

"This is all fluff, conjecture, lies, and you can't prove a thing," Arnold says.

I shrug my shoulders as best as I can. "There are two questions you might want to ask," I say. "How was Estalita able to get into the country escorting a coffin, and then able to stick around for months?"

No one speaks up.

"She got a Green Card. And how was she able to get a Green Card? She was promised a job in America. And where did she find the job? At AS Enterprises, where else?"

"This is ridiculous," Arnold says.

I pull out the envelope Kelly picked up from Herman and hand it to Ernie. "Here's the paperwork."

"How would you get that?" Arnold explodes. "That's classified."

"Let's just say, I can be a little 'seedy' myself, Arnold."

I put my hands out as if to say "That's all, folks."

Two sets of handcuffs magically appear from Jack and Ernie, and are slapped on Cato and Arnold.

Blanche and Travianna nervously ask, "Do we still have to move?"

"I don't know, but I would doubt if any sale of assets is allowed until all this is straightened out, which, with all the lawyers involved, could take some time."

"Whew!"

The show is over. Time to go home.

"Wait," Bree screams out. "You never told us what made Buck disappear."

"Care." I motion for her to announce.

"He won the lottery!"

"What?"

Shock on all, especially Cato.

"Yep, Buck picked enough correct numbers for a six-million-dollar payday. Knowing the money might be more trouble than it's worth, he takes his time collecting, then changes his name, cashes out of everything except his property, and disappears without a trace. Smart guy, except like most disappearing people, he makes one mistake. Women. We found him on a dating site searching for *the nature girl of his dreams.*

"Where is he?" Cato asks.

"Your guess is as good as mine," I lie.

Hey, nobody's perfect.

## CHAPTER 37

"**H**e's dead."
"Dead?"
"Suicide."
"Jupiter, I'm so sorry."

It's ten the next morning. Jupiter's in my apartment, crying her eyes out. The kids are still asleep.

"The FBI called and said they found his remains."
"The FBI?"
"He killed himself on federal land."
"Where?"
"Yellowstone."
"What was he doing in Yellowstone?"
"Killing himself."

Jupiter breaks down. She can no longer speak. I give her some time.

Yellowstone?

Twenty minutes go by. I do my best to comfort her, but there is little I can do.

It is said the most painful thing in life is to lose a child, and at this point, I believe it to be true.

Kelly and Care get up and see Jupiter. I head them off before they reach the front room.

"What happened?"
"Is Draconian here?"
"He died."
"Died?"

I have two stunned kids.

We all enter the front room. I sit next to Jupiter, the girls on the other side of the room.

"Tell me what they told you."

Through the tears and sniffles, Jupiter does her best. "The guy calls and says that my boy jumped into an open geyser."

"An open geyser?"
"Yes."
"Are they sure?"
"He left a note."
"Oh my God."

Jupiter chokes up. I place my arm around her and do the best I can to ease her pain.

"I have to go there, Sherlock," she manages to get out. "I have to see for myself."

I give it a few minutes.

I tell the girls, "Get Tiffany on the phone."

My daughters scramble. Kelly comes back first, holding the phone towards me. "Dad, Tiffany says—"

I take the phone, move into the kitchen. "Tiffany, listen to me." The tone of my voice must be convincing because she doesn't speak. "I need the use of your company plane. This is an emergency. If you want to take it out of my pay, I don't care. I need a plane and I need it today."

"Is it a matter of life and death, Mr. Sherlock?"

"Half of that."

***

Hours later, the five of us arrive at a private landing strip in the exclusive Yellowstone Club. We are met as we deplane.

"Sherlock?"

"That you, Romo?"

Romo Simpson was—and remains—the quintessential G-man. I previously knew him in Chicago on a murder case I investigated years ago. Back then he was angling for a promotion. If this is what he got, I'm not sure he got promoted.

"What are you doing here?"

"The usual," I answer. "What are you doing here?"

"I head up the bureau's office up here."

"Congratulations."

"I was hoping for New York, and this is where they put me," Romo confesses.

I introduce the rest of my crew.

"Come on," Romo says. "I have a car waiting."

There isn't much chatting on the way into the park. With Jupiter continuing to cry her eyes out, it's a little hard to chat up the Big Sky scenery.

The geyser in question is about a mile from Old Faithful. The area has been roped off.

"One of the rangers found him yesterday and called us," Romo tells us.

We go under the yellow tape. I allow Jupiter to go first and we lag back.

Romo keeps his voice down. "Actually, this happens a lot up here."

"Really?"

"It's over 200 degrees inside a geyser. You die instantly and burn up completely."

"Sounds like hell on earth," I comment.

I watch as Jupiter finds Draconian's storm trooper boots and cape beside the hot hole in the ground. She removes a page of paper and reads. Jupiter faints.

I run to pick her up. The three girls follow. I sit her up and try to get some bottled water into her, but she's out cold.

I pick up the paper and read:

"It is time for my life, as I knew it, to come to an end. It is the best for all concerned. I hope to find myself in a better place.

"Draconian."

Jupiter lies in my arms. Kelly pats her forehead with a wet cloth, and Care tries to get water down her throat.

Something's wrong. I can feel it.

Jupiter regains consciousness.

"Help her back into the SUV," I tell Kelly and Care.

"This is like totally weird, Mr. Sherlock," Tiffany remarks.

"Tiffany, does your phone work up here?"

"My phone would work on the moon if I ever visit there."

"Let me have it."

I walk off to the side, see a few buffalo grazing, and walk the other way. I dial the phone. The next voice I hear is filled with excitement.

"Tiffany! How great of you to call."

"Herman, it's not Tiffany. It's me."

"Sherlock, darn. I thought my fantasy was finally coming true."

"I need you to do something right now."

"I'm busy."

"Put down the rice bowl, Herman. Here's what I need you to do."

"What?"

I specifically state my need and end with "I'll hold."

"You want me to do it right now?"

"Yes. Go."

In the next five minutes, I can see my girls helping Jupiter.

Tiffany is chatting with Romo Simpson, who gives her an official FBI cap to try on.

"Sherlock—"

"Yes."

Herman speaks slowly. "You got a pen?"

"No, but I got a great memory."

"Here's the address. He bought the ranch six months ago."

I hurry back to Romo's SUV.

"Do you know where Hungry Joe, Montana is?" I ask.

Romo answers, "No, but I got a GPS."

"Let's go."

"Wait, wait," Romo says. "The FBI isn't some taxi service."

"Romo, if my hunch is right, I'll give you all the credit, and your next promotion will be that much sooner."

"Everybody in the car. That's an order from the FBI."

\*\*\*

Hungry Joe isn't much more than a blip on a map even Google couldn't find. It takes about eight seconds to drive through. We find the ranch ten minutes later.

The sign on the gate reads: *Private Property,* but that doesn't stop the FBI. Romo drives in, through a half-mile of forested land, until the property opens up to a massive fenced-in pasture. There must be sixty brown cattle grazing on the green grass.

"Those are funny-looking buffalos," Tiffany, who now looks very governmental wearing her FBI hat, remarks.

"Those are cows, Tiffany."

"Oh yeah," she says, "the kind that make chocolate milk."

As soon as I see the house and barn, I tell Romo, "Pull over behind those trees."

As soon as the SUV is hidden, I ask, "You got binoculars?"

"Of course. I'm the FBI."

"You people stay here. We'll be right back."

Romo and I get out of the car and position ourselves behind a tree. I take the binoculars and focus them on the house. We wait.

"What are we doing, Sherlock?"

"Raising the dead."

"From this distance?"

It doesn't take long before I see two people emerge from the home.

"Go get Jupiter," I tell Romo.

I watch as two guys hook up a trailer to the back of a pickup truck.

Jupiter and the rest of the women arrive with Romo, who explains the additional women: "They wouldn't listen to me."

"Welcome to my world."

I continue to peer through the binoculars and then put them down.

"Jupiter, I don't want you to freak out, scream, or go running off, but I'm going to show you something that might be a little unsettling."

I hand her the binoculars.

She peers through the lenses, adjusts the focus, and screams, "That's my son!"

Thank God she's too far away for the guys to hear.

"He's fine. He didn't commit suicide," I tell her and add, "at least in the physical sense."

Jupiter drops the binoculars and is about to run screaming towards the two, but I hold her back.

"Now is not the time to break a bond that's been a long time forming, Jupiter. You have to give them time."

Jupiter ceases all motion.

"Your son is fine. He's got a new life. Let him get used to it before you remind him of his old one."

Jupiter knows I'm right. After a huge sigh of relief, she walks back to the SUV with Tiffany and my girls.

"Who are those two?" Romo asks.

"The older guy is Bob Smith, the younger one is his son."

"And what's Bob Smith's rank and horsepower?" Romo asks.

"When it comes to disappearing, or faking your own death, nobody does it better."

# CHAPTER 38

I take the girls back to their mother's house on Saturday morning.

"Give me a kiss."

They both reluctantly smooch me.

"Don't forget to tell all your friends you got to visit Yellowstone on your vacation."

"Twice," Care says.

"Yeah, we're the only people on earth who visited Yellowstone on two consecutive day trips," Kelly qualifies.

"It's not the amount of time, Kelly, but the experience that's important."

"Yeah, right, Dad."

The front door of my once house opens. The kids grab their stuff and start to scramble out.

"And at your new schools on Monday, don't forget: Learn something new every day!"

"Yeah, right, Dad."

Their mother waits with open arms at the door.

I look, but can't see Mom's new or improved aura. Maybe she should try a different camp next summer.

## THE END.

It is a fact that on average, 90,000 Americans disappear each year, mostly for financial reasons. Over 99% get caught or decide the grass isn't greener on the other side of the fence.

If you are considering disappearing or faking your own death, do yourself a favor and first pay a visit to Manila in the Philippines. Whether you need a phony death certificate, forged documents, or a warm corpse, you'll find it in Manila, the world's capital for such activity.

Unfortunately, a number of people have died in Yellowstone National Park by falling or jumping into active geysers. This is not a fact often seen in brochures titled, *Fun Things to do on Your Visit to Yellowstone.*

Sekhmet, the Egyptian goddess of Power, is not a god you want mad at you. As a protector of the Pharos, Sekhmet got so angry once, she almost destroyed all of humanity; only a drunken wine binge halted her wrath.

From ancient Egypt to the present, many cults have formed to honor and pray to Sekhmet. We can only hope the members of these cults are also among the 1%, who successfully disappear each year.

Thank you very much for reading The Case of the Dearly Departed. I certainly hope you enjoyed my novel, and if you did, please let others know of your good reading fortune. The easiest way being through cyberspace via social media networks such as Amazon, Facebook, LinkedIn, Goodreads, and Twitter. Please put in a good review to the above and to your friends, contacts, and fellow readers. It will be greatly appreciated.

## About Jim Stevens

Jim Stevens was born in the East, grew up in the West, schooled in the Northwest and spent twenty-three winters in the Midwest. Jim Stevens has been writing for over thirty years. Usually without much success, but for some reason he keeps writing. Jim started writing TV series specs in the 1970s and went hungry. He segued into spec movie scripts and starved. He went into the corporate world for a twenty-five year career in broadcasting and advertising, but just couldn't drop his pencil. He found time to write plays in the Chicago theater scene, wrote, produced, and directed numerous short films, videos, and TV commercials, created TV pilots, and even optioned a few movie scripts that never saw the glare of the Klieg lights.

Jim has been writing novels for the past seven years. His Richard Sherlock Whodunit series has ranked him in the top 10% of Amazon authors. He is also the author of *WHUPPED*, a reverse romantic comedy from many different points of view, and *WHUPPED Too* its sequel. His novel, *Hell No, We Won't Go, A Novel of Peace, Love, War, and Football* is his first writing of a 'serious' nature.

Jim loves to hear from his readers, especially the ones who enjoy his books. He can be reached at JimStevensWriter@gmail.com

If you would like to be the first on your block to get all the up-to-date news on the detecting of Richard Sherlock and whatever Jim Stevens has to say, please sign up for Jim's email list. All you have to do is drop a line to JimStevensWriter@gmail.com to join a very select and fun-filled group. Don't delay, do it today!